Praise for
The Haunting of Maddy Clare

"A compelling and beautifully written debut full of mystery, emotion, and romance."

—Madeline Hunter, *New York Times* bestselling
author of *The Surrender of Miss Fairbourne*

"*The Haunting of Maddy Clare* is a novel of chilling romantic suspense that evokes the lost era between the World Wars that so wounded the lives of the young men and women of England, and adds to the mix an inventively dark gothic ghost story. Read it with the lights on. Simply spellbinding."

—Susanna Kearsley, *New York Times* and *USA Today*
bestselling author of *The Winter Sea*

"*The Haunting of Maddy Clare* is a compelling read. With a strong setting, vivid supporting characters, and sympathetic protagonists, the book is a wonderful blend of romance, mystery, and pure creepiness. Simone St. James is a talent to watch."

—Anne Stuart, *New York Times* bestselling author of *Shameless*

"Compelling and deliciously unsettling, this is a story that begs to be read in one sitting. I couldn't put it down!"

—Megan Chance, national bestselling author of *City of Ash*

"With a fresh, unique voice, Simone St. James creates an atmosphere that is deliciously creepy and a heroine you won't soon forget. *The Haunting of Maddy Clare* promises spooky thrills and it delivers. Read it, enjoy it—but don't turn out the lights!"

—Deanna Raybourn, *New York Times* bestselling author of the
Lady Julia Grey series and *The Dark Enquiry*

"Fast, fun, and gripping. Kept me up into the wee hours."

—C. S. Harris, author of the Sebastian St. Cyr Mystery series

Titles by Simone St. James

THE HAUNTING OF MADDY CLARE

AN INQUIRY INTO LOVE AND DEATH

SILENCE FOR THE DEAD

THE OTHER SIDE OF MIDNIGHT

LOST AMONG THE LIVING

THE BROKEN GIRLS

THE SUN DOWN MOTEL

THE BOOK OF COLD CASES

The Haunting of Maddy Clare

SIMONE ST. JAMES

BERKLEY
New York

BERKLEY
An imprint of Penguin Random House LLC
penguinrandomhouse.com

Copyright © 2012 by Simone Seguin
Excerpt from *The Book of Cold Cases* by Simone St. James copyright © 2022 by Simone Seguin
Penguin Random House supports copyright. Copyright fuels creativity, encourages
diverse voices, promotes free speech, and creates a vibrant culture. Thank you for buying
an authorized edition of this book and for complying with copyright laws by not
reproducing, scanning, or distributing any part of it in any form without permission.
You are supporting writers and allowing Penguin Random House to continue to
publish books for every reader.

BERKLEY and the BERKLEY & B colophon
are registered trademarks of Penguin Random House LLC.

ISBN: 9780451235688

The Library of Congress has catalogued the
New American Library trade paperback edition of this book as follows:

St. James, Simone.
The haunting of Maddy Clare/Simone St. James.
p. cm.
ISBN 978-0-451-23568-8
I. Title.
PR9199.4.S726H38 2012
813'.6–dc23   2011033391

New American Library trade paperback edition / March 2012
Berkley trade paperback edition / October 2022

Printed in the United States of America

Book design by Elke Sigal

The Haunting of Maddy Clare

SIMONE ST. JAMES

BERKLEY

New York

BERKLEY
An imprint of Penguin Random House LLC
penguinrandomhouse.com

ISBN: 9780451235688

The Library of Congress has catalogued the
New American Library trade paperback edition of this book as follows:

St. James, Simone.
The haunting of Maddy Clare/Simone St. James.
p. cm.
ISBN 978-0-451-23568-8
I. Title.
PR9199.4.S726H38 2012
813'.6—dc23   2011033391

New American Library trade paperback edition / March 2012
Berkley trade paperback edition / October 2022

Printed in the United States of America

Book design by Elke Sigal

For Adam

Chapter One

CS

The day I met Mr. Gellis, I had been walking in the rain.

In the morning, unable to face another day alone in my flat, I wandered through the bustle of Piccadilly, the collar of my thin coat pulled high on my neck. The air was swollen with cottony drizzle that did not quite fall to the ground, and pressed my cheeks and eyelashes. The lights of Piccadilly shone garishly under the lowering clouds; the shouts of the tourists were loud against the grim silence of the businesspeople and the murmurs of strolling couples in the square.

I stayed as long as I could, watching the bob of umbrellas. No one noticed a pale girl, with cropped hair under an inexpensive and unfashionable hat, her hands plunged in her pockets. Eventually, the mist resolved itself into rain and even I turned my reluctant steps home.

Though it was only noon, the sky was near dark when I opened the gate and hurried up the walk to my small and shabby boardinghouse. I climbed the narrow stairs to my room, shivering as the damp penetrated my stockings and numbed my legs. I was fumbling for my key with chilled fingers and thinking of a cup of hot tea when the landlady called up the stairs that there was a telephone call for me.

I turned and descended again. It would be the temporary agency on the line—they were the only ones with my exchange. I had worked for them for nearly a year, and they sent me to one place or another to answer phones or transcribe notes in ill-lit, low-ceilinged offices. Still, the work had dried up in recent weeks, and I was painfully short of funds. How fortunate I was, of course. I would have missed their call had I come home only five minutes later.

In the first-floor hallway, the house's only telephone sat on a small shelf, the receiver lying unhooked where the landlady had left it. I could already hear the echo of an impatient voice on the other end.

"Sarah Piper?" came a female voice as I raised the receiver to my ear. "Sarah Piper? Are you there?"

"I'm here," I said. "Please don't hang up."

It was the temporary agency, as I had suspected. The girl sounded flustered and impatient as she explained what had come up. "A writer," she told me. "Writing a book of some sort—needs an assistant. Wants a meeting with someone today. He wants a female."

I sighed, thinking of fat, sweaty men who liked a succession of young ladies in their employ. Normally I'd be sent to an office to begin work right away, not to a personal meeting. "Is he a regular client?"

"No, he's new. Wants to meet someone this afternoon."

I bit my lip as my stomach rolled uneasily. Temporary girls were easy targets for any kind of behavior from a man, and we had nearly no recourse without getting fired. "At his office?"

She huffed her impatience. "At a coffeehouse. He was specific about meeting in a public place. Will you go?"

"I don't know," I said.

"Look." She had an edge in her voice now. "I have other girls I can call. Are you going or not?"

To meet a man alone in a coffee shop? Yet my rent at the boardinghouse was two weeks past due. "Please," I said. "This isn't a matchmaking service."

"What's to lose?" she replied. "If you don't like it, I'll give it to the next girl."

I looked out the window, where rain now streaked down. I pictured the girl at the other end of the phone, bored and brassy and fearless. A girl like that wouldn't think twice. It was girls like me who thought twice—about going back out in our only good set of clothes, about meeting unknown men in unknown places. About everything.

I took a breath. I could go back to my damp little flat, and sit at my window, thinking and drinking endless cups of tea. Or I could go out and meet a stranger in the rain.

"I'll be there," I said.

She gave me the coordinates and hung up. I stood for only a moment, listening to the water on the windows and the sound of coarse laughter in one of the first-floor rooms. Then I went back out to the street.

ക

"I don't suppose they told you much," the young man across from me said as he poured his tea. "I told them as little as I could."

He was nothing like I had pictured: young, perhaps twenty-five, the same age as I. His dark blond hair was not slicked down as was the fashion, but worn longish and windblown, as if he combed it in the morning and forgot about it. Quick intelligence gleamed in his gray eyes, the wry set of his face, and the eloquent movement of his hands. The coffeehouse he had brought me to was in Soho, and the bohemian atmosphere of it matched his style—an olive green coat of soft well-worn wool over a white shirt unbuttoned at the throat. He blended perfectly in a place like this, with its offbeat paintings and thin, sullen waitresses.

It was I who was out of place here. I never came to Soho; its reputation was too wild, too artistic for me. But as I sipped coffee that made my mouth burn with flavor and watched Mr. Gellis' fascinating smile, I ceased to care. I wrapped my cold hands around the cup, curled my sodden toes in their cheap shoes, and managed to smile back.

"Not much," I agreed. "They said you are a writer."

He laughed. "I hope you didn't get too excited. I don't write lurid books or anything of that sort. Just dry academic books."

"I don't read lurid books."

"You won't be disappointed, then." He dropped a lump of sugar in his cup. "A lady who doesn't read lurid books is promising. I asked for someone intelligent."

I blinked. The agency thought me intelligent? I doubted it; likely I had been chosen because I was currently available. Still, the compliment warmed. I took off my hat and quickly ran my fingers through my earlobe-length hair, which was curling a little in the damp. "Do you require a secretary? I can transcribe."

He leaned back in his chair. "There may be some of that." He tapped his fingers on the tabletop and looked out the window, as if thinking. I watched his clean, debonair profile with the

beginnings of warm pleasure. His presence was so comfortable, so easy, I was suddenly glad I had come.

Mr. Gellis tapped his fingertips on the tabletop again and turned to me. He seemed always in motion, as if his thoughts could not sit still. "I confess I'm not entirely sure how to approach this. What I need done may seem rather strange."

Some of my happiness drained away. "Strange?"

"I met you in public for a reason," he went on. "I specifically need a female, and I did not want you to feel uneasy, presented with something that might frighten you."

I was cold now. "I beg your pardon?"

He reddened. "I'm terribly sorry. That came out wrong. I don't get out much socially, you know." He sighed. "I'll let my notes do the explaining."

He pulled a large notebook from the leather satchel slung over the back of his chair and slid it across the table to me. The notebook was well used and full; I could see corners turned down, the edges of glued-in clippings, extra pages folded and stuffed between leaves.

I opened it to the first page, which contained a newspaper clipping about a haunted house in Newcombe. In the margin next to the clipping was a neat set of handwritten notes. I turned to the second page and found more notes, in a careful hand that was squared and bold and masculine.

I read the notes for a long moment; then I looked up. "This is—"

"Yes."

"An eyewitness account of a ghost."

"Yes."

I felt his gaze on me as I flipped through more pages. It was a notebook of hauntings, one after another. "So—you research ghosts?"

"I document them." He rubbed a hand through his hair. "Well, what do you know? I'm so used to it I don't really think of it anymore. But it sounds strange said out loud, doesn't it?" He dug into his bag again and handed me something else—a book. I took the slender volume and read the title.

Accounts of Haunted Properties in the North of England, by Alistair Gellis. I looked up at Mr. Gellis, who was staring modestly down and stirring his tea with a spoon. "You said you write dry academic books," I accused.

"I certainly try to." He shrugged. "I travel to haunted places and test the veracity of the claims. I use technology to document them, or debunk them, as the situation calls for. Then I compile all of my conclusions into books filled with citations and footnotes. As dry as I can make it, really."

It was all too wild for me to take in. "You believe in this?" I said without thinking.

He frowned, and I wished I could swallow my words. Of course he believed in ghosts, or he would not write about them. "It isn't a matter of believing, really," he said. "I believe what I see."

"But surely some of these are hoaxes?"

The corner of his mouth curled. "Yes, some of them are hoaxes. Many of them, in fact. The hoaxes go in the books, too. But some of them . . ." He paused, then shrugged again. "What can I say? Some of them simply are not."

I put the book down on the table. This was surely the strangest assignment any temporary girl had ever been given. I did not know what to make of it. Mr. Gellis seemed young, intellectual, and even eccentric: the type of person who could fall prey to charlatans,

I thought. It had not escaped my notice that his clothes, for all their casual elegance, were more quietly expensive than those of anyone else in the room. Likely he attracted liars like magnets.

"You think I'm mad." When I looked up, he was smiling, amused and a little rueful. "You can say it. You think I'm barmy. Most women do."

"No," I protested. "No."

"A liar, then."

I was shocked. "No! Of course not."

"Very well, then. You simply don't believe in ghosts."

"I don't—" I shook my head. "I don't know. I've never thought of it. I don't know what I believe." I took a breath, traced a finger along the edge of the small book in front of me, trying to put into words what concerned me. "I don't have an opinion about ghosts. It's people I don't believe in, I suppose."

"What a very unusual girl you are," he said.

I looked up, surprised. Mr. Gellis sipped his tea, his eyes watching me calmly over the rim of the cup. I talked through my confusion. "So—the, ah, job. I am guessing you need someone to organize your notes?"

"Yes, yes." He put down his cup and sat forward. "I have an assistant. He takes my notes for me and keeps everything organized. That is his notebook there."

He gestured to the fat notebook on the table between us, and I pictured a serious and bespectacled man, meticulously keeping all of Mr. Gellis' clippings in order and writing notes with that neat, sure hand.

"His name is Matthew Ryder," Mr. Gellis went on. "But he is away this week, visiting his sister who is having a baby. Normally I would not need a replacement, but I find that this week I do."

I nodded. Taking notes, organizing clippings—it was easy enough. "Certainly I'll help you," I said.

He held up a finger. "Ah—I haven't finished. Don't agree just yet. You said you have no opinion on the existence of ghosts."

"I've certainly never seen one," I conceded.

His smile was like sun breaking through the clouds. "How lucky for you, then. Because you're going to see one this week. For me."

Chapter Two

❧

There was sharp laughter at the next table, but I barely registered it as I stared at Mr. Gellis. "You wish for me to witness a ghost?"

"I hope so," he replied, as if we were discussing everyday business. "If the lead I have is authentic. I've done this long enough to believe it is."

A hard, cold lump formed deep in my stomach. A waitress came by, and Mr. Gellis took another cup of tea. When she turned to me, I shook my head, embarrassed, as there had been no discussion of who was paying and I did not have enough money for a second cup of coffee. "I don't understand," I said when she had left.

"Then let me explain." Mr. Gellis rubbed his hands together and a glint of excitement came into his eyes. "I assume you are not familiar with the famous ghosts of England?"

I shook my head.

"Of course not. As you see here, I've documented many of them. There are a lot of ghosts in England, but there are a few of us writing books like mine, and we tend to cover the same ground. It's inevitable. The challenge is to find something new—an entirely unseen haunting that has never been written about before. And just this week, I've finally found one." He gulped his tea, swallowing nearly half the cup's hot contents, and I realized he was truly excited. "Just a few days ago a vicar contacted me. He had been living in a tiny town called Waringstoke, where a local family asked him to attempt an exorcism. This was several months ago. The exorcism failed spectacularly—not only did the ghost not leave, but according to this vicar, she physically attacked him. A physical attack, Miss Piper! It is entirely extraordinary."

It was the first time he had said my name, and I dropped my gaze to the table, embarrassed that I had noticed. "What kind of physical attack?"

"Throwing things, mostly. Heavy things. He told me he felt the disturbance almost immediately; he described it as a feeling of rage. He said he's never felt anything like it before, and hopefully never again."

"And why did he contact you?"

"Why, I offer money for tips, of course."

I looked up again. Mr. Gellis waved a dismissive hand, and I knew he was one of those people born to money, so effortlessly gifted with it that it meant nothing to him. "That is neither here nor there. He was so rattled by the experience that he got a new living and moved away. He still has nightmares. I've met many liars in my life, and I don't believe he is one of them. I immediately wrote the family living in the house and asked their permission to come. They agreed, but on two conditions."

"And what are those?"

"First, that we do what we can to make contact with the spirit and get her to leave. I'm no priest, but I've been asked for this type of thing before, and I can promise to try. And second—" He leaned toward me, and I could see the dark lashes around his eyes, the clean-shaven texture of his jaw. "Apparently the family believes, in hindsight, that allowing the vicar to come was a mistake. Because they now believe their ghost dislikes men. And so they will only allow a woman to see her."

As I stared at him, my jaw slightly fallen, he finished the last of his tea and looked out the window. "The rain has stopped. Perhaps we can take a walk, and I will explain the rest."

The rain had indeed stopped, though the streets were grimy and dull as we wound our way along Berwick Street. It was near suppertime, and the faces that passed us looked drawn and hurried, bleached by the rain. Mr. Gellis had paid the bill at the coffeehouse, tossing the coins on the table without counting them. Now he shoved his hands in the pockets of his coat and resumed his story.

"The ghost in Waringstoke is female," he explained. "She was, apparently, a servant girl who worked for the family. She hanged herself in the barn at the age of nineteen."

"How sad."

"Yes. According to the vicar she was a strange girl, somewhat off in the head. She rarely left the house. Mrs. Clare—that is the lady of the house—told me the girl was afraid of men, and found their presence upsetting. She had not thought the girl's ghost would take the same exception—who would be able to predict such a thing? In any case, she will not agree to another man in the barn, where the haunting is based. She is most adamant on this point. And if I want to document this ghost before anyone else does, I have to agree."

"This is completely strange to me," I said. "But perhaps you deal with this kind of situation all the time."

"Not at all. It's downright crazy. Mrs. Clare could be lying, or as off her head as her maid supposedly was. But the haunting is on private property, and I have to see it. What can one do?"

I bit my lip. "And so I come in."

"I suppose it's daunting."

"What if—" It felt strange even saying the words aloud, as if concern over a ghost were an everyday event. "What if she attacks me the way she did the vicar? What if I'm in danger?"

He frowned and ran a hand through his hair. "Well, I suppose I don't really have an answer for that. Are you afraid she'll throw things at you?"

"I don't know. It sounds silly to be afraid of having a few things thrown at me. What if she truly intends to hurt me?"

"It's unlikely you'll be in any real danger." He was looking down as we walked, thinking. "It sounds like what the vicar experienced was closer to a temper tantrum than a true attack. I've seen poltergeists behave that way. It's more like an expulsion of energy than true malice." He shrugged, the movement rolling in time with his easy gait, and glanced at me. "I suppose I can't guarantee anything, though. This is the paranormal, after all. You will have to be prepared to take the risk."

We wound our way into a small square lined with trees. I noticed he had a slight favor to his left leg as he walked. We were only four years from the end of the Great War, and Mr. Gellis was in his twenties. For all of my adult life I had lived in a world of men with injuries; only old men and boys were unscarred in the London of those days. It seemed that being a rich, charming eccentric had not excluded Mr. Gellis from seeing battle like everyone else. I let this settle in, let it alter my opinion of him. I did not ask him, of course—one simply did not. But as the corner of his mouth turned down and his face set with creeping pain, Mr. Gellis did not seem like a gentle eccentric at all.

I stopped walking, and he followed suit. I stood where I was for a long time, my hands in the pockets of my thin raincoat, feeling waves of chills come over me, rippling from the crown of my head to the pit of my stomach. We had all gone through so much death in our lives. This was a real girl, a real suicide, and—possibly—a real ghost he was asking me to see.

"I don't think I can do it," I said.

He turned to face me. "Miss Piper," he said softly. "Do not be afraid."

"If it isn't a hoax, if it's true, you are asking me to—to see a dead thing." Even to my own ears, my voice quavered.

He looked away from me and up to the sky. We were surrounded by small and undoubtedly expensive town houses, their walks behind low black iron fences. The noise of the city receded here. Overhead, the clouds refused to disperse; they hung like a low, dark ceiling, swirling in the sky. The trees rustled wetly in the breeze. Somewhere, a lone bird gave a cry and was quiet.

"I have seen many ghosts," Mr. Gellis said finally. "It is so hard to explain. We're frightened of them, but most of them are simply—lost."

I stared blankly at the houses. My father and mother came unbidden into my mind. I was sick to my stomach, humiliated to find myself near tears. It seemed I suddenly couldn't control my emotions. "The dead should stay dead," I said. I pushed my parents away. "Death is not a lark, or a hobby."

"Miss Piper." His voice was warm, resonant. "Look at me."

I raised my gaze to his. He was standing squarely before me, his hands in his pockets, the wet wind gently ruffling his hair. The humor from the coffeehouse had long gone and his face was still grim. "Do you think I do not know what death is?"

I thought of his limp, and was ashamed.

"I will be there," he went on. "You won't be alone. We will work as a team. I know we have not met before today, but you are the right person for this. I know you are. You know you are."

I could have wept. I could not remember the last time anyone had spoken to me with care, or kindness. I had walked the streets of this city, unseen and unnoticed. I had flitted in and out of jobs for a week at a time. I had no friends, no relatives, no men to notice me. I should say no; it was dangerous. And yet, now that I'd met him, the thought of going back to my flat, living my life, was intolerable. I wanted to be where he was.

I blinked back my tears and took a breath. I would have to take the risk, as he said. I could do it.

"When do I start?" I asked.

Chapter Three

Three days later, we began the drive to Waringstoke. The June weather had turned clear and crisp, with a breath of warmth in the air. Sunlight glinted off the windows of London's buildings and the chrome of the motorcars in the streets. In my tiny room, the sun penetrated only far enough to highlight the dusty streaks on the windows and the mildew darkening behind the wallpaper of my kitchen.

I packed most of my clothes in a small valise, leaving behind only my shabbiest items, whose seams could not be mended yet again and whose stains would not come out. I wore my best skirt, carefully brushed the evening before, and the newest blouse I owned. I could not help the condition of my coat, but Mr. Gellis had already seen it. It would have to do, as it was my only one.

Mr. Gellis estimated we would be gone a week; he said I did not need to bring anything but my belongings, but I felt the need to spend a few of my remaining coins on a crisp notebook and a new pen. I felt more of an assistant if I was prepared to actually work. I put the notebook and pen in my handbag, on top of my other items, and I felt better, like a professional woman on her way to a job.

I took a last look around my flat before I closed the door behind me. There were the gummy tiles on the floor, the sagging sofa—and, beyond, the tiny bed, made neatly with its threadbare and mismatched sheets. I had spent many hours alone here, looking out the window and pretending to read a book, or simply sleeping. I was tempted to feel excitement now, as if I would come back a different person—a new person. Perhaps, my excitement whispered, I would not be back at all. But of course, it was foolishness. I would be back in a week, looking out the window at the world as I always had.

Mr. Gellis owned his own motorcar. I had thought we would take a train; I had almost never sat in a motorcar in my life, and certainly I had never seen one as fine as his. I hardly dared to touch the clean, soft leather upholstery in the passenger seat. There were no streaks on the windows here. I could see London as it disappeared before my eyes, as the road slid smoothly away from us. I dropped my gaze to the frayed cuff of my coat where my hands clenched in my lap and thought I must look pinched and shabby.

After our initial greeting, Mr. Gellis drove in silence, the sun catching highlights in his hair. He did not look at me for a long time; finally, he said, "Don't worry about it."

"I beg your pardon?"

"The motorcar," he said. "My father died in 'sixteen. I came home to quite a bit of money, as it turned out. No one expected it less than I."

Came home from the war, of course. I didn't know what to say, so I looked out the window.

"My books do sell a few copies, but I couldn't make a living if

I had to." He seemed in the mood to talk, with little input from me. "My father was in banking. I never had the urge to go into it myself, so I've no idea how he made so much money, I'm afraid. Still, I'm lucky. I'm not sure how well I would have done, trying to find an occupation." He flashed me a smile. "The only thing I've ever been truly interested in is ghosts."

"Why is that?" I turned back to him.

"Why ghosts, you mean?"

I shrugged. "I wonder how you came to be interested in something so morbid."

He was looking at the road ahead. He was quiet for a long moment, and I began to think he wouldn't answer. "Well, then," he said at last. "It started with an experience. These obsessions often do." He lifted one hand from the wheel, ran it through his hair, and replaced it. "I was sixteen. Away at boarding school. I was spending Christmas holidays with a friend of mine, named Frederick Wheeler." He shook his head. "Old Freddy—I wonder what happened to him. We were good friends at the time, the way boys are. He was a good chap. Had a lick of blond hair that came straight down over one eye, no matter how he slicked it—it drove him crazy. We wanted to keep our hair long, of course, because we thought it would attract girls."

He cut a glance at me and must have seen something in my face, because he gave me a warm, genuine smile. "Don't worry; this story doesn't end badly for Freddy, or me. Our unhappy ending was not having any girls notice us."

I felt myself smiling. "A fate worse than death."

"Truly." He had turned back to the road now. "I had been there a few days, knocking around the big drafty old house with Freddy and his parents. There wasn't much to do, but we managed to entertain ourselves. Skating on the pond, climbing the roof of the old folly, eating everything in sight—those kinds of things, you know. Well, one night something woke me—I was never sure what, but I had been dreaming about footsteps, stealthy shuffling ones, and I thought, as I was lying there, maybe I had really heard them. I thought perhaps Freddy was awake. So I got up and went down the hall, to Freddy's room."

He glanced at me again, perhaps to see if I was still listening. As if I could do anything but hang on every word of this story.

"Freddy's door was ajar," he continued, turning back to the road again. "I peeked in, thinking maybe he was asleep after all. And he was. He was asleep in his bed, and there was something standing at his bedside, staring down at him."

A small gasp escaped me. "No."

"Oh, yes. It was a figure—a person, I thought, but indistinct. It was standing there, motionless, and the head was tilted down. It was certainly facing him, and staring down at him."

"What did you do?"

"I stood there for a long time, frozen in my tracks. I couldn't breathe, I tell you—I was so startled. The thing wasn't moving; it didn't seem like it had seen me, or perhaps it didn't care. All it cared about was Freddy. It just stared at him, its hands at its sides. I could see its legs, so I thought it was male, unless it was a female wearing trousers.

"I didn't know what to do. I wanted to run more than anything, but what if the thing meant Freddy harm? Should I wake Freddy, tell him to run? Chase it away myself somehow? I was paralyzed with sheer cowardice. As I stood there—it must have been only seconds, though it didn't feel like it—the thing turned away and disappeared. It never looked at me, and I never saw its face. It just turned and was gone. I made my legs move and nearly stumbled back to my room.

"I lay awake the rest of the night, staring at the ceiling, sweating, jumping at every sound. It was years and years until dawn. By then I was half-convinced that the figure would come back, that I'd left Freddy to a horrible fate and we'd find him dead in his bed. But he came down to breakfast, well rested and right as rain."

"Did you tell him of your experience?"

"I couldn't. I was too ashamed. I was sure they'd think me delusional. No one seemed in the least perturbed. It started snowing that day, an awful wet-rain snow, and we had to stay inside. We banged around the house, and in one of the corridors I'd never seen before, I found a painting. It was a portrait of a young man, with floppy blond hair like Freddy's and a serious look on his face. Freddy said it was his older brother, who had died when he fell from the loft in the barn at the age of seventeen, three years before.

"Something about it reminded me of the figure, though I couldn't say what. And suddenly, I realized two things. First, I had seen Freddy's dead brother, watching over Freddy while he slept. And second, I wanted to know more. Where the ghost had come from, where it had gone, why it was here. What it could tell me. I was still terrified, but I was fascinated, too.

"That was the start of it. Not right away, of course. I finished school, though I snuck all the books I could find about ghosts. Then I went to France." He shrugged one eloquent shoulder as the corner of his mouth turned down. "I guess anyone would think I'd had enough of death over there. But what I do is different. It's difficult to explain. Besides, I didn't know what to do with myself after I came home. This is the only thing I want to do." He glanced at me again. "Well, now you know all about me, I suppose."

"Yes," I said.

"And what do you think?"

I bit my lip.

He turned back to the road, but he was smiling now. "Come, now, you can say it."

"It's just—" I shifted in my seat. "I can't help but wonder—you said you'd never seen the portrait before. But you'd been in the house for a week. What if you had seen it, and didn't remember? What if it was in your mind, the night you went to Freddy's room?"

"Ah, now." He tapped his fingers on the steering wheel. "I hadn't, but I can pretend along with you. Let's say I had. I didn't know who it was. That much was certain. Why would I see him in Freddy's room?"

"Easily. You said it looked like Freddy. It would be simple to assume the portrait was a family member. And if it were modern, that would be another clue. And you admit you never saw the apparition's face."

"So my unconscious mind manufactured the entire thing?"

I suddenly realized what I was saying, and pressed my hand to my mouth. What had gotten into me? This was the first job I'd had in weeks, and Mr. Gellis was nothing but kind. How could I let my tongue run away and insult his experience? He could fire me on the spot and turn the car around anytime he wanted. "I'm sorry. I truly am. I am truly thoughtless. I know nothing about it, of course."

But he laughed. "It's perfectly all right. You're doing just fine, Miss Piper. I find it useful to have someone challenge the appearance of things, especially on a sighting expedition. I'm used to Matthew filling the role."

I recalled the assistant I was replacing, the man with the neat handwriting. "So he is a skeptic, then?"

Mr. Gellis laughed again. "I'm not sure exactly what Matthew is, but if I figure it out, I'll be sure to let you know."

I didn't know what to make of that, so I said, "Still, I should hold my tongue."

"Your point is taken," said Mr. Gellis. "But, Miss Piper, I must insist. I know what I saw. I simply know. If you ever see an apparition, a true one, you will know what I mean."

⚬

We stopped at a pub in a small village at midday, where Mr. Gellis purchased us sandwiches and bottles of milk. We ate quickly, as we needed to get back on the road, Mr. Gellis said, to make Waringstoke by evening.

As we ate, I thought about what he had said, that pursuing ghosts was the only thing he wanted to do. He had the freedom to do anything he liked. If I could idly pursue anything I wished, what would it be? I couldn't think of anything.

"You seem pensive," he said as we finished. "Are you regretting our agreement?"

"No. I'm sorry," I said, standing and brushing the crumbs from my skirt. How selfish of me, to sit moping. "I'm not much used to company."

"Neither am I." He smiled at me. In fact he was so much more at ease than I that he could have been lying; but I sensed an awkwardness in him, deep beneath the surface, and I knew he told the truth. "Female company, especially. Men tend to lose their polish when they know only other men for company."

"You are doing perfectly," I said with truth, as we walked back to the motorcar. "It is I who need to remember my manners. Tell me, does Mr. Ryder share your passion for ghosts?"

"No one quite shares my passion for ghosts, Miss Piper." He handed me into the car and closed the door. He came around to the driver's seat and got in. "But Matthew is a valuable assistant. It isn't just the notebooks; he usually handles the logistics of trips like these. I'm hopeless with maps. He handles the technical equipment as well."

I sat up straighter. "Technical equipment?"

"The camera. The film. We try to document each manifestation, though photographing a ghost is nearly impossible. Did you know that?"

"I can imagine, I suppose."

"Still, we try. Matthew is good with a camera. He also runs the sound recorder."

I stared at him. "Sound recorder?" I had never seen such a thing; I would have no idea how to use it. I felt the chill of true alarm. As it was, I would bumble the camera badly enough.

Mr. Gellis smiled. "It's a massive contraption—cost me an arm and a leg. I had it specially made. I've no idea how it works, really. Matthew knows. He took it apart and put it back together again the first day I got it. I don't think I've ever seen him so excited."

"Mr. Gellis, I really—I don't—"

"Please, don't worry." He took one hand from the wheel and waved it at me. "I've no expectation that you would know how to work it. Matthew taught me enough that I can make it function, at least rudimentarily for this one assignment. I can show you how to turn it on and off—since you will be the one trying to record the Falmouth House ghost, not me. Though the equipment hasn't mattered very much so far." He sighed. "As much as I would like to record an actual haunting, we have never yet succeeded. All I've ever recorded on that thing is static, the sound of wind, and my own voice."

"Perhaps this will be the time," I said.

He laughed at that. "Don't let Matthew hear you say so. He did not want to miss this assignment at all—if you record a haunting your first week on the job, he may have to strangle you."

"Have you known Mr. Ryder long?" I asked.

He cut me a look. "You are asking a lot of questions about him, you know."

I smiled and shook my head. "It's just that different pictures are going through my head. A young man, or an old man? Fat or skinny?"

"He is my age—nearly two years younger. Neither fat nor skinny, I suppose. And yes, he is very interested in ghosts. Though I think perhaps for different reasons than I."

I had no time to ask him to explain this, as he began to tell me some of his experiences in hunting ghosts. He was an excellent storyteller; he had a talent for building his tale, giving just enough detail and leaving just enough suspense to keep his audience interested. I leaned back in my seat and listened, thinking that I must ask him, sometime, if he had copies of his books for me to read. He was probably a skilled writer.

The stories themselves were terribly sad. A child killed in a carriage accident; a young man disappeared in the marshes, whose body was never found; an old woman, haunting her last residence, enacting the same simple tasks she had performed when alive, over and over, as if unaware she was dead. Most ghost stories, it seemed as I listened, were tales not only of death but also of unfathomable misery and despair. Happy people did not leave ghosts; or perhaps they left quiet ghosts, who sat in their favorite corners or wandered the banks of their favorite streams, never bothering the living. It was deeply strange to listen to such chilling tales of hopelessness and pain as I sat in my comfortable passenger seat, watching the perfect English day begin to recede into a warm, glowing English sunset.

"Are you never frightened?" I asked him, as the sun sank below the horizon and dusk began to envelop us.

"No," he said, his expression honest. "Ghosts, Miss Piper, are frightening at first—they are, after all, our dead. But ghosts are helpless. They can touch physical things—slam doors, break crockery, turn taps on and off. There was even a ghost I visited who pulled the bedcovers from the beds during the night, while the living were sleeping—as terrifying an experience as you can imagine. But they are trapped, performing the same acts over and over, unable to think or communicate. Do they have true awareness? Did Freddy's brother choose to be there, or was his spirit ruled by base, inescapable compulsion? Are they imprints left behind of those who have gone—like a shadow, or an echo? The answer to that question is what has driven me for five years. If a ghost exists that possesses awareness, I want to meet it."

"And you think you will meet such a thing at Falmouth House," I said.

He smiled. "I hope, Miss Piper—I always hope. But I do not make conclusions until I see the proof. And speak of the devil—we are approaching Waringstoke even now."

C&

I could see very little of Waringstoke through the twilight: a few small houses, a church and churchyard. The road we traveled now was rutted and narrow. I saw no evidence of other motorcars, or any other type of vehicle. The few houses were old, set well back from the main road on winding drives; they were small, wood and stone, well maintained, with warm yellow light in the windows. We were in a very old part of England, though not a rich one. It was a great contrast to London, with its metal and glass. Beyond the small village I could see rolling fields, green hills, and dense woods.

At length Mr. Gellis stopped the car. He came around and opened my door for me. I stepped out, stifling a groan as my legs cramped from the long drive. I stood in the sudden fall of silence and looked about me.

We were in the courtyard of a small inn; I could see a swan on the sign over the door, though I could not read the scripted writing in the dark. The inn stood two stories, one lumped atop the other, with sloping gables and mullioned windows from which dim light winked. I felt gravel through the thin soles of my shoes. The silence was absolute; not a sound could be heard but the faint rush of a breeze in the treetops and the faraway cry of a bird. After the noise of London, then the rumble of the motorcar all day, my ears were ringing, and as the darkening gloom settled over the landscape and the wind hushed through the far-off trees, it seemed eerie to me, as if the world had ended and all humanity had disappeared.

I turned to see Mr. Gellis looking at me. There was an expression of good humor on his face, mixed with a keen observance that I was learning to find familiar. "Lovely spot, isn't it?" he said.

The wind touched my hair, and I pushed a few stray locks from my forehead. "I don't know. I've never been in the country."

His eyebrows went up. "Never?"

I shook my head. "I was raised in Brixton. I live in the city now."

"A city girl," he said, opening the boot of the motorcar and removing our bags. "Never to the seaside on holiday? Never to a cousin's house on school break?"

I shook my head again.

"Well, then, I suppose this will be good for you." He closed the boot, and I paid silent tribute to his tact in not mentioning my lack of family and friends. "Fresh air, and all that. What is it they say? It will put some color in your cheeks?"

"Mr. Gellis." A man came toward us from the inn, tugging on an overcoat and a gray cloth cap.

"Yes," said Mr. Gellis. "You must be Mr. Ahearn."

The man nodded, but did not smile. "Yes, sir. You may leave the bags there. I have a boy who will bring them upstairs for you."

Inside, we passed the wide entrance to the taproom, which was beginning to fill. I caught a glimpse of low, dark wooden beams on the ceiling, heard a few chortles of male laughter and the clink of a glass. But I had no desire to go farther, and at a nod from Mr. Gellis I followed a maid up the stairs and to a small room, where my bags had been laid, and I could at last rest and freshen myself.

There was not much I could do. My blouse was hopelessly wrinkled, as was my skirt. My stockings needed rinsing, but I was not ready for bed just yet. I went to the small basin and splashed water on my face. In the cloudy mirror I did my best. I had my dark hair cut in a bob, as was the fashion of the time; and though, like most girls, I wished I could put my hair in pretty curls, styled close to my head, the way the movie stars did, I could not afford the style, the marcel iron, or the tins of gloss and packets of pins needed to maintain it. I also, in my low state of mind lately, could not bring myself to spend an hour a day on my hair, no matter how stylish I wished to look.

And so I had a simple bob, cropped below my earlobes. My hair was a chocolate brown color, nondescript, I thought, and it sat straight without much fuss, except when the breeze blew it into my eyes. On such occasions it was just long enough that I could tuck wayward strands behind my ears, if the wind was not too strong.

I combed a little water through my hair, trying to make it look fresh again. I had but a few cosmetics, dearly bought and sparsely used, so I did not use any now. My face would simply have to be good enough.

I was tired, and I briefly considered staying in my tiny room; but, looking around its sparse furniture, lit dimly by one shaky electric light in the corner, I changed my mind. The exhaustion in me fought with another emotion, a thrill of excitement that was unfamiliar to me. I wanted to know what came next. I needed direction from Mr. Gellis, anyway, as to what he would expect of me in the morning.

He was in the taproom. He had not, like me, gone to his room, and he was sipping a beer, making quiet notes in a notebook, his golden brown head bent to his work.

He smiled up at me when he saw me, a smile that was so easy and handsome it made my heart flutter in my chest. "There you are," he said. "Fresh as a daisy. Have a seat, and order some supper. We need to go over some details for tomorrow."

I sat. I had to admit I was very hungry, but pride still held me back. "This doesn't seem right, your paying for all of my meals. Shouldn't you insist I pay for myself?"

He lifted a brow. "Of course not. You are here on my assignment, as my employee. You're my responsibility. Besides, what kind of a gentleman lets a lady pay for her own supper?"

"I am a modern girl, you know." I felt myself smile. I could not quite believe he was flirting with me. Even less could I believe I was flirting back.

"So I've noticed." He smiled again. "You may be entirely too modern for Waringstoke. Everyone in the room has noticed you. I believe they expect you to begin smoking cigarettes and dancing on the tables at any moment."

I, too, had seen the glances from all the others in the taproom—the innkeeper, Mr. Ahearn, darting looks at us as he bustled about his business; the barkeep bending his head to whisper with his patrons as they talked in low voices; the glances from the men at tables in all corners of the room. But the tension had already been present when I entered, so it was foolish to think any of it was caused by me. "It isn't me they are looking at. It's you."

He leaned closer to me and spoke confidentially. "You must get used to it here. We're far from London, you know. This is a small community. Everyone knows everyone, and most know everyone's parents and grandparents as well. I've found that outsiders are not well received in most of the villages and towns I've been to in my line of work."

"I noticed the innkeeper was not particularly welcoming."

"Ah, you're perceptive, then. I did try to put a few questions to him while you were upstairs. I believe there's a statue of Wellington in my garden at home that is more forthcoming."

We were nearly whispering. I was listening closely, leaning forward. I caught sight of an aged man in a dark blue coat from the corner of my eye. He sat on a stool at the bar, tankard of beer in hand, and looked at me with an unmistakable expression of knowing disapproval. As I glanced at him, he met my gaze squarely and did not look away. I realized how it looked—Mr. Gellis and I, sitting intimately at our table, leaning toward each other. To any onlooker, we looked exactly like lovers. I reddened slightly and the man in the blue coat changed his expression to a sort of small, petty triumph. I looked away.

Mr. Gellis leaned back in his chair and signaled to someone behind me. A waiter—the bar's only one—approached and Mr. Gellis ordered my supper for me along with his own, with hardly a look in my direction. Beef, potatoes, stewed vegetables. As the waiter disappeared, Mr. Gellis looked at me a little apologetically.

"I realize we just agreed that you're modern," he said, "but it doesn't hurt to appear a little old-fashioned here."

As my surprise faded, I supposed I could see his point. Ordering my meal for me had been a display, meant for everyone but him and me. Still, I had been living by myself for some time and I wasn't used to having a man do anything for me. "I understand— but if you're going to make it a habit, I'll have to protest."

He smiled at me, easy again. "Clever girl. Now, let's go over our plans for tomorrow."

We spent the next hour or so talking of what would happen the next day. My supper arrived, and though it was the largest portion of food I had ever seen, I found I was hungry enough to make respectable work of it, causing Mr. Gellis to tease me about the effects of "fresh country air." He even persuaded me to have a small glass of beer. Our plans were relatively simple: Mr. Gellis had already sent a message to Falmouth House, and received a reply that we were expected tomorrow morning. We would interview Mrs. Clare and the old housekeeper about their deceased servant, Maddy. And then, if all went well, I would take the camera and recording equipment, go to the haunted barn, and see if Maddy would show herself.

The prospect was so strange, so unlike any job I had ever thought to have, that I could hardly fathom it. The excitement I had felt on leaving my flat possessed me again, mixed with not a little fear. At some moments it seemed as if ghost viewing would be like a scary parlor game, creating a chill but still merely amusing. At other times I remembered that I would be in the presence, supposedly, of someone from beyond the grave.

And in the back of my mind, worry scrabbled. What if I saw nothing? What if there was nothing to see? I'd be sent home, and this all would be over. Could I really be hoping to see a ghost?

Mr. Gellis and I made a continued stir by sitting so long at our table. I should be embarrassed; everyone, by now, must assume we were a couple. And yet I could not feel as I was supposed to. I had to admit a shallow trickle of selfish pride, that anyone would think a man as handsome and obviously blessed as Mr. Gellis would choose me for a partner. So what if he had found me at random through a temporary agency? So what if he thought of me as nothing but a simple employee? No one in the room knew that, at least not yet. And besides, did stranger things not happen every day? Was it such a complete impossibility, given how closely we were to work together? I was unattached, and Mr. Gellis wore no ring, and mentioned no wife. But this was getting ahead of myself. I made myself put such thoughts away.

But later, as I climbed the steps to my room, exhausted, I admit that for the first time in years—perhaps since my parents had died—I abandoned good sense and let silly, girlish fantasies take full rein in my mind. He seemed to like me, and we would be alone together very much, after all. When I look back on it, it is amazing that such silly, frivolous ideas were foremost in my thoughts. I wasn't a normal girl, but I was a girl, after all; and I would spin pretty romantic stories, for the last time, unaware of the hell that was about to descend upon me.

Chapter Four

*T*he next morning dawned dreary and wet; the sun disappeared. From the window of my room I saw a thin mist clinging to the ground, damp and silent. It seemed appropriate weather for ghost hunting.

I dressed quickly—despite the wet weather, the room in this tiny inn was cozy, and my stockings had already dried—and went downstairs to the taproom. I did not see Mr. Gellis. The innkeeper, Mr. Ahearn, approached me with a cup of tea.

"Morning." He nodded curtly. "Your fellow's already been. He's out front."

"Thank you." I would have preferred coffee, but I did not want to argue. I drank the tea as quickly as I could, and found my way to the front vestibule, where I took a moment to take my coat from over my arm and slide it on. I also put on my favorite dark brown felt hat.

I tugged the hat down over my ears and paused. Through the pane on the front door I could see Mr. Gellis, standing in the courtyard, the large suitcase that signaled the recording equipment on the ground at his feet. He wore his olive green coat, his hands shoved in the pockets, as he had looked the day we met. And he was talking to a woman.

She was tall and stylish, with the slim figure and long, slender legs that were the raging fashion of the time. She wore an expensive wrap, a perfectly vogue hat on her head, and looped in one slender hand was the lead of a small dog, who sat patiently by her ankles. As I watched, she handed Mr. Gellis a cigarette, then leaned forward to light it for him; her eyes, as they met his, were alight with intimate humor. She straightened and lit a cigarette for herself, still looking steadily at Mr. Gellis.

I felt my stomach twist, but I knew the innkeeper was watching me, so I could not stand there forever. I pulled on my gloves and stumbled out the front door to the courtyard.

Mr. Gellis turned as I approached. He had put on a cloth cap in the wet weather, and it only served to emphasize the squareness of his jaw, and the perfect set of his dark-lashed gray eyes under the brim. "Ah. Miss Piper."

"Good morning," I managed.

There was a brief, awkward pause. Mr. Gellis turned back to the woman, and for the first time he did not seem at ease. "This is my assistant," he said.

I blinked, stung, but did not move. I felt the warmth of my cheeks against the mist in the air, and hoped the low brim of my hat would hide the miserable look I knew was on my face. The woman regarded me with calm, and I saw she had a face that was nothing short of ravishing, her skin flawless white, her lips lush and beautiful, and her eyes heavy-lidded with the sort of sensuality Greta Garbo exuded, a world-weary, carnal knowingness that attracted men like flies. The dark hair visible from under the hat was crisply marcelled and complemented her creamy complexion. She held herself with careless confidence, her shoulders down, one hand lightly placed in the pocket of her wrap, so one could see the delicate suede cuff of her glove against the perfect whiteness of her wrist as it disappeared into her sleeve. Her other hand held the dog's leash and the newly lit cigarette. She gave me a desultory smile.

"I see," she said, speaking not to me but to Mr. Gellis. "I didn't know ghost hunters had assistants."

Was she making fun of him? Of us? With her dry tone, it was impossible to tell. Mr. Gellis looked at her and looked away. "In this case, yes. Miss Piper, this is Mrs. Barry—one of the local residents."

"How do you do," the lady said smoothly.

I had interrupted something; I could feel it. Mr. Gellis stared out into the drizzling rain, his body hunched with tension, his cigarette clutched between the curled second and third knuckles of his hand. I had not known he smoked. He certainly had not smoked at all during our long trip yesterday. It seemed I had not known anything. I looked at Mrs. Barry and thought of my stupid fantasies of the night before, and knew that in a world with such women, girls like me simply did not exist. I had always known it—why had I forgotten? I would never be such an idiot again.

I found my voice. "I didn't—I wasn't aware that you knew the residents here."

Mr. Gellis did not turn his head, so Mrs. Barry answered me herself. "It is purest luck," she said, tugging the leash gently as her little dog tried to walk away. "We met many years ago. Before the war." She turned to Alistair. "New Year's in 'fourteen, was it not?"

Her tone was airy, but I saw her take him in, her eyes traveling his shoulders and the line of his profile, and I knew she knew the answer very well.

"Yes," he said, giving her only the briefest of glances before looking away again. "New Year's in 'fourteen."

"And not again until I passed by this morning. Imagine my surprise." She turned back to me, took a slow drag on her cigarette, and gave a smile with the corner of her flawless lip. "Life has such strange coincidences, doesn't it?"

Some sort of wrenching unhappiness flashed across Mr. Gellis' face. He buried it quickly before turning back to us, but I had not missed it. "We should be on our way," he said.

"I wish you both luck," Mrs. Barry said, her tone almost as neutral as if she were talking to the postman. "It's nice to see you again, Alistair."

He nodded and walked away, plunging ahead into the mist as if setting off to sea. I hurried to keep up with him. Mrs. Barry soon disappeared in the white threads behind us.

My misery was acute. I tried an awkward attempt to cover it. "I thought you said the locals would not be friendly," I said, my voice a rasp.

He was quiet for a long moment as we walked, the wet mist creating damp goose bumps on my shins through my stockings. Finally he dropped his cigarette and looked at me, surprised, as if he had forgotten I was there. "Pardon? What's that?"

I looked away. "Nothing," I said. "Nothing at all."

☙

Falmouth House loomed in the fog before us soon enough. It stood in a small hollow, as if cupped in the palm of a hand, surrounded by tall oaks and a few poplar trees that broke upward out of the mist. It was white clapboard from the past century, its shutters painted glossy black. I noticed, as we approached more closely, that the heavy water in the air condensed and rolled down the lacquered shutters, as if they were weeping.

I was struck again by the deep quiet of the countryside, the absence of any human sounds; my mind still expected the clamor of cars, voices, all the clatter of nonstop human movement. Here was only the hushed patter of the drizzle, the call of birds in far-away trees. The air was impossibly sweet, like wine. A crow called from somewhere, its voice dark and throaty.

We ascended uneven steps to a stone porch and Mr. Gellis set down the suitcase containing the sound equipment. He looked at me briefly. "You must let me do the talking. I have experience with these situations."

"Of course," I said.

He knocked on the door, and we waited. I looked up at the house rising above me. It was not tall, two stories only, and it had no ostentation. It was a modest, faintly run-down house of white-washed wood, the house that a long-ago farmer who had begun to prosper would aspire to.

I could not see the barn from where we stood.

The door opened and a woman met us—sixtyish, with wiry curled hair pulled strictly back and the complexion of her nose and cheeks splashed with red, as if the skin was irritated. She gave us a brave smile. "You must be Mr. Gellis, sir."

"I am," said Mr. Gellis.

"I'm Mrs. Macready, the housekeeper," she said. "Please come in."

She showed us into a small sitting room off the front hall. Mr. Gellis introduced me, and set down his suitcase again.

Mrs. Macready said she would send in Mrs. Clare, the lady of the house, and she left the room.

Again we waited, in the small sitting room this time. Neither of us sat. An unlit fireplace did nothing to alleviate the damp chill. I looked at the cheap print of a gaudy pastoral scene over the mantelpiece and did not look at Mr. Gellis. The quiet stretched until Mrs. Clare came.

She was older than Mrs. Macready: over sixty, I thought, or perhaps even seventy years of age. She was very small—slightly built, for certain, but also painfully thin, as if she had been ill. Her eyes, large and vivid blue even in her advanced years, were sunk slightly in her skull. She wore a modest blue wool dress that matched the color of her eyes and contrasted smartly with the white of her hair. She had her hands folded primly in front of her. "Good morning, Mr. Gellis."

Mr. Gellis introduced me yet again, and Mrs. Clare turned her bright blue gaze in my direction. "Ah," she said softly. "You are the girl, then."

I nodded. I knew what she meant, of course; she had told Mr. Gellis he could not come to Falmouth House unless he brought a woman with him, and so I was an object of some interest to her.

"Are you an assistant?" asked Mrs. Clare.

"She is," said Mr. Gellis before I could speak, and I remembered he wanted me to say as little as possible. I nodded at Mrs. Clare in agreement.

Mrs. Clare looked from me to Mr. Gellis and back again. "Have you experience in this line of work?" she asked me.

"She hasn't much," said Mr. Gellis, again before I could answer. "But I have filled her in on the details."

Mrs. Clare's gaze passed between us again, and this time I

could see a glimmer of distaste. She seemed to straighten. "Let us sit, then," she said. "We haven't much time."

I followed Mrs. Clare's lead and sat on the thin, uncomfortable sofa. Mr. Gellis chose a chair in the corner. He removed his cap and leaned forward, his forearms propped on his knees. "What do you mean, we haven't much time?"

Mrs. Clare sat on the opposite end of the sofa from me and gave a quick sigh. "We are in Falmouth House, Mr. Gellis, and you are of the male sex. I believe I have explained why this is a problem."

"I thought your manifestation only haunted the barn."

"Maddy is not a *manifestation*." Mrs. Clare seemed to find the word insulting. "She is a spirit, as I have much occasion to know. And yes, she stays in the barn, but she has an awareness of what goes on in the house as well. A man in the house will upset her. It's best if we conclude our meeting and you return to your inn before she discovers you've been here."

"What does she do when she's upset?"

Mrs. Clare looked out the window at the dripping trees. "She can make things very unpleasant. In a variety of ways, I suppose. She gets—agitated." She looked at us again. "That is not what I wish to discuss right now, however. We have other ground to cover."

"Certainly," said Mr. Gellis. His voice was gentle, but I sensed he was not exactly agreeing to leave the topic alone. "What is it you wish to discuss?"

Mrs. Clare looked at him squarely. "After you contacted me with your inquiry, I researched you, Mr. Gellis. I read your books. They gave the impression that you are a man of some intelligence and compassion, instead of a thrill seeker. That is one of the two reasons I agreed to this meeting at all. I expect discretion. I don't want Maddy turned into an object of public curiosity, or a tourist attraction. She is nothing of the kind. She would hate it, and—this may sound strange to you—she does not deserve it. You cannot imagine exactly how difficult a life she led. I want her to have a measure of peace."

"You are protective of her." Mr. Gellis could not keep the surprise from his voice.

Mrs. Clare smiled thinly. "Perhaps it's strange to you. But then, Mr. Gellis, for all your experience, you have not seen a situation like ours. You have not seen a spirit like Maddy's before. Alive, she came to us as a stray—she appeared on our doorstep one rainy night, injured and unable to speak. She had been abused beyond any sort of average comprehension. My husband and I took her in. I tried to heal her for seven years." Mrs. Clare looked down at the hands clenched in her lap. "I tried my best, as did Mrs. Macready. But we failed. Perhaps success was not even possible. I will never know that. And since she died, Maddy has only gotten—worse."

Mr. Gellis had pulled a small notebook and pencil from his coat pocket and was writing. "You mentioned your husband, Mrs. Clare. May I speak with him as well?"

"He passed on in 'fifteen, the year after Maddy came to us. Our only son died long ago. There is only Mrs. Macready and me."

"I see." Mr. Gellis made a note. "And what was the second reason?"

"I beg your pardon?"

He looked up at her. "You said there are two reasons you allowed me to come. One was the impression you received from my books. What is the other?"

Mrs. Clare turned her gaze to me, then back to Mr. Gellis.

Her eyes, behind their brittle dignity, were tired and sad. "The other reason is that I've come to realize we need help here. Rather desperately so, I'm afraid. I cannot stand it anymore. My health has suffered. I don't know how it's done—whether you can banish her, or simply persuade her, or even if it's possible—but Maddy has to leave. She has to go. I want your young lady to do something about it."

My cheeks prickled as all attention in the room turned to me. I stayed silent.

"Miss Piper does not have experience with that sort of thing," said Mr. Gellis with a frown.

"I can't imagine it takes any sort of training." Mrs. Clare's tone was haughty. "Simply ask her, or tell her, to leave. Over as many visits as it takes."

"It may not be possible," he protested.

"It is not optional, I'm afraid, sir. Unless Maddy is gone by the time you leave, you do not have permission to publish your findings."

Mr. Gellis' expression, normally so easy and handsome, was bemused and even a little angry. "That's unheard of. I can't guarantee that kind of thing. I do not have control over the supernatural."

The request made sense to me; if Mrs. Clare wanted privacy and discretion, yet she had invited someone here who intended to put Maddy in a book, it only followed that she expected that Maddy would be gone by the time the book was published, or it would not be published at all. But I kept silent.

"That is just as well, sir, as you will not be in contact with Maddy anyway. Your assistant will be." Mrs. Clare turned to me. "I have begged her to leave, of course. So has Mrs. Macready. But she doesn't listen to us. I'm not certain she knows we're here. That's why we called in the vicar, and we all know what a disaster that was. I feel so terribly sorry for her—but I've done all I can. She needs to go. Do you understand?"

I pressed my knees together. "I understand," I whispered.

Mr. Gellis looked from Mrs. Clare to me, and back again. "I still have a great many questions about this manifestation. I need details. How often she appears, what she does. There may be a pattern. And I need to know more about what she was like in life."

"You'll have all of that, Mr. Gellis. But your assistant should see Maddy first." Mrs. Clare closed her eyes briefly, as if tired, and opened them again. "It will be so much easier if she has simply seen her. You must go back to the inn and leave your assistant here. I will send her to you when she is finished."

Mr. Gellis stood, obviously reluctant to be banished to the sidelines. "I'd like an interview with both yourself and Mrs. Macready. They will be separate, and quite lengthy. I would like your promise on this before I go."

Her mouth pursed, but she nodded. "Very well. Tomorrow. I will make sure Mrs. Macready is apprised. Now, please—you must go before she notices you."

Mr. Gellis looked at me with a question in his eyes. I nodded at him; I was so terrified, I could not rise from the wretched sofa, but I would not let him see it. I was as ready as I would ever be.

"Send her to me, then," he said, and he left the room.

Chapter Five

Mr. Gellis had prepared me for the use of the sound recorder on the previous evening. He assured me he would take care of the technical preparations, including the winding of wire on the two large reels, and its threading through the complex parts between. We had opened the suitcase and he had shown me what to do, his agile hands pointing out the interlocking pieces, and the activation switch I would need to move from OFF to ON. The machine ran on a battery that lasted some twenty minutes—not long, Mr. Gellis said, because the battery had to be made small enough for the machine to be portable. My instructions were to place the recorder in the center of the barn, turn it on, and attempt to draw the ghost as close to the machine as possible in my twenty-minute span.

I had received similar instructions for the camera. I had seen cameras, of course, though I had never owned one. Again Mr. Gellis patiently explained the workings of it. He himself took the idea of capturing the ghost with some cynicism; he had never succeeded in doing so, mostly because of the limitations of the technology. The camera required a large amount of light to take a photograph, light that was rarely available in the dim houses he had investigated. Ghosts were inevitably chased away by the flashes required to get a proper picture, and in any case the bright illumination of the flash would wash out, in his opinion, any delicate ghostly image that was present in the first place. It was his frustration with the camera that had led to his commission and purchase of the special sound equipment, at great cost. He was very excited about the possibilities of capturing his ghosts by sound.

I picked up all this technology—the camera on a loop of cloth about my neck, the recording machine in its suitcase—and stood. I was trembling with fear, but there was nothing for it. I had been hired for this one task, after all, and there was nowhere to go but forward.

But Mrs. Clare stood and looked only at me. Mrs. Macready came back into the room, and the two women stood together. Now that Mr. Gellis had gone, neither seemed in much of a hurry. And now I was ready to go, my courage screwed up as high as it would ever be.

Mrs. Clare's gaze traveled me up and down, cool and assessing and, I thought, not entirely disapproving. "My dear, I hope you are more intelligent than your employer makes you out to be. You look perfectly terrified."

I said nothing.

"She should be there," said Mrs. Macready. "Sometimes she's quiet, but not these days. I heard her in there yesterday. I've removed the lock from the door."

"You heard her?" I said. "Do you not go in?"

The housekeeper looked pained, with a deep, heartfelt grief. "I can't bear it," she said simply.

"Don't judge her too harshly," said Mrs. Clare, and it took me a moment to realize that she spoke of the ghostly Maddy, not Mrs. Macready. "She may try to frighten you—play tricks. She likes to do that. She doesn't mean anything by it. If you knew her in life, you would understand how truly harmless she is."

"You defend her, and yet you wish to be rid of her," I said.

A look crossed Mrs. Clare's eyes that mirrored the grief on her housekeeper's face. "Come to me after you've been in the barn," she said. "Perhaps then you'll understand."

The barn was only a small distance behind the house, down a rough-worn path. The mist had not dissipated; it curled around my ankles and calves as I walked, and I was glad I had kept on my coat and hat against the chill. There was no sound but the scratch of my footsteps and the dripping of water from the trees. I longed to hear even a single birdsong, but none came.

The building itself was just large enough for a few horses, now long gone, and the food and other necessities to keep them. It was well built, snug, and tidily painted, placed against a backdrop of trees like a piece of jewelry in a silk setting. I realized I had been expecting a run-down, ancient structure, listing perhaps, in keeping with a space that was supposed to be haunted.

I stopped before the big wooden double door and listened, but all was silent. I pushed the heavy arm up from its latch, opened the door, and stepped in.

It was as if I had stepped into an entirely different building.

I looked around in wonder. In contrast to the tidy exterior, a hurricane of destruction had come through here. The stalls for the horses had been all but destroyed, burst apart and flattened close to the ground, their doors leaning crazily from their remaining hinges. Some powerful force had touched nearly everything, exploded bales of hay, torn slats from the half wall separating the storage area from the barn proper; tackle lay flung about the floor, some of the heavy leather ripped to pieces. Dim, gray light came through the high windows; it did little to illuminate the ruined interior, creating only dark blue shadows and looming shapes. The silence in the barn was utterly deadening, so quiet I imagined I could hear my blood beat and a ringing in my ears.

I looked about, a little wildly, imagining movement from the corner of my eye. I could see nothing. I closed the door behind me, shutting out the wet outdoor light, and took a tentative step forward, then another. No sound; nothing moved. There was only the damp smell of old horses, mixed with a strange metallic scent. I did not have the courage to wonder what the metallic smell was.

Suggestive power, I thought bravely to myself, thinking of Mr. Gellis and the portrait. *They have told you this place is haunted, and so you will believe it so.*

My knees were trembling, but I made my way forward, into what I estimated was the center of the barn. My footsteps sounded loud on the soft earth floor. I set down the suitcase and, with shaking hands, opened it and set up the recorder. *Suggestive power,* I thought again to myself. But I would not let myself think that if there was no ghost to record, Mr. Gellis would send me back to London and my adventure would be over.

I turned the switch to ON with a sound that echoed in the stillness.

Something moved behind me.

I whirled. There was only the gloom, and the door of the barn, now seeming miles away. I wondered how long it would take me to run to it.

There was another movement, glimpsed this time from the corner of my right eye; again, I turned, and again, I saw nothing. The hat I wore was of the day's style, with a low brim pulled close around the face, like a bell; I felt a stir of panic that I could not see properly from my peripheral vision. I quickly pulled off the hat and set it on the floor next to the recorder.

I pushed strands of wayward hair from my face and looked around again. It was warm in the barn; whether unnaturally so, or whether I imagined it in my panic, I could not tell. I shakily raised the camera and placed my finger on the button.

Did something move? What was the creaking sound I heard, faintly over the ringing in my ears? Why was a clammy sweat forming on my skin? Why could I not breathe? The tension snapped in me and I took more steps forward, toward the ruined stalls, unable to bear it. "Hello?" my voice croaked into the stillness. "Hello?"

I heard the creaking sound again; this time, I saw the source. One of the stall doors dangled from a half-ruined hinge, suspended from the upended timber of the destroyed frame. As I watched, the door began to sway, deliberately—forward, and back, and forward again. There was not a breath of air to stir it.

This, then, was the Falmouth House ghost at last. I stumbled forward a few more steps, toward the swinging door. I raised the camera and clicked it blindly, unable to think in my panic of what the lens might see. The door continued to move, forward, back, forward, back again.

It began a sort of mesmerized panic in me, the rhythm of that swinging door; I stared at it, unable to look away. I was still terrified, and yet I was strangely soothed—perhaps a little like a rabbit looking into the eyes of its predator. My heart beat wildly in my chest. And yet I stepped closer, crouched lower for another angle, wound the film, raised the camera, and clicked the shutter again. A swinging door, after all—isn't that what one would expect at a haunting? It was not so outrageous a thing to see. I would document it. If the photographs did not show anything, then the creaking of the door must surely be audible on the recorder. Mr. Gellis would—

There was another sound, behind me and to the right. The door stilled. I froze. The sound was coming from the direction of the window, and it was strangely familiar. I could not turn my head; I only stood paralyzed, watching the door as it slowly swung to a halt.

Thump-thump. Thump-thump. A familiar sound, but my brain was too wild to place it. It grew louder. I couldn't breathe. As I gasped silently for air, I realized the metallic smell had grown stronger. And I began to shake with terror as I finally recognized the sound.

Heels, barefoot, kicking against the wall. Something sat in the sill of the high window, and kicked its heels as it dangled its feet.

It was behind me, only six feet away.

I could turn. Now I could turn. I could see it. All I had to do was turn.

I couldn't move. I felt a strangled sob come from my throat. The heels kicked louder—summoning me, demanding my attention, wanting me to turn and see. I sobbed again. What kind of thing would I see, sitting in the window? Would it even be human?

Thump-thump. Thump-thump. I could not do it. It wanted me to look; *she* wanted me to look. But I could not. Sobbing again, I stood where I was and closed my eyes.

The heels continued. The heat rose; I was not imagining it now, nor the metallic smell. I clenched my eyes shut, willing them not to open. Why? I didn't know—only that at all costs I must not do it, must not turn and look. To turn and look would be a mistake. Every nerve in my body screamed it.

Abruptly, the thumping stopped. A low sound came from the window, the echo of an angry groan, deepened by a muffling gurgle. It could have been a voice, but it was no voice any human had ever emitted. It gurgled wetly for a long moment, hissed, and was silent.

I opened my eyes.

The walls of the barn *pulsed*; there was no other way to describe it. They gave a great, fleshy bow inward, then out again. I stared in terror before I realized the heat was pricking my skin, becoming unbearable. Sensing the thing was gone from the windowsill, I finally turned around.

The barn was on fire.

Flames licked the walls, climbed to the ceiling; the ruined bales of hay were catching. As I watched, the flames raced toward the front of the barn; in seconds, they would engulf the only door.

I screamed—something, I know not what, came from my throat—and finally unfroze. I scrambled toward the door, realizing as I ran that I would be leaving the recorder to burn.

I stopped, undecided. The fire was licking the doorframe now, though the door was still passable; I might, perhaps, have a few precious seconds. I turned and ran for the recorder. Would someone come? Couldn't they see the fire from the house? I reached the recorder, which had stopped itself—how long had I been in here?—and slammed it into its suitcase, gripping the heavy handle with my slick hands. A sound came from overhead, and I looked up to see that fire had engulfed the roof, and one of the flaming rafters was falling straight down toward me.

I started to run and lost my footing. My legs slipped out from under me and I landed hard on the floor on my left hip. The camera banged on my chest. The suitcase hit the floor next to me. I screamed and curled, covering my head with my arms in a futile attempt to guard myself, and waited for the blow to fall.

And waited.

Nothing happened.

Perhaps, by some outrageous stroke of luck, the beam had missed me. I uncovered my head and prepared to run for the door again.

I looked around me. The fire was gone; I was in the cool, silent barn again, alone, with wet mist on the windows. The flames, the burning beams, all of it had utterly disappeared.

I looked up. The roof was as it had ever been, rafters intact. Stupidly, my panicked brain began to slow and calculate. Somehow, despite what I had just witnessed, there had never been a fire.

I sat gasping, nearly sobbing with the fear that had not yet left my veins, my hip throbbing. Slowly, I stood. I collected the suitcase again. I looked about for my hat.

Mrs. Clare's voice came into my head. *She may try to frighten you—play tricks. She likes to do that.* My God, my God. How was such a thing even possible?

Giving up on my hat, I hobbled for the door. The heat was

gone now, as was the smell; *she* was somehow gone, though I could not know where. From the corner of my eye I saw a familiar piece of fabric and I limped over to it, picked it up. It was the remains of my hat, torn utterly to ribbons.

I looked at it for a long moment, as the last waves of terror washed over me. Then I turned and ran for the door.

Chapter Six

I have very little memory of my return to the inn. I have a brief picture of myself stumbling through the tattered mist, unaware of my direction, my dress soaked with perspiration turned icy cold. I was shivering convulsively, despite my thin coat, though from fear or chill I cared little.

Mr. Gellis found me, I believe. I have a memory of his voice, his hand on my elbow. He relieved me of the suitcase with the recorder in it and I felt weightless without it, as if it had been anchoring me to the earth and I could now float away on my terror like a helium balloon. The world seemed far, far away.

My next memory is of sitting on a chair at the inn, my forehead in my hands as Mr. Gellis spoke softly to me. "You'll be all right," he was saying. "There, now. That's a girl."

I lifted my head and looked around. We were in a small room furnished with a table and four stiff-backed chairs. The window, behind a heavy velvet curtain tied back, showed the day still gray and dismal. "Is this a private room?" I asked through the cotton in my mouth.

"Yes. I've hired it for the week," said Mr. Gellis. He was setting the suitcase on the table and opening it gingerly. "I thought it was best, though it wasn't easy getting Mr. Ahearn to agree."

I sat straighter. I was still light-headed, but the world was beginning to look a little more real around me. I had never been so happy to see the streaks on the thick windows, or the dried rings of water left on the table from drinks past. It was prosaic, blessed sanity.

"I'm gathering you saw something," said Mr. Gellis. He had stopped fiddling with the recorder and was standing over me, looking at me intently. "You appear rather shaken."

I nodded, unable to speak.

His gaze glittered. "You must tell me everything. Every detail. I need my notebook—yes—here it is. My pen. I need to get every impression while it's fresh in your mind. It's the best way. I've ordered some tea. Would you like some?"

"Yes, I think so."

Mr. Gellis pulled up a chair and sat, with notebook and pen. He bent and started writing, perhaps some sort of preliminary notes of his own. Before we could begin, a barmaid came in with a pot of tea and several cups on a tray. She set everything down on the table and left.

Mr. Gellis did not look up. He kept writing. The pen was loud in the stillness of the room. I looked at his bent head, waiting.

In a moment he gestured quickly to the tea tray. "If you'd be so kind," he said, and bent back to his writing.

I sat stupidly for a long moment. Then I stood, on shaky legs that would hardly bear me, and made my way to the tea tray. My hip throbbed, and my shoulder ached where I had somehow wrenched it in my terrified escape. But, I told myself, Mr. Gellis knew none of this. Of course he would expect me to serve tea. I was his assistant, and I was here on his charity, so the least I could do was—

The door smashed open with a bang. A man stormed into the room—he looked like a thief: quick, dangerous, dark-jawed, and rough-dressed. A charcoal-colored cap was pulled low over his eyes. He didn't see me, but made straight for Mr. Gellis.

"Alistair," he said. His voice was low gravel. "Did I miss it? For God's sake. Was there something? There was, wasn't there? God-damn it to all fucking hell."

Mr. Gellis had looked up from his notebook; there was no fear on his face, only faint amusement. He tilted his head in my direction, indicating me to the madman.

The man whirled. His dark eyes took me in. I realized I had backed up to the window, where I stood, trying not to shake. His entrance had been yet another blow to my nerves. There was spilled tea on the tray.

The madman seemed to take in all of this in an instant. He reached up and pulled the hat from his head. Despite the gesture of deference, his expression held only a cool contempt, mixed with, I thought, a tinge of anger. "Oh. Hullo," he said to me.

I nodded at him.

Mr. Gellis was still amused. "Miss Piper," he said, "please meet the man you have been replacing—my assistant, Matthew Ryder."

❧

I stared at Mr. Matthew Ryder in shock. I had pictured another eccentric intellectual, like Mr. Gellis—bespectacled, perhaps shy, the type of man who could understand complex recording equipment and quietly organize his employer's notebooks. I could not reconcile the man before me to that picture.

Perhaps he wasn't a madman or a thief, as I had first thought him, but he did not seem to be very far from either. His quick, dark gaze missed nothing, and some dangerous emotion crackled under its surface. He did not stand still. His accent, in his low gravelly voice, held a lower-class twang, bespeaking his origins; and seemingly aware of this, he was brash, rude, and insolent, as if daring Mr. Gellis to take offense. Mr. Gellis, far from rising to the bait, kept an air of amused tolerance. I could tell from the first moment that their strange acquaintance was a long one.

"What are you doing here?" Mr. Gellis was saying to him now. "You're interrupting me frightfully. We were just about to begin. You're supposed to be gone until the end of the week."

Mr. Ryder shrugged. "Charlotte had her baby. Everything seemed fine to me. What do I know about it? So I got out. I drove all night to get here. Didn't want to miss a minute of it. What's been going on?"

"I sent Miss Piper in this morning, but have not examined her yet, thanks to you. You should have taken a few days off."

"Like fucking hell. You should have told me about this one earlier or I would never have gone. Did it come out?" He turned to me, his black gaze burning. "Did you see it?"

Something in his foul-mouthed insolence awakened some anger in me. I was tired of being spoken of as if I were an object in the room. I met Mr. Ryder's gaze with my own. "It saw me," I said.

Mr. Gellis' head jerked up, and Mr. Ryder stepped forward. They were both avid on me now, alive with an obsessive curiosity I had never seen before. I suddenly felt the imbalance, a female now outnumbered by two young, strong men in the room, both of them staring at me with fascination. I looked from one to the other.

"What does that mean?" Mr. Ryder said. "Did you see it or didn't you?"

"She—she wanted me to look at her, I think. I couldn't do it." I thought of the heels banging on the wall, the gurgling sound, and suddenly I was weak again. I pressed a cold hand to my forehead and sagged against the window. "Mr. Gellis, did you say this girl Maddy hanged herself?"

"Yes," said Mr. Gellis.

That horrible, horrible gurgling sound, as if she was unable to speak. Again I imagined what I would have seen, had I turned around. "Oh God," I said quietly.

"Miss Piper." Mr. Gellis' voice was quiet, soothing. "You must have a seat. Mr. Ryder has interrupted us, and for that, he apologizes profoundly." I highly doubted such a thing, but Mr. Gellis went on. "Now—we must have the full account from you, while it is still so fresh in your mind. It's time to tell us what you saw."

"What I saw *isn't possible*," I said.

He still soothed me. "We see ghosts for a living, Miss Piper. I've seen dozens. Nothing you can say is strange. Anything is possible—anything at all. Now, please have a seat, and relieve us both of this torturous curiosity."

I left the window and made my way back across the room. I could not help limping; Mr. Gellis had turned back to his notebook and did not see, but I looked up to see Mr. Ryder watching me, a sharp look in his eyes. I felt as if he were cataloging me, measuring me somehow in his brain, and finding me wanting. My stomach churned in uneasiness at the sight of him, and I looked away.

I sat down. Mr. Gellis pulled his chair close to mine. Mr. Ryder, still restless and unable to stand still, paced out of my line of vision—he stood somewhere else in the room; I knew not where, perhaps back by the window where I had just been. I did not turn to look. I looked at Mr. Gellis, whose dark gray eyes were on me, the sweet crook of a smile on his mouth. I smiled weakly back at him.

"Now, begin," he said. And I did.

It took a long time. Despite Mr. Gellis' assurances, I could hear the words as they came from my lips, and they sounded insane. I sounded like a delusional woman who has had a waking nightmare. I pushed away the thought and kept on, forcing the mad words out one after another. I looked at the ground as I spoke, so I would not have to see the expression on either man's face.

Partway through my recital, I heard a soft clicking, and a cup of tea was put before me. I raised my eyes. It was Mr. Ryder, his face a careful blank. I murmured a soft thanks and reached for my cup. As he pulled his hand away, I noticed a flat, dark pink scar on the back of his hand, winding up beneath his cuff and into his sleeve. A burn scar, a large one. So Mr. Ryder was, like Mr. Gellis, likely a veteran of the late war. It wasn't a certainty, of course—perhaps he had received his scar some other way—but I had not seen a young man in years who had not been to war.

"Please go on," said Mr. Gellis, and I realized I had stopped cold in the wake of my contemplation of the scar. I looked up at both men anew. Mr. Gellis was sitting easily in his chair, one leg crossed over the other, notebook poised on his thigh, ready to continue writing, looking at me with a polite expectation that only barely hid the obsessive gleam in his eyes. Mr. Ryder was still standing, though he had stepped back after serving my tea and was leaning against the table, balanced on one hip, his arms crossed over his chest. He, too, looked down at me with a gaze that did not blink or look away. I thought of how both men had been in battle, had seen, likely, death many countless times—violent death that disregarded a man's personal worth or morals, how many loved ones he had, whether he was good or proud or bright or adored. These were men who had contemplated their own deaths, and come terribly close. It somehow seemed more comfortable to speak of the ghosts of the dead with such men.

I took a sip of my tea and continued. When I finished, Mr. Gellis put down his notebook and pen and leaned forward, his elbows on his knees, and his hands cradling his forehead. He looked at the floor for a long moment.

I looked at Mr. Ryder, but he was turned away.

"Am I mad?" I asked.

"No," said Mr. Gellis, without looking up.

"Have you seen such a thing before?" I asked.

He gave a low chuckle that sounded distinctly bitter. "No," he said.

"A hallucination." Mr. Ryder was looking out the window, unseeing, his thoughts racing, speaking nearly to himself. "It can give hallucinations. I've never heard of anything like it. It's incredible." His voice was soft. "Alistair, we've got to get into that barn."

Mr. Gellis shook his head, which was still cradled in his palms. "There's no way. I've looked at the angles. Mrs. Clare won't allow it. The barn is locked tight. They're never from home."

I was mildly shocked. Mr. Gellis had thought to break into the barn? For a ghost?

"At night, then," said Mr. Ryder.

Alistair shook his head, still cradled in his hands.

Mr. Ryder scowled, acquiescing only for the moment. "Maybe the photos will have something. And I'll check the recording."

"I'm sorry," I said to them.

Mr. Gellis raised his head. They both looked at me.

"I know you hired a woman because the ghost does not like men," I said. "But I seem to have—agitated her. I know Mrs. Clare wanted to avoid that. Perhaps she won't let any of us back in. I don't know what I did, but that's what has happened. It seems it would have been all the same if one of you had gone in the first place."

Mr. Gellis frowned, but Mr. Ryder turned from the window to me. "Miss Piper, it's been a long morning. We'll order some food, and I'll check the recording. Maybe you'd like to take a small rest?"

"I don't know," I said. "I don't know if I could. But I could freshen up." A splash of cool water on my face suddenly sounded like heaven.

Mr. Ryder nodded. "Take your time."

As I left them, and made my way slowly up the stairs, there was absolute silence behind me. Neither of them said a thing.

I went to the washroom on the second floor and washed my face. It felt just as good as I had imagined. On impulse, I pulled off my blouse and sponged myself off with the hottest water the tap would afford, soaking away some of the tension, dried sweat, and—I imagined—fear. Then I looked at my discarded blouse and realized it was scuffed and dirty from my flight from the barn. My skirt was the same.

I pulled on the blouse again and went to my room. I changed into a soft, flowered shirtdress from my suitcase, my favorite garment, unfashionable but comfortable and easy to wear. Putting it on felt like a hug from a friend. Only a woman can truly understand the feeling of her very favorite item of clothing.

Comforted, I looked at the bed. Yes, I could likely sleep—but

I discovered I was suddenly hungry. Mr. Ryder had mentioned food. Forgoing the bed, I left my room and went back to the stairs.

I stood on the step for a moment, gathering my courage to continue down. The two men below made me feel a little like a finch in a den of lions; Mr. Gellis, for all his easy ways, was a man obsessed, and Mr. Ryder was simply—all my instincts told me—outright dangerous. There were deep currents between them I could not fathom. I took a moment to gather my courage, and I looked out the window.

A man stood there.

I was on the second floor, so he was not close; still, he was close enough. He stood beneath the trees, just where they thinned out at the edge of the woods beyond the inn. He wore a large great-coat and a wool cap against the damp, and I could not clearly see his face, which was shadowed. But I could discern enough to see he was looking at me. His gaze was fixed directly on my window, and it did not waver.

My breath stopped. I suppose my nerves were still on edge, for at that moment I truly thought I was looking at another ghost. Were there ghosts everywhere in Waringstoke? But the man put a cigarette to his lips, and I distinctly saw the glaring red of the tip as he inhaled. After a moment he dropped the cigarette and ground it out with his heel in a gesture that made me think of my father so strongly, I could nearly smell the smoky tang of the old hand-rolled tobacco my father had smoked.

I turned away from the window, still shaken, and continued down the stairs. Who would want to watch the inn? How long had the man been there, in the trees, and what had he hoped to see? I was still pondering it when I came to the bottom of the stairs and heard Mr. Gellis' and Mr. Ryder's voices discussing me.

The door to the inn's private room had been left ajar, and their voices were clear.

"It's practically criminal, Alistair." This was Mr. Ryder's distinctive, rough voice. "You don't need me to tell you that."

Mr. Gellis sounded stiff. "I don't know what you're talking about."

"Don't pull your stick-in-the-arse act with me. I've known you too long." There was a soft clacking as Mr. Ryder, I assumed, did something with the recording machine. "Where did you find her?"

"An agency sent her," said Mr. Gellis.

"My God. An agency girl, that's all? A secretary?"

"It isn't as if there is an agency for girls experienced with the paranormal, you know. It's a little difficult to come by. And who would you rather I hired? A brassy thing with a movie-star obsession and a mouth like a sailor? A girl who can't put two words together intelligently to save her life?"

"That girl"—Mr. Ryder's voice sounded tight—"has the fewest defenses of any girl I've ever seen. She's got a soft shell, Alistair, and you well know it. And you send her alone in the barn with that thing."

"Goddamn you, Matthew, I needed someone sensitive. You heard her report—it's extraordinary. It's the only way it would work. She's ideal. The minute I met her, I knew."

"Ideal, my arse. Send her home."

"Are you worried she'll take your job? You needn't be, you know. We've been through far too much. I'd never do such a thing."

"I don't need your pity, Alistair, or one of your sanctimonious speeches. I say send her home."

"No. Not as long as Mrs. Clare refuses to let one of us into that barn."

"You're going to kill her," said Mr. Ryder softly.

"I believe that's a little dramatic," said Mr. Gellis. "I've never known you to be Lancelot, Matthew."

"Shut up." There was a small silence. "I can hear something."

My heart stopped. I had been perfectly still in my spot on the stairs—how had they heard me? I reviewed my options. To retreat would be obvious, and foolish. I quickly decided to go forward, making a normal amount of noise, as if I had just come down the stairs and heard nothing.

I clattered forward into the room. "I'm terribly sorry I—"

Neither of them saw me; neither of them heard me at all. They were both hunched over the recording machine, Mr. Ryder with some sort of small speaker pressed to his ear. Mr. Gellis was staring in utter concentration.

I hear something had not referred to me at all. I reddened.

Send her home.

I looked at Mr. Ryder. He was in profile to me, listening to his earpiece with utter focus, his lips slightly parted. I noticed, in the dim light of the room, with the leisure to look at him without his terrifying gaze on me, that his lashes were thick and black.

Mr. Gellis turned, saw me, and silently motioned me over. I took my gaze from Mr. Ryder and moved in.

Mr. Ryder sagged, gave a small gasp, and took the speaker from his ear. He turned the dials on the recorder, rewinding the wire, and gave the earpiece to Mr. Gellis without a word.

It was Mr. Gellis' turn to listen as Mr. Ryder played the sound. He, too, dropped the earpiece and moved away, as if upset.

Mr. Ryder picked up the earpiece and handed it to me. He turned the dials again. I felt strange, as if I was both disregarded and treated as an equal; for the moment, it was as if I were a man like one of them. I pressed the speaker to my ear, and Mr. Ryder played the recording.

It was muffled; there was a long space of hissing sound, and then a voice I recognized—my own—saying, "Hello? Hello?" I remembered saying that as I moved toward the horse stalls, clicking the camera. My hands began to shake.

A long silence again; then some sounds, as if from far off; and then, incredibly, a shuffling sound, crisp and clear, directly next to the machine's microphone. I knew, at this point, that I was somewhere near the stables, beginning to feel warm, perhaps trying not to look at Maddy, or perhaps already not looking at her. And this sound, at the same time, was next to the recording machine.

A shuffle again, arrhythmic and uneven; a pop, a bang that hurt my ear; and a blast of sound, white prickly static, on and on—and then, silence.

I put the earpiece down. Tears pricked my eyelids. I was suddenly tired, and weary, and so very, terribly sorry.

The ghost had found our machine, and somehow, she had broken it.

Chapter Seven

❦

There is little to say about the rest of that day, or so I sometimes think to myself. That is to say, we did not have any further supernatural visitations, and no more strangers appeared at the window. And yet there is one incident from that day that I have left to tell. It seemed like nothing—should have been nothing—and yet I find it nearly the hardest to tell.

Mr. Ryder worked furiously, and with a great many obscene oaths, to fix the machine's recording apparatus. He didn't succeed. Mr. Gellis retreated to his room to type his notes. We ate. At some point, I went to my bed and slept.

I did not dream of ghosts; instead I dreamed, strangely, about Mrs. Barry, the fashionable woman I had seen walking her dog that morning. In my dream she stood at the edge of the woods where the strange man had been, holding a cigarette, but I knew the cigarette was somehow terribly dangerous, and she should not touch it. As she raised it to her lips, I tried to scream.

I woke groggy and confused. The light in the room was failing around me, and as I wiped the sweat from my face, I realized it was nearly night. My body felt heavy and my head ached. Reluctantly, I got out of bed.

I stepped out into the hallway, heading for the washroom. The inn was very small, and we were the only guests; though the place was usually quiet, it was especially so now. It was the end of the dinner hour, and from the soft murmur of voices from the downstairs common room I could tell that everyone in the building except myself could likely be found there. The guest hallway was utterly deserted.

I padded down the hall under the dim light, touching the dark oak walls with my fingertips to guide my way. The quiet settled about me, the comfortable peace of a house inhabited by people in a far-off room, and I felt very private, as if I were invisible.

The washroom door stood ajar, with no light within. I approached silently and pulled it open. Then I stood, rooted to the spot, taking in what I saw there with a shock that reverberated through all of my body.

There are large moments in life; but sometimes it is the small moments—the casual moments—that change everything. The second's absent wandering of attention before an accident. The choice to take one road, instead of another. I could not pinpoint exactly how everything changed the second I opened that washroom door; I knew only, and instantly, it seemed, that nothing in my life would ever be the same.

Mr. Ryder stood in the washroom. He was standing before the mirror, a flannel in his hand. He had the flannel pinched between his forefinger and thumb, and pressed tightly between his eyes, to the bridge of his nose. His eyes were closed, his jaw clenched, as if he was in the extremes of pain.

He wore only trousers; his feet and chest were bare. He was turned partly away from me, and did not see me in that first instant. I glimpsed his discarded white shirt, tossed carelessly over the old radiator. But, mostly, I saw him.

Spread across his sleekly muscled back and down his right arm, which pulsed with lean, raw strength, was an enormous, dark pink burn scar. It ravaged the skin of his shoulder blades, up to the close-cropped hair on the back of his neck; it twisted its way down, through the dip of his lower back, to the waistband of his trousers. The flesh even on his rib cage and under his arm was tortured with fire, and the arm itself was scored and angry, the skin tight and painful, down and down unto the wrist and the back of his hand, the edge of which I realized I had glimpsed as he handed me my cup of tea.

It was hideous, horrible, the most terrible scar I had ever seen, marring his body so utterly that it looked as if he were even now consumed with flame. The image of him shocked me—nearly naked, utterly still, his body a testament to unimaginable torture. I stepped back, and my back hit the wall. I may have made some sort of sound. Mr. Ryder opened his eyes, and lowered the flannel, slowly, I thought—he seemed to force himself to come back from wherever he had been, to come away from whatever private and lonely hell of pain he had inhabited and return to the here and now. He turned and looked at me, registering me, pressed back against the wall, my lips parted, a look of horror undoubtedly on my face. A swift expression came into his eyes—anger, and, underneath it, a terrible despair. Our eyes held for a long moment.

"I'm sorry," I murmured.

He reached out and closed the door.

I could not breathe. I should knock—speak to him—tell

him—what? I had seen something so intensely private to him, he would likely never forgive me. In that one moment I had opened the door, it seemed probable Mr. Ryder would hate me forever.

I made my way back to my bedroom, quickly undressed, and lay on my bed in my slip, hugging my knees to my chest. Yes, he would hate me now. Despite our brief acquaintance, and our mutual antipathy, I still felt the loss of it. Even more, I felt the loss to him, of whatever horrible thing he had gone through, to receive such scars on his body. I felt the loss to a strong young man, to his life and vitality, to be injured so.

But more, even more than those things, I felt a keen loss at our misunderstanding. Because he had turned and seen me at exactly the moment of my first surprise, and my expression must have been one of, he would think, revulsion. Though he did not like me, it had cut him to the quick to have a woman look at him in horror. It would cut any man. Even I knew that.

And as I lay there, I knew he had misunderstood. When I closed my eyes, I could see the image of him burned behind my eyelids. When I opened them again, I could see nothing but him, standing before me. There was a knot deep in my stomach, bruised and painful, a deep tug of longing that would not go away. Again I saw him turn to look at me, and I knew the longing would never be gone. I was doomed to it. For there was no way to convince him that, with all his scars, the terrible truth was that he was still the most beautiful thing I had ever seen.

Chapter Eight

The next day, as planned, we interviewed Mrs. Clare and Mrs. Macready. We used the inn's private room again; it was here that my secretarial skills came into use, as Mr. Gellis conducted the interviews, and I sat nearby, transcribing everything in my tidy shorthand. Mr. Ryder sat in the corner of the room, again out of both my sight and the interviewees', and listened. If he had any opinion of my taking on the task he would normally do, he did not voice it.

I could not look at Mr. Ryder, and he did not look at me, but I was painfully aware of his presence. He wore a white shirt this morning, under a corduroy jacket of deep brown that looked well-fitted and well-worn. He wore no tie, of course—he had not worn one the previous day either, and I had the impression it was not his usual practice. He had not shaved, and his jaw was dark. This was all I allowed myself to see before I turned away.

Mr. Gellis, in contrast, was trim and shaven, his shirt crisp and pressed, his hair neatly combed. He sat calm in his chair, the picture of utter focus as the lengthy interviews went on. I was starting to see how clever he was—with his clean good looks, he could hide a skillful interview behind the blandness of polite conversation. In essence, he could efface himself when needed. One could know this only if one had seen him at other times, when his passionate obsession was roused, or when he was somehow painfully conflicted, as he had seemed when smoking a cigarette with Mrs. Barry. He had a great deal of charm and charisma, too, when he wished—charisma he could just as easily tamp down and put away.

Mrs. Clare came to be interviewed first. She gave Mr. Gellis a look of curiosity that was tinged unmistakably with approval. "You didn't mention in your letter that you are acquainted with the Barrys."

Mr. Gellis, who had been settling down with his notebook in avid anticipation, paused in surprise. "I beg your pardon?"

"The Barrys," Mrs. Clare replied. "You had a conversation with Evangeline Barry yesterday morning. It seems you have known her some time?" She smoothed her skirt absently, not seeming to need an answer. "I myself know them only slightly. They've never made much effort, I have to say, though of course they could have, as my husband was the magistrate. They're known to be rather standoffish. I've heard that he's no better than he should be, for all that they have money." She looked up at Mr. Gellis again. "It goes to show that money, especially new money, simply does not equal class."

We were all quiet after this extraordinary speech. I could not read Mr. Gellis' expression to see what he made of it. Who had seen the conversation yesterday morning, and gossiped around town about it? The innkeeper, or his family, perhaps? I turned to look at Mr. Ryder in his corner. His eyebrows were slightly elevated and he tilted his head. He was evidently seeing something in Mr. Gellis' face that I was not able to see.

I turned back. Mrs. Clare looked only at Mr. Gellis, as if she had decided there was no one else in the room. She had recognized Mr. Gellis as of her own class of gentry, based on his acquaintance with the richest couple in town, and the concept seemed almost a relief to her; though, of course, she had had to make certain he understood that her own status was based on quality, and not on something as vulgar as money. Mr. Ryder and I, possessing neither, were not worthy of notice.

"Ah, well," said Mr. Gellis. "My acquaintance with Mrs. Barry is from years ago, I'm afraid, and I know her husband not at all."

"They're not seen much, as I said. The house was empty for years until he inherited it, and they only lived there a few years after they married. They went to London and came back after the Armistice. The women here have tried to feel some sympathy for her, not having any children, but she hasn't been very receptive. As for him, money is about all the good anyone can say for him. No one even knows what his father did."

Mr. Gellis rubbed his temple, bemused and perhaps a little embarrassed. "Well," he said.

But, having had her say on this topic, Mrs. Clare had turned to me. "You," she said, her eyes piercing me. "You did not come to me yesterday. I told you to come to me after you'd been to the barn."

I reddened. "I apologize. I hardly knew where I was going. I was rather agitated."

Mrs. Clare nodded in a sort of resignation, and the Barrys were forgotten. "So she did show herself, then. We suspected so. We could hear things. What, exactly, did she do?"

"There were several aspects of the manifestation." Mr. Gellis took over, back on his favorite topic. I was actually grateful, as I wasn't sure I could go through all of it again. "Sounds. An attempt, we think, to speak. She interfered with our recording equipment."

"Maddy can be mischievous," Mrs. Clare said.

"So it seems. But I am particularly interested in one aspect. Has Maddy ever created a sort of hallucination before?"

Mrs. Clare looked at him. "I beg your pardon?"

"She seems to have created a nearly perfect illusion in Miss Piper's mind that the barn was on fire. Miss Piper was convinced of it, and accordingly terrified. Has she ever done anything like that before?"

Mrs. Clare's gaze turned to me, and she thought for a long moment. "How extraordinary," she said. "No. No, she has never done it to me, or to Mrs. Macready as far as I am aware. How did she do such a thing to you?"

"Perhaps Miss Piper is somewhat sensitive," Mr. Gellis offered. Of course. I had a soft shell.

But Mrs. Clare was frowning. "I am more concerned with the illusion itself," she said. "It's strange. Does it mean Maddy plans to burn down the barn? If she wanted to, she could have done so a thousand times already. Or was she simply playing games?" She looked worried. "I do hope Maddy is not going to burn down the barn."

"I will help you get to the bottom of this," said Mr. Gellis smoothly. "As promised. Let's start the interview, so I can get a better picture of Maddy herself."

And so we started. Mrs. Macready came in the afternoon, and though she contributed a good many details Mrs. Clare hadn't known or offered, she did not say anything that contradicted any of Mrs. Clare's facts. Both women were clear speakers, firm, and rarely emotional. Over the course of the day, a picture began to form of Maddy and her history—far from complete, and far from conclusive, but as detailed as we were likely to get with such a complicated subject.

The story went something like this. As Mrs. Clare had told us, Maddy had appeared one rainy night on the Clares' doorstep, weakly knocking at the door. She was filthy, bedraggled, soaking, and barely clothed; she could speak only in low, hoarse cries of distress. Mr. Clare, the local magistrate, had still been alive then, though very ill, and he had given permission for the strange girl to be taken in, at least until they could deliver her home.

It was obvious something was terribly wrong with the girl, but it was Mrs. Macready who explained, as she had been the one to give the girl a hot bath. The stray girl had bruises everywhere on her body—up and down her arms, about her throat, and, most tellingly, on her breasts, legs, and thighs. When probed for details, Mrs. Macready admitted that the bruises had been fresh and pink. There was blood dried into the remains of the girl's dress, blood in her hair. She had not wanted to be touched. It was impossible to ask her what had happened to her, or where, or by whom, as she would not speak.

They had given her dry clothes and food, and in the subsequent days the Clares had begun to make inquiries in all the surrounding towns, asking about any girl who had gone missing. The girl did not seem genteel; they guessed she was perhaps a servant. It was impossible to tell how long she had been walking barefoot through the woods, or from how far away she had come. She still would not speak. Mr. Clare sent inquiries to his fellow magistrates farther and farther afield.

Though she did not talk, the girl was not mentally deficient. She understood what was said to her, and watched all that went on around her with a sort of wild intelligence. Mrs. Macready, especially, felt that the girl was as normal as any other, underneath her terrible distress. She took the girl under her wing and gently put her to work under the servants' stairs, peeling a few potatoes at first, or washing a few pots. "It helped to keep her busy, I thought," said Mrs. Macready. "She seemed a little calmer somehow, though she were never truly calm. I didn't give her much that was hard. She could take an hour to slice a few apples, and I wouldn't mind. I did it mostly to keep her near, to keep her company, like."

It was here that Mr. Gellis asked Mrs. Macready to describe Maddy. Mrs. Clare had given the same description: young, perhaps about twelve; pale, with long, ink-dark hair. Her eyes had been gray. Mr. Clare had thought she was Irish, an idea both women instantly adopted and still believed.

The strange girl had been afraid in Mr. Clare's presence; she had shied uneasily away from him, and would not look at him. But it was as nothing compared with the unreasoning terror she had shown when the milkman came by, or the gardener. Indeed, when any man, of any kind, came to the house, the girl would disappear, to be found later, crouching in her room with the door locked, again mute.

For by this time, she had slowly begun to speak. She said her name was Maddy, though she wouldn't, perhaps couldn't, give a surname. Eventually, the Clares had given her their own name, and she came to be known as Maddy Clare. Mrs. Clare shrugged at the strangeness of the idea. "She would only say one word when we asked her name," she said. "Maddy. What were we supposed to do?"

After a time, it came to seem normal to have Maddy in the house. Their inquiries had come to nothing. No one wanted the girl, and she had nowhere to go. There was talk at first about her, and speculation around town; she was the object of a little gossip, especially as she never left the house, even to attend church with the other servants. But the Clares' class and reputation were sterling, and the talk died down when the next topic came along.

Maddy still spoke only rarely, and could still be terrified into days of mute silence. Still, she worked steadily, as if she felt the debt she owed to the kind family who had taken her in. All would have been quiet, except for Maddy's rages.

The rages, according to both women, were infrequent—perhaps once yearly. And they were truly terrible. In a rage, Maddy would rip her clothes to shreds; she would break furniture and crockery; in one of them, she had gone to the back kitchen garden and torn up every plant there, demolishing each plant even unto pieces, until her hands bled. Mrs. Clare had made her repair the damage for that one, and replant every plant in the garden. Her rage past, Maddy had done it with eerie calm.

"What would set her off?" Mr. Gellis asked.

Mrs. Clare took a long time, rubbing her fingertips tiredly on her forehead. "I don't know. As God is my witness, I don't know. The first was after Mr. Clare died—we thought it had to do with that, but then it happened again, and—I just don't know. I never crossed Maddy, Mr. Gellis. I was never unkind to her. I never punished her or disciplined her. I pitied her too deeply for that. There was never anything I could think of to make her so enraged."

"Nothing," Mrs. Macready said more succinctly to the same question. "Nothing at all, sir. Maddy didn't need anything. She just wasn't right in the head, that's all. She'd go off, and it was

terrifying, I don't mind telling you. Mrs. Clare would tie herself
up over it, but I never did. I loved Maddy like a daughter, in my
way, but sir, she was a little bit mad. Mrs. Clare don't like to hear
it, but it's the truth."

And so, though Maddy lived in the Clare household for seven
years, she remained essentially a mystery to those who knew her.
Who she was; where she had come from; what had happened to
her; what enraged her so; whether she was sane or not; what her
deepest feelings, thoughts, or questions were—even Mrs. Clare
and Mrs. Macready, who mothered her as much as she would let
them, never knew.

And after seven years, on a day when Mrs. Clare went to an
acquaintance's for tea and Mrs. Macready went to the market for
a few fresh pieces of fish for supper, Maddy went to the barn, took
a rope that was used for the horses, and hanged herself from the
rafters. She left only a badly scrawled note, placed on the floor
beneath her dangling feet. Each word of the note was set on its
own line. The note read:

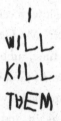

By their estimate, Maddy Clare was nineteen years old. They
had not known she could write.

Mrs. Clare looked out the window as she told this; she was the
picture of a woman keeping her emotions only barely in check,
her face a mask of despair, the words forced out one at a time, like
an automaton. Her eyes were dry.

There was a long moment of silence. I felt sick to my stomach, but I did not look up from my shorthand. Mr. Ryder was still and silent in his corner.

"I did not know there was a note," Mr. Gellis said softly.

"No one knows there was a note, Mr. Gellis," said Mrs. Clare, "except myself and Mrs. Macready. We put it away when we found it—found her. The magistrate did not even see it."

"What did it mean?"

Mrs. Clare shook her head. "I don't know. Once again, Mr. Gellis, when it comes to Maddy, I simply don't know."

Again, Mrs. Macready had a simpler answer to the question of the note. "You're looking literal, like," she chided. "Trust me. I knew Maddy, and I've thought about this. The note didn't mean nothing except that Maddy was in hell. She was in hell when we found her, and she stayed in hell, though we tried our best. God knows what she thought was true when she wrote that note. She was in hell—that's the only truth that matters."

The haunting had started within weeks. They knew it was Maddy, of course; if anyone would rest uneasy, it would be she. They tried everything to put her at peace—séances, Ouija boards, attempts to commune with her, to tell her to move on. Nothing worked. Then they had called in Mr. Pelham, the vicar, and Maddy had flown into something that resembled her mad rages when she lived. She had remained terrified of men until the day she died.

It was as the interview concluded that Mrs. Clare asked Mr. Gellis what he intended his next steps to be. Mr. Gellis closed his notebook and put down his pen. "My assistant, Miss Piper, will go to the barn again tomorrow. It seems to me that Maddy has found Miss Piper to be rather receptive; this time Miss Piper will try to gather more information, and communicate directly with Maddy if that's possible. Is that agreeable to you?"

Mrs. Clare nodded, then looked at me. I sat frozen, my fingers aching as they clutched my motionless pen. I was trying to breathe.

Mr. Gellis also turned to me. He was all business. "Can you do it, Miss Piper?"

The back of my neck was frozen cold. "Yes," I said.

They turned away, and I risked a glance at Mr. Ryder. His eyes were on me, his expression unreadable. Then, like the others, he turned away.

Chapter Nine

We rose early again the next morning. Now the day dawned differently, the sky clear and blue, the breeze warm and promising spring and, soon, early summer. The wet mist of the previous day had dissipated.

I looked out the window at the top of the stairs for the man at the edge of the trees, but he was not there.

I found both Mr. Gellis and Mr. Ryder in the common room, drinking coffee. I poured a cup for myself and joined them. I felt strangely disembodied today, nearly giddy, in a way that was almost frightening. I should be terrified of Maddy Clare and the barn. I should be solemn after the recitation of Maddy's tragic story—indeed, I had felt grief for her late into the night, until I fell asleep. I should be again wary of the two men who sat at a table in the common room now, looking, mostly, at me.

I did not feel any of these things—or if I did, I was only vaguely aware of them. Mostly, I felt a sort of readiness.

We drank our cups in silence.

Mr. Gellis spoke at last. "Miss Piper, do you think you are capable of going in there this morning?"

I put down my cup. "Yes, Mr. Gellis."

"You remember the words?"

He had given me suggestions of what to say to Maddy's ghost, should she appear—a set of lines, much like a theater script. I had everything committed to memory. "Yes."

"The recorder isn't fixed yet," Mr. Gellis continued. "There will be no camera this time either. I rely on you to take accurate mental notes. We'll need to debrief you the minute you get out of there, so please try to stay collected. Do you think you can do that?"

"Yes," I said.

"Very good."

I stood and took my empty cup to the sideboard. I stood there for a long moment, with my back to both men. I had not looked at Mr. Ryder, and likely he had not looked at me, but I was so painfully aware of his presence that my equilibrium was beginning to crack. Just the knowledge of him in the room made the knot of longing in my stomach unbearable.

"Mr. Ryder—" I began.

"For God's sake." His voice was low and rough. I could not remember the last time I had heard him speak. "My name is Matthew."

I turned and looked at him, surprised. He was scowling at me with his dark eyes that missed nothing. He pointed at Mr. Gellis. "And that is Alistair. If he won't put a stop to this *Mr. Gellis* nonsense, then I'll do it myself. It stops here."

Mr. Gellis frowned for a moment, then shrugged. "It doesn't seem a bad idea, I suppose. And we'll call you—" He cocked his head at me. "What is your first name, Miss Piper?"

It took a moment to realize that neither of them would ever have heard my name. "Sarah," I said.

Mr. Gellis—Alistair—suddenly smiled at me, one of his sweet, lopsided smiles. "Lovely. Now, Sarah, we have to go. Are you ready?"

I smiled back at him, relieved to see his charming side. "Certainly."

"Very well." He stood, and came toward me. To my surprise, he took me gently by the shoulders and looked into my eyes. "I know I can be rather distracted at times," he said sincerely. "I don't suppose I'm as kind as I could be. I warned you when we met, I'm not much used to female company, so I must apologize for my boorishness."

"Oh," I said, helpless.

"You have done very well, you know. You did well your first day in the barn, and yesterday with the interviews. Very well indeed. I wanted you to know that."

I was blushing now. "Oh. Well."

"You're brave to go again. Most girls would have been running straight back to London by now." He gave me another smile, and as I felt rather warmly toward him, I returned it. To my shock, he pulled me gently to him and gave me a hug—a chaste one, to be certain, but still a hug. His arms came around me and his hands pressed my back, as I felt myself flush down the front of him and I turned my cheek to rest briefly on his collarbone. He smelled of tangy cologne and clean wool. My arms were pinned under his, so I did not have the chance to raise them and hug him back. Before I could respond, he had let me go.

I was blushing furiously—a fact that I knew well would be misinterpreted by both men. I looked at Mr. Ryder—Matthew— but his face was a careful blank, and he simply sipped his coffee. Alistair was looking kindly at me. I blushed harder. Alistair was terribly handsome, a fact I had known from the first moment I saw him. Handsome, and smart, and easy to be around. But my crush of the first few days had been exactly that—a temporary crush. As much as I liked Alistair, the physical closeness of the hug had only brought home the fact that I felt nothing more than amiable friendship for him. It was Matthew who kept me awake at night, whose image I saw constantly in my daydreams. But to blush at Alistair's hug meant I must be smitten with him, and both men would think it so.

I did not know what to do about Matthew thinking I had feelings for Alistair. Perhaps he simply didn't care. It was too difficult to untangle, and too embarrassing to contemplate. Besides, I could not think of it right now. Maddy Clare awaited me in the barn, and today I had something to say to her.

&

The barn was again silent when I went inside. Mrs. Clare did indeed leave the barn locked, as Alistair had said; with more of my senses about me this time, I noted that she—or Mrs. Macready— would come to the barn, unlock it, and go away again before my arrival. Neither Mrs. Clare nor Mrs. Macready ever went inside anymore.

I had nothing with me this time. My hands were free, and I had left off my coat and hat. *I am becoming experienced at this,* I thought wryly. *An experienced ghost hunter.*

I stood in the barn for a long moment, looking around at its abject destruction and listening. Though it was a beautiful day outside, there were no swallows in the barn. There was no sound at all.

I closed my eyes. I had no sense of Maddy's presence, but I plunged ahead nonetheless.

"Maddy," I said aloud, and my voice sounded small in the dense air. "It's me again. My name is Sarah. Sarah Piper."

There was no response.

"You played a little joke on me, last time," I went on. "It was well-done indeed. Perhaps I offended you with my camera and recorder. I've brought neither of those things this time. It's just—you and me."

Still no sound, but—oh, yes, the air was growing closer, closer by the minute. My breathing grew shallow. I made a note of it. *Maddy's presence makes the air like breathing clotted cream.*

She was around me now, somewhere. A quiet scuff behind me. I did not turn.

There was no heat, no sense of danger yet. Just a waiting, and a very vigilant watching. I could feel her eyes on me.

I began to shake. My giddiness was gone, and I was feeling the fear now, the fear of truly—without any sort of doubt—being in the presence of an undead soul. *My God, she is actually here, actually listening to me.* It was terrifying, and yet, for the first time, I could see a glimmer of what powered Alistair's obsession, what drove him to seek ghosts at any cost. What made him wish so terribly to be in my place at just this moment.

He had given me lines to say, so I took a breath. "Maddy, your work in this world is finished," I said from memory. "You must let all of this go. There is somewhere else for you, somewhere that is waiting for you. If there is a light, Maddy, you must go toward it."

I scrambled and tried to remember the rest, but behind me was another sound, a quick scraping, and an old lantern, which had been lying in a corner, sailed through the air from behind me, high in an arc, and hit the back wall of the barn with a terrifying crash. The glass of the lamp blew to pieces.

My heart was pounding in my chest. I would take it, then, that

Maddy did not much like my little speech. I closed my eyes. She was still listening, I could tell. I had no idea how I knew—perhaps Alistair was right and Maddy could channel into me somehow—but I knew she still listened, that she was not angry, not yet.

I deviated from the script. I had a question of my own to ask her. "Maddy. What does *I will kill them* mean?"

A dead silence.

"Who?" I continued. "Who will you kill? I don't understand. Or did you kill someone already? When you were alive? What did it mean?"

A small scuff, not a foot behind me; she was close, then. I closed my eyes. The air was so thick I could not breathe, and I realized I could no longer speak even if I had wanted to. She was too close.

There was a trickle of icy air on the back of my neck. I felt the hairs stand up like tiny pins, painful on my skin; a swift unearthly inhalation, choking and clogged.

And then she grabbed me.

I could not scream. I tried and tried, my mouth open, as I gasped for air; tried and tried and tried to scream, in a terrible pantomime I would relive in my nightmares for months to come. I was frozen, unable to move or run, and an icy grip took my upper arms, and lifted me from the floor.

The grip pinched; it was so cold, it pierced the skin of my arms with pain. I kicked my legs, only faintly, as I could hardly move, and tried to wriggle from the hold, but it was like iron. I was lifted, suspended, unable to get away. It was like being caught in a giant spider's cocoon, invisible and inescapable.

There was a voice, but it was not human. It was not a voice. It was in my head, deep inside my brain, and it was indescribable.

I can smell him on you, it said.

I tried and tried to scream.

The grip pulled me higher.

I can smell him. A man. I can smell him ON YOU.

Through my haze of panic I thought briefly of Alistair, hugging me before I came here. That simple, friendly hug. It was a lifetime ago.

Who is he? Who is he? Who is this man who smells so?

By pure, terrified instinct, I tried to shut my thoughts down. I would not think of Alistair—would not give him to her. I shut my mind, thought of nothing.

There was a low, sickening chuckle deep in my brain. I thought I would go mad.

You smell of man, little girl. You smell of man. He's all over you.

And then: *Bring him to me.*

I tried again to kick my legs. Oh God, oh God—

The grip let go and I fell to the floor. My feet went from under me and I landed on my knee. I had not realized how high I had been, but the fall told me I had been hanging some five feet in the air. I scrambled back up and ran for the door.

Nothing followed me; there were no visions this time. I had my orders. Maddy Clare let me escape the barn, where I could finally scream and scream.

Chapter Ten

❧

Bring him to me.

How strange it must have seemed on that beautiful spring morning, to see a woman run from the barn at Falmouth House, screaming hoarsely into the warm air.

I ran up the rise past the house on legs that shook. I was as near to hysterics as I have ever been; I could still feel the clammy invasion of Maddy inside my head, and every time I thought of it I wanted insanely to shut off my brain, to scratch through my skull with my fingernails. My arms were seared with pain. She had *touched* me. The tears on my cheeks were icy.

Over the rise I stumbled into something hard—a man, steely and warm. He gripped me about the waist. I thrashed away from him, and he let me go only to regrasp me from behind, his arm under my rib cage. A large hand touched my face, gently worked my gasping jaw shut. His voice came near my ear.

"Hush," he said. It was Matthew Ryder.

I quieted at the sound of him, still heaving for air. His arm tightened about my waist, and I was pressed full against him, so much so I could feel he was out of breath, too. I felt him exhale against my neck.

"Are you hurt?" he asked.

I shook my head. The feel of him was making me sane again. My body was quieting against his.

"My God," he said. "I was waiting for you back there and you started screaming. You terrified the hell out of me."

"Maddy," I managed. My throat hurt.

"Yes," he said quietly. "She's gone now. Do you hear? She can't hurt you. We'll go back to the inn."

I nodded. My body was relaxing against him. His arm still pressed around my waist. My breathing slowed. He didn't move, and we stood there for a moment, pressed together. I was aware of the warmth between us, the cool air around us, and for a long moment I simply let the feel of it wash over me, the feel of being close to him for the first time.

You smell of man, little girl.

The thought made me stiffen and he let me go, probably thinking I was pushing him away. We would never understand each other, it seemed.

He came in front of me and looked me over. His dark eyes took me in. His soft, sensual mouth was pressed into a grim line, and I knew he had been truly worried for me.

"Thank you," I whispered to him, but he had already turned away and walked over the rise.

❧

Alistair was waiting in the private room at the inn. He took one look at Matthew, striding toward him, with me trailing behind, and his expression grew taut. "What happened? Did she appear?"

"I would guess so," said Matthew. He went straight to the sideboard, where a pitcher of water had been set out, and poured a glass. "You'll be hearing from the Clares in a moment unless I miss my guess. She came screaming out of the barn."

I dropped into a chair, relieving my shaking legs. Alistair looked at me. "Are you all right?"

"Yes," I said. "Matthew is right, I'm afraid. I was screaming. I may have made something of a spectacle. I'm sorry."

The familiar gleam came into Alistair's eyes and he picked up his pad and pen. "Tell me everything. Now, before any of it leaves your mind."

I shuddered involuntarily. "None of it will ever leave my mind."

"Then go."

I looked at him. I realized I would have to tell Alistair that Maddy had told me she wanted him to come, and for a moment I seriously considered not telling him. What did Maddy want him for, after all? To kill him? It would be better if he didn't know. I could simply say that Maddy had grabbed me, lifted me, thrown me down. That she had not spoken to me at all.

But how foolish was I, to think that Alistair needed my protection?

Alistair lifted his eyebrows at me, and Matthew put a glass of water on the table. Reluctantly, I put the idea of lying away. These were grown men, experienced men, men who had been to war and seen unspeakable things. Why be afraid of a ghostly shadow? How could I think I could protect them—I, who was so afraid and unworldly next to both of them? Stupid to think that I could simply face Maddy Clare on my own.

"She spoke to me," I said.

Alistair's eyes widened in excitement. "My God. What did she say?"

And I started from the beginning, and I told them everything.

When I finished, Alistair stood and slammed his notebook to the table with a bang. He paced the room, running his hands through his hair. "Incredible," he said. "Incredible. This is the most advanced manifestation anyone has ever seen. This is more than just a shadow. It's what we've been looking for, Matthew. It's *awareness*, don't you see?"

Matthew, leaning against the sideboard, looked down into his empty water glass and said nothing.

"Five years," Alistair went on. "Sixty-four confirmed manifestations I've witnessed in the last five years alone. And nothing ever, even remotely, like this. This is the greatest discovery in the history of the field. Physical manifestation. Voice. Reaction to stimuli." He shook his head. I had never seen him so excited, so happy. He could not stand still. "This will make our names, all of us. There's no way it can be faked. How to grab a human being and levitate her into the air? It can't be done. This is a true manifestation, fully documentable." He turned to us, eyes alight, and said what I most dreaded. "I'm going into that barn."

"You can't!" I said.

He turned his gaze on me, though he was hardly seeing me. "She asked for me. How can I not go?"

"It doesn't sound like a good idea, Alistair," Matthew added.

"I'm going to document her," Alistair went on as if we hadn't spoken. "I'm going to record her and get photographs and fully document this. She can't escape me." He grinned, a narrow grin that unsettled me. "I'm going to hunt her down."

The chill his words gave me made me almost physically ill. My mind was groggy and throbbing, the way it is after waking from a nightmare, thrashing and still unsure of reality. Cold sweat ran down my temples. I pictured Alistair going in there, Maddy seeing him. I felt something yawning and avaricious inside me, something almost gleeful—not my emotions, but Maddy's, as if she were somewhere inside me. The thought was so horrifying I pushed it from my mind.

"Sarah," came Matthew's voice from somewhere over my shoulder. "Are you quite all right?"

I put my hand to my forehead. "I really think I might lie down a moment."

"Of course, of course," said Alistair. "I will have some tea sent up—"

A short, sharp knock sounded at the door. Without a pause for an answer, the door opened and Mrs. Clare stepped in. Her face was haggard and alarmed.

"This is terrible," she said without preamble. "What happened in there, Mr. Gellis? You promised us you would not go in the barn yourself. I only saw Miss Piper from the window this morning."

"I assure you I did not, Mrs. Clare. What do you mean?"

Her tired gaze turned to me. "Maddy is as agitated as I've ever seen her. What did you say to her?"

I shook my head. Alistair spoke for me. "It seems Maddy was in an angry mood. We are still debriefing Miss Piper."

How smooth he was! How honest he sounded! He wanted to shield Mrs. Clare from the truth, it seemed. Perhaps to hide his own intentions of getting into the barn despite her orders.

Her eyes, lined with exhaustion, never left me. "The noise is going to drive me mad if it keeps up. Thumps and crashes—I didn't think there was anything left to destroy in there. Several paintings fell from the walls in the house this morning, and crockery was broken in the kitchen. She never comes into the house anymore, not like she did at first. You said something to upset her."

I looked at her helplessly. *Lock your barn,* I thought. *Please, lock it—though perhaps it is too late.*

"I'm sorry," I said. "I told her my name. I hardly had a chance to say more. I can't think what set her off."

Her eyes narrowed, and I knew she didn't believe me. I stood on my unsteady legs. "If you'll pardon me. I must go lie down."

"By all means, Miss Piper," said Alistair.

I looked at him and saw nothing but bland politeness on his face. Alistair, so friendly and sweet, and, I was discovering, so capable of deception in pursuit of what he wanted. I looked at Matthew, seated in the corner with one ankle crossed over the other knee, but he was staring down at his boot and frowning. He did not look at me. I turned away and left the room.

As I approached the stairs, a man descending them brushed past me. His shoulder jarred mine, and as I turned to look at him, he lowered his face. He wore a cloth cap and a gray jacket, and he disappeared quickly out the door.

I slowly ascended the stairs. I went to the washroom first, where I splashed warm water on my face and hands. Despite my manufactured excuse, I found exhaustion was indeed weighing on me, and I wanted nothing more than to lie on my bed. I dragged my aching limbs down the hall to my bedroom and opened the door.

The entire room was in disarray. The drawers were pulled from the dresser and overturned, the nightstand pitched against the wall. My valise had been opened and everything inside pulled out, and—I let out a cry at this—my clothes were shredded. Every piece of clothing I owned—paid for with pennies earned one by one—every skirt and blouse, so painstakingly packed by the naive version of myself who thought this to be a wonderful paying job, torn to pieces.

I thought of the man in the cap and the gray jacket. He had ransacked my things.

I should have screamed; I should have run for the landlord. I could do nothing but stare in a sort of sickened, exhausted horror that left me without the will to move. One of the maids found me there, five minutes later. I remember nothing of it, though later she told me I was weeping.

Chapter Eleven

*T*here was an uproar, of course, though I hardly recall it. The employees at the inn were questioned. They had seen nothing, no strangers or suspicious men. I was repeatedly asked for a description of the man. I could not give one. I had not seen his face, and there had been nothing distinctive about him at all.

Someone suggested the constable be called—there was none in Waringstoke, but someone could be summoned from a neighboring town, some sort of representative of law and order. Alistair turned the idea away. He took pity on my embarrassment and told the innkeeper that no harm had been done, that it need go no further than it already had. He requested I be given a new room. He said he would replace my things himself.

That broke me from my exhausted stupor. "You can't," I protested.

"You are here at my discretion, Sarah," he said gently. "I've put you in this predicament myself. I feel terrible, if you want to know the truth. Of course I'll replace your things."

I was proud, but what choice did I have? I was alone with nothing but the clothes I wore, and hardly a penny to my name. I had to accept. Secretly I hoped it would be a loan, that I would be able to repay Alistair someday.

Everyone listened to Alistair, of course. He had a way of easy authority about him. The curious patrons drifted away and the innkeeper and his wife set to work moving my room, no longer panicked. It was easy to believe everything would be all right when Alistair said so.

I knew better. Nothing would be all right. My upper arms hurt where Maddy had touched them, and I rubbed the skin gingerly through my sleeves, my arms crossed over my chest. The rubbing only made them feel worse.

Somewhere in the madness, Mrs. Clare had disappeared. I vaguely wondered when she had left.

My things were moved; the inn had only six rooms, so I had been moved down the hall, closer to the washroom, while the latch to my original room was repaired. Alistair steered me down the hall. "Are you certain you're quite all right? You've had a few shocks today. Should I send for a doctor? Some food? Tea?"

"There's only one thing she needs," said a familiar voice from behind me. "A ticket out of Waringstoke."

I turned. Matthew had put his cap on, and was leaning against the wall, his hands in his pockets. "I'll be fine, thank you."

"I don't think you will." Matthew's face was inscrutable, but his voice was cocky, and I suddenly sensed he was mocking me. "Or did you not notice what just happened here?"

I took a step forward in a genuine spurt of anger. "You'd like that, wouldn't you? If I left? Then you'd be free of me."

"Now, now," said Alistair.

Matthew's face darkened. He ignored Alistair and spoke straight to me. "It isn't that I would like it. It's only that this doesn't seem like a good situation for a woman, and it gets worse by the minute."

Outrage made my face hot. "And that's your objective opinion, is it? That I should step aside and get out of your way? I already know you want me to go. You needn't bother to deny it."

"That's ridiculous." He was flushed now. "You're in danger, that's all. Something you seem too stubborn to figure out. If Alistair had any sense, he'd send you straight to London on the next train."

"*Send* me!"

"Hey—both of you." Alistair raised his voice. "What's gotten into you?"

I backed up a step. Matthew took off his cap and scrubbed his forehead with the heel of his hand, the scar plainly visible from under his cuff. I shook my head, assuring myself I'd be a fool to entertain, even for a second, the notion that Matthew was truly concerned about me. He only wanted me gone. "I'll be in my room," I said.

It was hard to believe I was tired, but for once my body overtook my overwrought mind. After I was left alone in my new room, my shredded things piled in a suitcase on the dresser next to me, I sat on the bed and removed my shoes. I lay back, looking at the old oak-paneled ceiling, trying to catch my thoughts and pin them down, but they would not stay still.

I was, in fact, afraid. I knew it was dangerous, that things were starting to spin out of control. I realized now that a wild kind of alchemy had happened that morning between Maddy and me. She had awareness, *thoughts*, not just rage. Mrs. Clare said I had upset her, but I wondered if it was so simple, if there was not worse to come.

And now there was the man. Matthew was right about that—it wasn't safe here. If I was logical, I would leave.

But if I was in danger, then so were the others. Lying there on the bed, I decided I would not leave. We had all been through a war, after all. I knew of so many men who had never come home. After that, what was dangerous to any of us anymore?

☙

I must have dozed, for I opened my eyes to see that dusk had fallen. My room was quiet. My mind drifted; my thoughts slowed.

I had just washed my face and brushed my hair—my hairbrush, at least, had not been damaged—when a soft knock sounded on my door. Assuming it to be one of the maids, I opened it.

Matthew Ryder stood there.

He fixed me with his dark gaze. His cap was gone, his hair tousled and damp, as if he had washed. He wore a clean white shirt that glowed a little in the dusk. He seemed huge and uncouth, his shoulders wide, the muscles flexed under the white fabric. His jaw was dark with stubble. I couldn't move, couldn't turn away or shut the door to save my life, as my heart jumped in my chest. In the stillness I could hear him breathe.

I tore my gaze downward with an effort and saw that he carried a small bag in one hand. A white cascade of fabric was draped over the other arm.

"I need to come in," he said simply.

I looked back up at him, shocked. The thought of letting a man in my room was strange enough, but it was a thousand times worse that the man was Matthew Ryder.

He saw my hesitation, and a look of stubbornness that I was

coming to recognize settled over his features. "Sarah. Are you going to play the coy maiden with me?"

I shook my head. Stupid, of course, to think that he would come to my room with any designs on me. He was here on an errand, likely one he didn't particularly want to do. I stepped aside.

He came in the room and set down the small bag. He unfolded the white fabric from his arm. "The landlady gave me this for you." He handed it to me and I held it up. It was a nightgown—old-fashioned and frilly, perhaps, but well made.

"How good of her," I said. "I hadn't thought of what I would sleep in tonight."

"Do you like it?" When I looked at him in surprise, he added, "She had several. I picked that one."

I looked back down at the nightgown, its high collar and extravagant sleeves. I'd be swimming in it, but I wasn't about to say anything ungrateful. I searched for something positive instead. "I won't be cold."

Surprise lit his eyes, then a quick, wry humor. The corner of his mouth quirked slowly up in a half smile of genuine amusement. I'd never seen him smile—a true smile, not a cynical grimace—and for a moment it robbed me of breath.

He saw how I looked at him, and the smile faded away. His eyes darkened, and a purpose came into his gaze, raw and serious. My heart thudded. I was irritated with myself; he fascinated me so, despite how he unsettled me, despite how I mistrusted him. I made myself remember that he didn't like me, that I was angry at him, and I put the nightgown on the bed.

Matthew picked up the bag again. His expression had changed, hardened into what I thought was almost derision, though I could not think why. "Your arms. Where Maddy touched you."

They stung, even now. "What about them?"

"I'm going to take a look at them. They're paining you, no?" He raised his eyebrows in a question, his gaze never leaving me. He must have seen me rubbing my arms earlier, though I was surprised he'd noticed. "I would like to see them, please."

Show him my upper arms? "Matthew, I don't think—"

"Sarah." His voice was rough like a cat's tongue. "Unbutton your dress."

My mouth opened in shock. "I beg—I beg your pardon?" I couldn't do it. I had a thin cotton slip beneath my dress, of course—I wasn't bare. Still, I simply couldn't.

"Unbutton your dress," he said again.

He could have left the room to let me prepare, or he could have sent for a true doctor. But of course he had no intention of doing either. I was in his place, in his job, and worse, the other night I had embarrassed him. I hadn't forgotten the look he had given me when he saw me in the hall.

"You're doing this on purpose," I said. "For revenge."

Surprise flitted again across his features; it seemed I had managed to surprise him twice tonight. He looked down at the bag, as if its contents were suddenly of high import. When he looked back up, the humor had returned to his eyes, touched perhaps with sheepishness. "All right—yes, there is that. I admit it."

I crossed my arms.

"But you're still going to do it."

My mouth opened, then closed. The smile still played at the edges of his lips, but there was no mistaking the seriousness of his voice, or the way his dark eyes regarded me.

He meant to have his little revenge, then, embarrassment for embarrassment. His gaze traveled over me, down my body, to my waist. I felt its appreciative slide like a hand, and I blushed. Something sluggish and warm started in my veins as we looked at each other. I felt it throb slowly over my skin, through my blood. The tips of my breasts tingled as if they were already exposed. I thought of what he had looked like, nearly naked, the thick planes of his muscles, his slim stomach, the powerful flex of his arms. I thought of that brief moment when he had held me as I ran from the barn, his arm roughly about my waist. I knew the feeling that overtook me every time I looked at him was something that could not be undone, put away, sent back to sleep. It was a threshold crossed, and there was no going back.

And suddenly, I *wanted* to do it. I wanted to do what he said, to surrender. But also, part of me wanted him to see how I felt, what I thought when I looked at him. Part of me wanted him to know.

"Very well, then." I reached for the buttons on my dress. Before the first button was undone, my hands were shaking and I dropped my gaze, unable to look at his reaction. A girl's bravery went only so far.

But he had seen *my* reaction, hadn't he? He had seen what he thought was disgust on my face at the sight of him. He'd had no choice. Did his revenge also mean I had to look up and see his derisive stare, even his laughter? I fumbled the second button, unsure.

"Sarah," I heard him say.

"Matthew, I didn't mean to," I blurted, still unable to raise my eyes. "It was an accident. I'm sorry."

He was silent, so I kept going. Finally I tugged the last button from its place.

The fashion of the time was a boyish look; dresses were cut in a straight silhouette, and ideal females—movie stars, fashion models, women in the advertisements—were slender and flat-chested, long-limbed and long-necked. I, like most girls, knew I did not fit the ideal. I was slim enough, but I was of medium height, not tall and willowy; and my breasts, though not unreasonably large, would protrude, no matter what I wore. The flat drapes of the dresses in the stores never sat right on me, to my frustration, and so I bought workaday shirtwaists and buttoned blouses, to at least cover my embarrassing shape. They were the best I could do, but they were unfashionable, and I wished hopelessly for a body without curves.

As underwear I wore cotton tops reinforced with a second layer of cloth over the breasts, to keep my chest from unsightly motion as I moved. It was modest as a bathing suit. I told myself this as I looked down at the gaping front of my shirtdress.

Get this over with. In a quick motion I pushed the fabric from my shoulders and down my arms. I stood there exposed, my gaze firmly on the floor, thinking of what he could see. The slope of the tops of my breasts. The rounded shape of their curved undersides through the cotton fabric. If he looked closely, the faint suggestion of nipples—or perhaps he would simply imagine that.

I heard him take a small breath—just a quick inhalation—and I cringed in embarrassment. This was revenge indeed.

"Your arms," he said.

I looked at them and shock hit me, overtaking the humiliation. My upper arms, where Maddy had grasped me, were circled in dark, mottled bruises. Cutting through the purple and black, the flesh had turned grayish and sick, the marrow of where she had touched me as white, as hard, as dead as chalk. A small sound of horror escaped my throat.

Matthew came close, sat on the edge of the dresser, and took my arm at the elbow, angling it in front of him. "My God. Does it hurt?"

"Yes," I said shakily. "What is it? What's wrong with me?"

"Damned if I know. Fu—" He glanced at me. "Devil take it," he finished lamely. He touched the skin gently with a fingertip, ran it lightly over the chalky flesh.

Something strange happened. For a second, the world disappeared. I saw, right before my eyes, green treetops, and, beyond them, a chimney of red brick, protruding from a house I could not see. I blinked and the image was gone.

"Sarah?" said Matthew.

I shook my head. It made no sense, and yet it had been there. "I don't know," I said.

He dropped my arm, rifled through his bag, put it down again. "Stupid—to think I have anything to treat this with. What should I do, do you think? Bandage it?"

"I don't know," I said. "Should we call for Alistair?"

Our eyes locked and we looked at each other for a long moment. For the first time, I knew exactly what he was thinking, because his thoughts echoed my own. Really, we should call Alistair. And yet Alistair would want to take notes; Alistair would want to interview me yet again. Worse, Alistair would want to get the camera, claiming we needed to document my bruises before they faded away. It was the right thing to do, and yet—and yet, Alistair would undoubtedly wonder what Matthew was doing alone with me in my bedroom late at night, with my dress at my waist and my nightgown forgotten.

Matthew cleared his throat. "I think I'll just bandage them."

I bit my lip and nodded. "Bandage them. Yes. If they're worse tomorrow, I'll tell Alistair then."

"Do you promise?"

I nodded again.

He bent his head to rummage in his bag. His game of humiliation was forgotten now, and he seemed a little ashamed. "I'm not a monster," he said after a moment, his voice quiet.

I looked at the wall as he unwound the bandages, and thought of the moment I'd seen his scars. "What happened?" I asked.

He followed my train of thought in a pause of silence. Then a low laugh came from him, a deep cynical chuckle. "Some other time, my dear, I'll tell you a bloodthirsty bedtime story. Not tonight."

I sighed. Our moment of intimacy was over, it seemed, even though I sat there in my undershirt. Still, I wanted to keep him talking. "Why do you think that man destroyed my room? I have nothing to steal."

"He wanted to frighten you," said Matthew.

"Truly? Do you think he—" Matthew touched the bandage to my arm, and again the room disappeared; again I saw that red-brick chimney, just past the treetops, under a gray sky. The vision came clearer this time. I could see the glossy wet leaves, glistening and bobbing gently, and just past them the chimney, its red brick stained to dark rhubarb in the damp. I felt an urgency come over me—there was something about it, about this mundane picture, that was important and just out of my reach. If I looked harder—

"Sarah?"

I came back into my little room at the inn, the dim gaslight, the heavy wood beams. This was getting embarrassing. "I'm sorry. What were you saying?"

He looked at me suspiciously, but did not press. "I said turn around. I'm going to do your other arm."

I did as I was asked, trying to put myself back into our conversation about the man in my room. "Do you think he was trying to make me think it was Maddy?"

"A ghost in your room?" He grunted. "It's possible. The real question is, why was he trying to scare you off?"

"Because of Maddy." This answer I knew. I tucked a stray lock of hair behind my ear. "It's the only answer. I've hardly even spoken to anyone here. There's no reason for anyone to know who I am, let alone wish me ill."

Matthew's voice was wry. "You know nothing of small towns, obviously. Sarah, everyone here knows who you are, who we all are, for miles around. I guarantee it."

I covered my shock. "Why would anyone bother?"

"Why not? What else happens in a place like this? We were already news, but after this morning's display we're probably a sensation."

He reached down and held up the top half of my dress for me to take. "Here. I'm finished."

I slid it over my shoulders, my self-consciousness forgotten as I thought over what he'd said. "We may all be a sensation, but it was I who went into the barn. And it was my room that was tossed."

"Exactly."

But why? Was it possible that someone wanted me to stay away from Maddy? Why, when she was just a ghost that most people didn't even believe in? What had the man thought he'd find in my room?

I remembered the strange flashes of vision I'd seen. They were so vivid. Could I actually smell the rainy air, or was that my imagination? The burst of longing, of frustration, had been so clear. It may as well have been a written message: There was more to find here.

I turned and looked at Matthew. "I know you want me to go back to London, but I won't. Not until this is over. I want you to know that."

I had expected an argument, but he snapped his bag shut and seemed to consider it. "Why should I leave it be?"

"Because there's more going on. Something important. And I can help you find it."

"Maybe you can, and maybe you can't. If—and I mean if—I leave it be for a few days, what exactly do you propose to do?"

"I want to know more about Maddy," I said.

He crossed his arms and regarded me. "As it happens, so do I."

Chapter Twelve

The next morning over breakfast, Alistair announced we were going into town. We had to buy new clothes to replace my ruined ones, and since Alistair had agreed to pay, over my objections, he would accompany me. That left Matthew.

"Will you come, then?" Alistair cut the last piece of his sausage and glanced across the table at Matthew. "Or will you stay and try to fix the recording machine?"

Matthew spared not even a single look in my direction. "I can't fix that thing," he grumbled. "I'll come with you and find something to distract myself."

Alistair looked at him with wry affection. "Not too many pints of distraction, now. It's not even ten o'clock. We have work to do."

"Yes, Mother."

This got a laugh from Alistair. He looked at me, merriment in his eyes. "You see what I have to put up with, Sarah? He'd better watch out—you're a much more polite assistant, and you're a hundred times better to look at."

I smiled back and wondered at these two men, so different and yet so obviously long acquainted. Suddenly, I was curious about how they met. I did not think Matthew would tell me, so I asked Alistair as we walked over the hill toward town, Matthew trailing behind us alone.

"We met in training, if you can believe it," Alistair replied instantly. "His bunk was next to mine." He glanced at me. "I don't suppose, when you look at us, that you think we have much in common. But we did. Matthew likes to get in trouble just as much as I do. And there are lots of ways to get in trouble in the army, especially if you haven't seen a battle yet."

I thought this over and decoded it. Alistair was saying they had been different men then. Young men who had never seen war. Men who thought enlisting to fight the Hun would be a lark. I had met other young men in London just like them in those early days, when it seemed as if every girl I knew wanted to set me up with a potential beau. I had been dragged to many parties with strangers, and everywhere one looked at such parties, there were soldiers and more soldiers. At first, the soldiers had shouted patriotic songs and made crude jokes about the Hun. Later, though, there were only men who looked at women with a strange sort of hunger, mixed with a separation of experience that could never be gulfed. Men who had come back shattered shells, if they had come back at all.

I tried to picture Matthew younger, carefree. The picture would not come.

"We even stuck together on the boat to France," Alistair went on. "But we were in different regiments, so I lost track of him over there. I fought in France and Belgium for three years, until I got shot in my leg. Bullet grazed the vein in my thigh and I almost died—would have, if I'd been standing half an inch to the left." His expression darkened, but he shrugged. "Still, it got me invalided out for a while to recover. I was sent to a home hospital in Essex. I slept for three days. When I woke up, guess who was in the bed next to mine."

"Matthew," I said.

But the good humor had left Alistair's face. I began to regret that I had broached this topic. "Yes, well. Matthew was in a bad way, much worse than me—that's all I'll say. What happened to him is his story to tell, not mine." He watched as the trees thinned around us on the road, as the small center of Waringstoke came closer. The sunlight dappled in his hair. He had begun to limp with the length of the walk. "They put me back together again, let me recover all the blood I'd lost, gave me a walking stick. Told me I was good enough to go back and fight some more. I was still waiting for the paperwork to come through when the war ended. I've always been a lucky bastard."

He sounded grim as he said it, and I didn't know what to say. Was he pleased to be free from the fighting, or had he been disappointed in not getting the chance to go back?

From behind us, Matthew's steps accelerated, bringing him closer. "Alistair. Remind me why we didn't bring the motorcar?"

"Because it's only twenty minutes," Alistair teased, moving aside and letting Matthew come next to him. The twinkle returned to his eye. "You, my friend, are getting fat and lazy on inn food."

"It's bloody hot," said Matthew.

He was right. The sun had burned through the morning mist, leaving a yellow heat that was wet and heavy. There was hardly a breeze to be had. Still, I was as glad of the walk as Alistair was. It was good to get away from the darkened old inn, from the shadow of Falmouth House.

We came to the heart of what Waringstoke called town—two streets in a simple X, lined with shops, a post office, a pub. Anchoring the end of the east–west lane was a church and churchyard, glinting gray stone set against the wet green of the grass. The churchyard looked overgrown. There was no one about, at least on the quiet streets. I thought of how different it was from shopping in London, at Harrods and the hundreds of large and small shops on every street, the windows filled with elaborate displays. I had so rarely had any money with which to buy anything, I was well acquainted with the window displays.

The night before, Matthew and I had quietly agreed that today would be a fact-finding mission about Maddy Clare. The locals must know something about her—she may have kept to herself, but she had lived at Falmouth House for seven years. Surely there was gossip about the mad girl who worked as the Clares' maid and never left the house? Surely someone, somewhere, had told stories she shouldn't have?

We split up, Matthew to his own business, Alistair and I to the few ladies' shops to replenish my suitcase. Mere days ago, I would have been paralyzed with terror at the thought of shopping with a man. I was still a little shy, but it did not take me long to feel relaxed again. I had been nearly undressed in front of Matthew, after all. And I had faced worse fears than having a man help me pick out underthings.

It still bothered me, however, that Alistair was paying for everything. He seemed to sense this, and in the way of his good-natured soul, he did not push me. He let me pick out only the least expensive items; he let me choose only the clothes that were practical, sturdy, in the simplest of styles so they would not be out of fashion in a year. He argued with me when I insisted I needed only one pair of stockings. I maintained I had more at home in London and did not need him to buy me a second pair. Eventually, I made him give in.

I had replaced everything but my favorite shirtdress. Alistair left me to try on dresses, saying he must make a stop at the post office, as he had forwarded his mail to Waringstoke. I shopped alone.

I selected a few—simple and serviceable, of course, and suited to my figure—and proceeded to the back of the shop, as directed by the saleslady, to try them on. I pulled the curtain and stood in the tiny dressing area.

My dress—the one surviving dress from my previous wardrobe—had sleeves to the elbows. I slid the dress off and looked at the bandages Matthew had fastened last night, circling each upper arm. They glowed eerily white in the gloom. My arms still hurt. Did they hurt more or less than yesterday? Did I even know?

Should I remove the bandages to look?

I had promised Matthew I would. I had promised him that if my arms were worse today than they had been yesterday, I would tell Alistair. And yet, I didn't want to. I simply didn't want to know.

What if the problem was serious? What if I needed medical attention?

Could any doctor possibly treat what was wrong with me?

As I stood in indecision, I heard the click of heeled footsteps approaching. I assumed it to be the saleswoman until I glimpsed the shoes beneath the bottom of my curtain. They were new, glossy, high-fashion heels, with a sleek buckle at the ankle. No saleswoman in Waringstoke owned shoes like that.

"Miss Piper," said a woman's voice.

I closed my eyes. I knew exactly who it was, of course. I had known the second I saw the shoes.

"Mrs. Barry," I said. The woman walking her dog the other morning. The tall, utterly beautiful woman who had shared a cigarette with Alistair.

"I'm sorry to bother you," she said in her strong, husky voice.

I stood in the gloom in my yellowed cotton slip, the bandages blazing from my arms, and wished more than anything that she would go away. Next to her glamour, I felt the day's confidence draining away. "How do you do, Mrs. Barry?" I managed.

"Listen." The shoes moved closer. I stared at them in envy; they had cost more than a month's wages at the temporary agency. "I have to confess something—I followed you here," she said, surprising me.

"What are you talking about?" I did not move closer to the curtain.

"It sounds horrible, I know. Crazy, in fact. But I have my reasons. Just listen a moment."

I pictured the morning I had found her talking to Alistair, how small I had felt. How she had looked at him when she lit his cigarette. How there had been currents of something I could not see. "Mr. Gellis is at the post office, if you are looking for him," I said smoothly.

"Please. Just listen."

I paused, thinking. "All right."

She sighed, and the shoes paced away. I pictured her in an exquisite dress, a matching hat, those soft suede gloves she had been wearing when I first met her. No. On second thought, she would be wearing a different pair of gloves, a pair for warmer weather.

I had been so very intimidated by her when I had first met her; now I was merely repelled. I shifted my weight to one foot, waiting.

"I want to know something," said Mrs. Barry. "This ghost. The maid. Is it true she talks to you?"

My jaw dropped. "What?"

"If it's true, I need to know. I need to know it." She sounded hurried, impatient, perhaps a little afraid.

"Mrs. Barry, perhaps you should tell me what you've been hearing."

She sighed again. I heard her pace across the floor. "It's all over town. That Al—that Mr. Gellis brought you here. That you are some sort of clairvoyant, called in particularly for your expertise in speaking to ghosts. That Agnes Clare let you into the barn to see the ghost. That you've been communing with that girl from the dead."

I pressed my hand to my mouth. I did not know whether I wanted more to giggle—me, a ghost specialist brought in by Alistair!—or gasp. I thought quickly and decided not to disillusion her—I would not lie, but it might be to my benefit to maneuver a little. "What do you know about Maddy Clare?" I asked.

"Please." Her footsteps came closer. "Have you been speaking to her? Truly?"

"She has spoken to me," I said carefully. This was true; I left out the part about being nearly driven mad by the sound. "Did you know her in life?"

"Oh, God." Mrs. Barry became still at the other side of the curtain. "What did she say? Was it about . . ."

"About what?" I prompted when she stopped.

"Miss Piper—did she have a message? Any kind of message? Please tell me."

I was firm. "Not until you tell me what interest you have in a message from Maddy Clare."

"I don't have time," she said hopelessly. "I have to go. I told Tom I would only be a moment, that I was looking at dresses. He'll follow me in here. Listen—I'll be walking my dog in the mornings. Every morning. There's never any suspicion in that. If you can tell me—please. Please meet me and tell me."

She sounded so very desperate. I wondered what was wrong, but I also knew I would not get it out of her. She was already turning to leave. "Please," she said again, and was gone.

I stood in the quiet for a moment, wondering if she would return, but she did not. *The maid,* Mrs. Barry had said. *You have been communing with that girl.* She had been unable to say Maddy's name.

Ignoring my bandages, I pulled the dresses from their hangers and began to try them on.

Chapter Thirteen

Waringstoke's pub was small and cozy. Except for the public room at the inn, it was the only place for the town locals to gather, so it wasn't a surprise to see it relatively crowded at the lunch hour. As we took a table, Alistair, in the midst of grumbling about Matthew's tardiness, froze midsentence at something over my shoulder.

"What?" I said. "What is it?"

He gained control of his expression and looked away. "Nothing."

I wasn't fooled. I angled myself inconspicuously in my chair and caught a glimpse of Mrs. Barry being seated at a nearby table with a man, presumably her husband. He was turned away from me, but I could see he was slender, dark-haired. I turned back to Alistair.

There was nothing in his eyes. He signaled for a barmaid. "I can't wait for Matthew. I'm hungry."

I waited until we had ordered, gathering my courage. Finally,

I plunged forward. "What is it about her?" I asked him. "About Mrs. Barry?"

He said nothing for a long time. In fact, our food had arrived before he spoke, and I thought he had resolved not to speak altogether. He dug into his ploughman's lunch, his eyes still carefully averted from the other table. "Sometimes, Sarah, you are far too observant."

"You can tell me," I said, stung. "I'm not a child. Are you—are you two—"

"Cuckolding her husband?" His cheeks had gone red, and he set his fork down. "No. We're not. Is that what you'd like to know?"

If you've bearded the lion in his cage, I thought, *there's nothing to do but show courage.* "Well, I didn't—I didn't mean that. It's just that it seems there's something going on."

He picked up his fork again, pushed his food around on his plate, just as I was doing. "I met Evangeline at a New Year's party in 1914, like she said. It was at a club in London. I danced with her twice, and I asked her to marry me."

I couldn't help a small sound of surprise.

He stabbed a potato. "I've never asked that of a woman before or since. It was stupid, but it was real. There was something between us, and nothing else in that moment, in any moment, made any sense. I simply didn't want to let go of her. And then she told me she was already married."

"Oh," I said.

He lifted his eyes to mine. "There you go, Sarah. Now you know it. I went off to war and I didn't see her again. I had no idea she lived in Waringstoke. I didn't know anything about her, except that I could never have her. And then she came by the inn that morning, walking her dog."

The pain in his eyes made my heart ache. I thought of the fear I'd heard in Evangeline Barry's voice. *I told him I would only be a moment. He'll follow me in here.* "Alistair," I said, leaning toward him, wishing I could put my hand on his. "Alistair, I think perhaps—"

"Well, well."

I looked up, my cheeks flaming. It was Mrs. Barry's husband, approaching our table. His dark hair was slicked back, and he had blue eyes fringed with dark black lashes. "It's the ghost hunters," he said, as if delighted. "Here they are, in person. How lucky we all are!"

Alistair and I exchanged a look, and he opened his mouth to say something, but Mr. Barry merely continued. "I beg pardon," he said smoothly. He placed a hand on the back of my chair and leaned down, his face uncomfortably close to mine. "I am Tom Barry." He held out his other hand to me. "How do you do?"

Startled, I put my hand in his. "Sarah—Sarah Piper."

"Miss Piper." He squeezed my hand, held it a little too long, then turned to Alistair, his hand still on the back of my chair. "And you, sir?"

Alistair frowned. Neither man held out a hand to the other. "Alistair Gellis. Is there something we can help you with?"

"You're ridding Waringstoke of its ghosts, are you not?" said Tom Barry, pulling up a chair and seating himself. He placed his hand on the back of my chair again. "I'd say that's damned helpful. But I'm here to help *you*. And so you must let me buy you a drink." He leaned in confidentially, lowering his voice so the other tables couldn't hear. "I hear you're from London. What a bloody relief! I lived there for a few years during the war, myself. Places like this, you know—" He shook his head, his glance indicating the rest of the room, and presumably all of Waringstoke. "Well, let's just say I'm overjoyed to have someone real to talk to."

I turned to look at Evangeline at the table behind me. She was sitting watching us, her legs crossed, a cigarette in one hand propped by the elbow on the table, her pose relaxed. She caught my eye and gave me an amused smile, an ironic wave. I stared at her, trying to reconcile this woman with the frightened woman who had approached me in the change room not three-quarters of an hour ago.

Tom Barry had turned his gaze to follow mine. "My wife," he said to me. "She's quite shy, and so she's staying exactly there, while the rest of us have drinks together."

"Really, there is no need," said Alistair.

"It's already done," said Tom Barry. "I've ordered us a bottle of whiskey. The finest this place has to offer. We'll drink a few toasts. And maybe we'll have a few ghost stories round the table."

Whiskey! It was barely one o'clock. I tried to protest, but the barmaid placed the bottle on the table, along with three glasses. Barry reached for it immediately and began to pour. "I'm sorry I'm so forward," he said, though his tone said he was not sorry at all. "I suppose it's a little surprising to a Londoner. But we're all friends here, you know, and I'm used to it. Besides"—here he lowered his voice again—"the villagers here are a little suspicious of you, if you don't mind my saying so. Narrow minds, and all of that. So I thought I'd lead the way. Break the ice, you know." He smiled at us; his smile was a little crooked, as if not drawn on his face quite right. He raised his glass, and used a voice that boomed through the rest of the room. "A toast!"

I didn't want any whiskey. I'd never had it in my life, and the thought of drinking down all that dark liquid—for Barry had filled our glasses quite full—made me slightly queasy. And yet, as I looked around the room, I saw that everyone was indeed looking at us, some of them directly, some with sideways glances. Even the bartender was watching us as he polished a glass. What if Barry was right? We needed these people, these villagers, to help us with the case of Maddy Clare. What if they looked to Tom Barry as something of a leader, as he'd implied? Nothing would get solved if no one would talk to us. Perhaps a little whiskey was a small sacrifice.

I caught Alistair's eye. He put his hand on his glass. I did the same.

"That's the spirit!" said Barry. "To our guests!" He drank his glass in one swallow.

I held my breath and tipped my glass to my lips, but the first swallow burned down my throat and I gasped. I put my glass down, coughing, my nose burning. I apologized, but Tom Barry was laughing.

"A virgin, eh?" he said. "We won't get through the bottle very quickly if that's how you drink. Give it another try."

"It isn't necessary," said Alistair. I noticed his glass was empty; he could drink just as effortlessly as he did everything else. "Sarah, don't worry about it."

"Be a sport," said Barry, with his crooked smile. "One more. Just one."

"I really don't—"

"She doesn't want it."

My heart stopped as I recognized the voice. Matthew stood by our table, his expression unreadable. He wore his cloth cap and was slouched easily into his corduroy jacket, his posture one of relaxed strength, like that of a boxer out of the ring. He had one hand in his pocket, and in the other he held a glass of beer. He must have been served at the bar, then, and I wondered how long he had been standing there, watching us.

Tom Barry laughed again and looked at Alistair. "Who is this, then? Your man?"

"You're in my chair," said Matthew.

Barry looked at him for a tight beat of silence. "Go away, my boy. We're having a drink here and you're not invited."

Alistair found his voice. "Matthew is a member of my team."

Tom Barry looked from one to another of us, each in turn. "Well, then," he said, as he read our faces. "I see."

"You've proven your point," Matthew said, nodding toward the whiskey bottle. "We have work to do here."

"Matthew," said Alistair.

"No, it's quite all right." Tom Barry stood. He looked at us with an expression that said we'd made an enemy. "I can see you don't want my help. Well, good luck without it." He brushed past Matthew and his eyes narrowed. "You think you're a strong one, don't you? I could take you on."

"You'd lose," said Matthew.

Barry motioned to Evangeline, who was watching the exchange with calm eyes. She put out her cigarette and stood. Without another glance at us, she followed her husband out the door.

Matthew took Tom Barry's vacated chair, swiveled it with one large hand, and gracefully straddled it backward, his forearms across the top of the wooden back. He adjusted his cap on his head and looked at us. "Well, then?"

Alistair sighed. "Matthew, we were trying to be political here."

"By making Sarah drink whiskey?"

I blushed and looked at the half-empty glass in front of me. The smell of it was unappealing, and I wished I could be rid of it.

"She didn't drink much," said Alistair. "He was willing to help us."

"No, he wasn't." Matthew took a sip of his beer. "He was willing to help himself. And you know I've no use for politics."

"A friendly gesture doesn't hurt. Not that I've ever been able to get that into you."

"You can't take me anywhere." Matthew's tone was almost nasty. "I guess your hired help needs better manners."

"That's uncalled for. I told him he was out of line."

"Funny, I didn't hear it."

"Stop arguing," I broke in.

They both looked at me.

My cheeks burned, but I went on. "Alistair, you could have stood up to him. Matthew is right—he was bullying us. It was a show in front of the rest of the town, though I have no idea what for. You were too flustered because he's Evangeline's husband."

"What?" said Matthew. He leaned back. "That was Evangeline?"

I watched the two of them exchange a look—so Matthew knew all about Evangeline, then. I pressed on. "And you," I said to Matthew. "Whatever you think of Tom Barry, you could have remembered that we're in public here, and we're strangers to these people. You've just made a lovely story that will be all over Waringstoke, if it isn't already. You yourself told me that we're already news in a small town like this. Now you've made a very nice stir."

I had never made a speech like it in my life before. For a second the three of us, including myself, sat surprised. Then Matthew spoke.

"I didn't know that was Evangeline," he said. He looked at Alistair. "Did you know she was in Waringstoke?"

"No." Alistair sounded tired. "Not until I saw her when we arrived."

"And now you've met her husband," Matthew said with sympathy. "Lucky you." He looked at me. "We should interview Evangeline."

I shook my head. "I don't think she'll see us. She approached me in the dress shop. I don't think she can get away from him except when she's walking her dog."

"She approached you in the dress shop?" Alistair rubbed his forehead. "Sarah, what are you saying? Do you think she is afraid of her husband?"

"I don't—" I bit my lip. "I don't know." I couldn't sort it out. Which had been the real Evangeline—the frightened wife, or the woman who had walked out with her husband? Had the scene in the dressing room been an act to get information from me?

"All right, then," said Matthew. "That's a dead end, at least for now. I've been doing some digging this morning. There are other avenues we could take to investigate."

"Investigate?" said Alistair. "I have no idea what you're talking about. We're ghost hunters, not detectives. I've no intention of doing an investigation."

"You have to," I told him. "You promised Mrs. Clare you'd try to get rid of Maddy. How are you going to do it if you don't know why she's here, or what she wants? Nothing about her story adds up. Where did she come from? What happened to her before she reached the Clares'? Why did she kill herself? Why does she haunt the barn?"

"Sarah," said Alistair, "it could be nothing to do with any of that. Do you understand? Maddy may just be a random phenomenon. Some ghosts are simply a concentration of energy, nothing more."

"But some ghosts are more," said Matthew.

Alistair looked from Matthew to me. "Ah, well." He leaned back in his chair. "I know when I'm outvoted. Very well, we'll try it your way and see." He crooked an eyebrow at me. "Sarah, since it seems you are in charge—what do you propose we do next?"

I ignored the tease, and pondered the question. "I noticed the churchyard as we came into town," I said at last. "I'd like to see her grave."

⊗

"Do you know," said Alistair as we entered the quiet, lonely churchyard, "I'm not even certain she's buried here?"

"Where else would she be buried?" Matthew asked.

Alistair shrugged. "I never asked." He slanted a look sideways at me. "It seems I should have let you run the interview."

We had stopped partway down the path, and I glanced around, wondering where to start in the overgrown grass, where gravestones both new and old poked through next to the Queen Anne's lace. A hot breeze blew against my legs and breathed across my sweaty neck. "I'm sorry about my outburst," I said now, meaning it. "I shouldn't have spoken like that. I also shouldn't have pried about Mrs. Barry. I apologize."

Alistair put his hands in his pockets and looked around along with me, while Matthew strode ahead of us down one of the paths and began to peer at stones. "You meant well," he said softly. "I had no idea you were so emotional."

"Neither did I," I replied. I caught his eye and nodded toward the church, where a figure was emerging from a side door and coming toward us. "Who is that?"

Alistair turned and followed my gaze. "My guess is the sexton."

The man came closer, and I was surprised to see that I recognized him. He was over sixty, the creases in his face deeply set, his sparse gray hair combed back from his browned forehead. He greeted Alistair with only a brief nod. As Alistair introduced us, and the man reluctantly told us his name was Jarvis, I finally placed the man in my mind. I had seen him in the taproom at the inn on my first night in Waringstoke, glaring at me in disapproval. He had been wearing a blue coat at the time. He wore an old sweater now, patched at the elbows, sagging over trousers that were none too clean, and work boots caked with mud.

His expression today was nearly as hostile as it had been that first night, especially when he directed it at me. "Help you with something?" he asked us, terse.

"Maddy Clare, the servant girl," Alistair said. "Is she buried here?"

The man grunted. "Back corner." He looked away, toward the trees. "Why they paid to bury a servant girl here is more than I know."

"They were fond of her," Alistair said mildly.

Mr. Jarvis grunted again.

"Did you dig the grave yourself?" I asked him.

Mr. Jarvis looked at me briefly again—the hostility in his eyes was unmistakable—and said, "I dig all the graves in Waringstoke, missy."

"Now, hear," Alistair chided him, but we were interrupted by a shout from Matthew. He was standing by a gravestone near the edge of the yard, where the trees began.

"She's here," he said.

Maddy's grave was untended and overgrown, though this was also true of much of the graveyard proper. There were tangled weeds around her gravestone—a simple lozenge set into the earth that proclaimed her name and date of death. We stood looking down at it, Matthew and Alistair and I, as the birds sang in the overhead boughs of the trees.

Finally I knelt in the prickly grass. I brushed the leaves and stems from the stone, cleared it all the way to the edges, feeling a twinge of pity that those who put this stone here had never known her birth date, or even her true name. They had had to do the best they could.

I thought perhaps I would get one of the vivid images in my mind, the way I did when the strange bruises on my arms were touched. I had no idea what those images were—or what the red chimney and the treetops were supposed to mean—but I felt they were significant.

But the silence stretched on, and nothing happened. I stayed kneeling, waiting. The men behind me were silent.

"Nothing," I said at last, with regret.

"It isn't surprising," said Alistair. "Haunting of grave sites is actually very rare. Most people are not emotionally invested in where they are buried, so their energy does not concentrate there after death. Actually," he said with wry humor, "if one wants to avoid ghosts, the graveyard is one of the safest places to go."

But still, I thought, the grave could have yielded something. Some echo of the person beneath. Even a quiet sense of stillness, of sleeping peace. I touched the gravestone again. My parents' graves had seemed sad to me, the only time I had been able to bear to visit them. There had been a quiet sorrow about the two graves, side by side, that had reverberated through the air as if reflecting the way they had died. Or had that been my imagination—my own mood, based on my memory of that horrible day in the summer of 1919?

I sighed and stood again. I caught sight of the sexton, Jarvis, retreated most of the way back to the church now, watching us. I remembered Mrs. Barry's belief that I was some sort of "ghost specialist" brought in by Alistair. Mr. Jarvis, perhaps, suspected the same thing. It would explain his interest in me. But did it explain his hostility? What did he think I was learning from my visit to Maddy's grave?

We turned to leave. We had left my packages at the pub, and we were to pick them up, and start the walk back to the inn while the afternoon held. Alistair said he needed time to go through his notes; he was undecided as to whether I should be sent back into the barn, or when. He was torn between the obvious danger to me and the incredible firsthand research I provided each time I encountered Maddy. He was still bent on documenting the haunting, and if I was indeed to be sent back into the barn, he needed to decide what equipment I might bring.

And so, Alistair planned to spend the evening studying. Matthew was to spend the evening trying to fix the sound recorder. And I, after the terrible excitement of having my room broken into the night before, was to be given the evening off. That I had no idea what to do with an entire evening, and that I was afraid of being alone, were not taken into account. I sighed. Perhaps I would find a book to read.

As we left the graveyard, we passed one grave that was immaculately kept. It was a large family monument, in pristine white stone, and the grass around it was trim and carefully tended—the only plot in the entire churchyard that was so. As I walked by it, I took in the name inscribed on the stone, and though I had not been able to help my curiosity, I found I was not surprised. The name on the pristine white monument, the only one tended by the greedy sexton, who was no doubt paid extra for the service, was *Barry*.

Chapter Fourteen

Alistair went to his room after supper. Though I knew he was going to study his notes, he also looked tired. His leg was paining him after the long walk. He was also, I believed, more upset by the encounter with Evangeline Barry and her husband than he let on. I was more convinced than ever that she had hurt him. Whether she had ever returned Alistair's feeling at all was a mystery. But she was married, and so it was impossible. I could only feel terribly for Alistair, and hope he could someday find some more worthy object and move on.

Matthew had gone to our small private room and shut the door, likely to repair the sound-recording machine as he had promised. Tired myself, and not wanting to venture out of the inn, particularly alone, I picked up the only book I could find— one of Alistair's books on ghosts—and began to read.

Alistair's writing style mimicked his personality: vivid, smooth, interesting, and fun. The book was filled with story after story of English hauntings, told in great detail, complete with interviews with survivors and witnesses, histories of the houses and the ghosts seen, diagrams of some of the interiors with locations of sightings marked with an inked X, and many photographs from the very camera I had learned to use. Some of the photos were clear pictures of the houses, interior and exterior, lit in broad daylight; others were dark, blurry renditions taken during the supposed hauntings in an attempt to catch the ghost on film, just as I had done with Maddy.

I had never been interested in ghosts before taking the job with Alistair, but now I found myself fascinated. I went back and forth through the pages, both admiring and puzzling over the body of work of these two men I had so inexplicably met, both of them so strong-willed and intelligent, yet so damaged, and pursuing such a strange line of work.

I found I had more questions at the end of the book than I had had at the beginning. I told myself I did not want to bother Alistair, that he needed rest, and study. I told myself that I needed some company, and perhaps even some protection, as my room had been violated the night before. I told myself that social interaction had never done anyone any harm. These were the excuses I made to myself for going down to the private room, knocking gently on the door, and approaching Matthew Ryder.

He was indeed repairing the recording machine. He was seated at the table, the machine in front of him, its side panels dismantled, its wires exposed. Parts lay on the table around him. He was looking up in angry disapproval as I came through the door, but when he saw it was me, his expression changed. I could not read it. There was some tiredness there. A careful control, for certain. And yet he watched me as I came in the room, his eyes never leaving me as I pulled out a chair and sat down.

He had washed. He was wearing a clean white shirt—I was starting to notice that Matthew's clothes were always impeccably clean, as if he was fastidious about it—the sleeves of which were rolled to the elbows, the better for him to work. The button at his throat was undone. His strong, muscled hands became still, and he watched me from his deep, dark eyes, with their dark lashes.

Before I could help myself, I glanced down at his bare forearms. The right was scarred worse than the left; this was the arm on which the scars traveled all the way down to the wrist and even the back of the hand. But the flesh on the left was mottled as well, partway down the forearm, even on the tender flesh of the inside of the arm. I could not imagine how painful that must have been. I jerked my glance away and looked back up into his face, caught him watching me steadily with unreadable calm.

I felt myself redden. After I'd been so bold as to intrude, my usual shyness came over me again. "Please don't let me interrupt you," I said, trying to sound casual. "I have just come in for some company. I hope you don't mind."

"You're wearing one of your new dresses," he said.

I touched my collar, self-conscious. I was indeed wearing one of the dresses Alistair had paid for—another shirtdress, serviceable like the one I had lost. The ladies of Waringstoke, it seemed, were much more impervious to fashion than the sharp ladies of London, and the dress was fitted for comfort, tapered in a little at the waist and sewn with enough room in the bodice. I had no need to flatten my chest or wear a confining girdle underneath. It was a relief, to simply wear something that fit my body as it was. It made me feel a little attractive, even though I was sure no one else would find the navy blue fabric with its pattern of tiny blue flowers more than modestly pretty.

"Yes, I am," I said to Matthew.

"It looks nice," he said.

I paused in surprise, and he looked away, dropping his gaze back down to the recording machine. He began to work again, his forearms flexing as he fitted two pieces together, and I tried not to feel too much shock—and happiness—at the compliment. Instead, I put my book on the table.

"I've been reading one of Alistair's books," I said. "It has Alistair's name on it, but I suppose you wrote it, too."

"I don't write," he said.

"Still." I watched his hands move. "The illustrations. They are your work, I think?"

He stopped in surprise again and looked up at me.

I shrugged. "A guess."

He grunted and returned to his work.

"I found myself wondering as I was reading," I went on, "why you and Alistair do what you do. What is so fascinating to you? What would possess you to travel the countryside, looking for what Alistair calls manifestations? It appears on the surface like a lark. Alistair has money, and it's easy to see him as an eccentric." I traced my finger around the edge of the book, thinking aloud. "But I've met both of you and it isn't a lark at all. You're both obsessed by it, looking for something in it. Why do you do it? Why don't you go home and start families and jobs like all the other soldiers did?"

It seemed the longer I stayed on this assignment, the bolder I was. But I wanted to know the answer, and I had nothing to lose. All Matthew had to do was tell me to go back to my room.

I thought he might, at first. He slid a piece into the recorder, picked up a small screwdriver, and began to secure it. "I suppose I could go home," he said at last, in his gruff voice. He did not look at me. "My father has a shop—men's tailoring. In a small town called Kingscherry, about an hour from Bath. Mother helps him, when she's well. We never got along, and I left home early. Still, that means nothing now. He'd like me to come home, take over the shop from him. I could have done that when the war ended."

He paused, thinking, and I nearly held my breath, hoping he would go on.

"Alistair has no one close—not really, you know. He inherited a big old house that he has no interest in—sloping grounds, ponds, a swimming pool. Not much fun if you're alone. He finished fighting and he just wanted to bang about. You can't imagine how hard it is to come home from hell and be expected to pick up the threads of a life. Apply for jobs, go to a factory, punch in, punch out. Put your lunch in a bag and get on the omnibus every day. Like nothing happened. *Nothing.*"

His eyes took on a faraway look—faraway and unpleasant. I knew he had gone somewhere I could not follow.

"Alistair was interested in these ghosts, even before the war. It was a lark then. Like a bunch of fools sitting around a séance table, pretending not to rap with their knuckles. Then we all went to France and ran for our lives through the mud with death at our heels. No parlor game—just death, breathing down your neck day and night. At first you're sick and then you're used to it, which is worse. And one day during one of those battles that never seemed to end, I started thinking about Alistair's ghosts."

He looked up at me, though I could tell he was seeing me from afar, as if he were looking through a lens. "There's a theory that when a person dies in great emotion, great unrest, or with something important undone in life—that is when a manifestation occurs. People come back, or their echoes. Alistair wants to know if it can be proven. And I stood to my thighs in mud as the shells flew overhead, and I thought—this battlefield should be full of ghosts. There should be thousands of them here. These lives are all cut short. Every one of them left things undone. Thousands at Ypres, thousands at Passchendaele. This field should be overrun. Why isn't it?"

We were quiet for a long time. Again I traced my finger over the cover of the book. *Ghostly Manifestations in the North of England.* Matthew's words hung between us, the war a chasm that could not be traveled. I could not go there; he could not come back.

"So you are trying to understand what happened," I said finally.

His eyebrow twitched in surprise, and he smiled. It wasn't a pleasant smile, but it was an improvement over the moment before, as I could see that at least he was back in the room with me. "When you say it aloud like that, we sound impossibly naive. I don't think I hope to understand it. I don't think it's possible. And yet, maybe a part of me still tries." He slowly rubbed his hand over his forehead, and up through his hair, a gesture I was starting to recognize. "What else is there to do, Sarah? I could go home and measure men's suits and continue to have screaming nightmares every night in my old bedroom. Alistair could go home and drink by himself and wish he'd ever had a pleasant word from his father—because Alistair has his demons, believe me, and don't let him fool you into thinking otherwise. He puts on a better show than me, that's all."

"The war and the ghosts," I said softly. "They are connected."

"I think the war annihilates ghosts," said Matthew. "If we have mechanized death—and we have; I've seen it—then where do the ghosts go? I find that most frightening of all. That the ghosts disappear with our humanity."

I thought about this, but I was already shaking my head. "It isn't so hopeless. I refuse to believe it."

He crossed his arms. "You still believe in humanity?"

I looked at him. He was so alive the room vibrated with it: a vital, fascinating, intelligent man, damaged perhaps in ways I did not understand, but also strong in ways I was only beginning to see. *You. I believe in you,* I thought, but could not say.

He caught my eye, and suddenly something else happened. The feeling was indescribable—a slow burn down my body, a melting of my bones. It was like the feeling in my room the night before, when he had challenged me to take my shirt off, but even stronger. The ache low in my belly came back. He kept looking at me, bold and unafraid, his eyes traveling me slowly, and my breath came short. It was time to admit to myself, if only quietly in my mind, that I desired to go to bed with Matthew Ryder.

I had a little experience. My mother would have been shocked, but she forfeited her authority when she left me in June of 1919. After she died, I had drifted back to London, signed with the temporary agency, and begun to earn my living. In every office I worked, there were girls; and where there were girls, there were parties, dates, every excuse to see men. Especially soldiers.

I had been dragged to more than a few occasions, under the guise of some coworker or other wishing to "set me up with a nice fellow." I usually did badly at such things, but sometimes there were men who were interested—I never knew why, whether their desperation or simple voraciousness made them turn their attention to me. For a shy girl unused to men, it is easier to hurl the moon from the sky than it is to turn away from a man who truly wishes to pursue her. And so I ended up on awkward dates, and engaged in awkward kisses. And sometimes I ended up, aimless, in their beds.

It had never been an enjoyable experience for me. It was wanted, expected, by the men, and at least it put me on somewhat the same footing as the young women I knew. I may not have had any pleasure, but by doing it at least I felt a little less strange, a little less alien to my own species. I supposed it was worth it for that.

But the thought of going to bed with Matthew made the blood rush in my veins. It suffused me with a kind of terror that was also sweet and had a keen edge of pleasure to it. It was immense, something I might not be able to handle. And yet I surprised myself by wishing to try.

I knew my face burned as we looked at each other, as that long moment spun out and out. I knew he was considering the same thing I was; his expression was not its usual cynical defensiveness, but a quiet speculation. He still sat back in his chair, arms crossed, the flex of his biceps visible beneath the fabric of his shirt in that pose. His tangy smell was in my nostrils, even from his side of the table. He broke the gaze and looked away. I was ten kinds of fool, of course, for even thinking he would consider going to bed with me. He had not even wanted me to see his skin.

We were interrupted by a knock on the door. Without waiting for an answer, Mrs. Clare came into the room. She was wrapped in a thin gray cardigan, her hair unkempt, her eyes a little wild. She looked between Matthew and me.

"Where is Mr. Gellis?" she asked.

"In his room," Matthew replied. He still sat as before, unmoved except to turn his head to look at her. "Is there something we can do for you?"

Mrs. Clare ran a palm over her temple. "I don't know. I'm not even certain why I came. I just thought Mr. Gellis might be able to do something. He said he would try."

Matthew frowned. "Do something about what? Is it Maddy?"

She shook her head. "Well—I don't know," she amended. "It must have something to do with her, but I don't know what. I can't remember when I slept last, and I've finally had enough. This is just the final straw. It's the crows, you see."

Matthew and I exchanged a quick, surprised glance. "Crows?" he asked.

"Crows," she said again, as if we had disbelieved her. "It was only a few at first. But now there are so many. They make such a noise all night long. Mrs. Macready hears them, too. I can't stand it any longer. Tonight I went outside and counted them." She ran her palm over her temple again. "I had to stop at three hundred and seventeen."

I stared at her. "You have three hundred and seventeen crows outside your window?"

Matthew stood. "I'll get Alistair," he said.

❦

Half an hour later we stood on a rise, looking at the Clare barn several hundred feet away. What we could see of the Clare barn. It was dark, but the moon was full, and with our eyes adjusted there was just enough light to see.

The barn was covered with crows.

Alistair raised his field glasses and whistled in low amazement. "Well, she wasn't bamming. I've never seen anything like it."

I didn't need field glasses to feel uneasy, looking at the writhing mass of black as it moved and twitched. Even from here I could picture the glistening black of the crows' wings, hear the dry rasp of their feet on the aged wooden roof. And the noise— the accumulated random squawking chatter of hundreds of birds. The trees surrounding the house and the barn were laden with black, as if someone had doused them in tar. Occasionally some internal argument would send ten or twenty birds erupting into the air, like the ominous breaths of a volcano.

Alistair passed the field glasses to Matthew. "Remember the McCarty house in Yorkshire? The ghost manifested itself in mice." He bent to pull the camera from its case, adjusted the lens.

"Mm." Matthew looked through the glasses. "Damn, I can hardly see a thing. I think the McCartys just had a mouse manifestation."

"Nonsense." Alistair lifted the camera. I thought I was completely forgotten until he handed me the elaborate cap for the lens. "Sarah—hold this."

"I snuck a glimpse at their pantry," Matthew was saying. "Really, Alistair. I wasn't surprised by the mice at all."

"This is a much stronger manifestation. I'll grant you that." Alistair had set the camera on a tripod and was busy tweaking the dials. "Roger Edmunds documented a ghost in Scotland that sounded like hundreds of rats scurrying in the walls. Or so he said—he couldn't record it, and no one could really say whether there simply were really rats in the walls. But this—this puts Roger Edmunds to shame."

Matthew lowered the field glasses and gave me a wry look. "Alistair hates Roger Edmunds," he explained.

Alistair depressed the camera trigger and the night exploded in a flash of light. I winced.

Matthew looked through the field glasses again. "Is the flash necessary?"

"Of course it is. It's dark out, Matthew. I've got no natural light here." He depressed the button again and the flash popped.

The sounds of the birds grew higher, the squawking and the

rustling of oily wings. "Perhaps we should come see them in the morning," I said softly, hating myself for a coward. But fear was trembling through me.

"They could be gone in the morning." Alistair smiled at me as he readied the camera. "It's an adventure, Sarah." He popped the flash again, stabbing the dark with its bright white light.

Matthew had not lowered the glasses. "An adventure," he repeated. "They're moving."

Alistair straightened. "What?"

Matthew handed him the glasses. "See for yourself."

Alistair took the glasses. "I'll look—you take a picture." He grinned as Matthew paused. "Afraid of a few birds?"

Matthew said a foul word and readied the camera. Alistair looked through the glasses, and Matthew pressed the button.

I gasped.

"My God," said Alistair.

I could see it in the flash of light: a plume of black birds, rising to the sky. The noise was incredible. The air filled with throaty, angry *caws*.

"They're moving because they see us," said Matthew.

"Do it again," said Alistair.

Matthew did, and this time I made no sound, as the fear had frozen my throat. The birds were flying toward us. In seconds I heard their wings, heard the rustle in the trees overhead as they landed heavily in the branches. They flapped and shouted at us.

"Can we go now?" I said.

Alistair was quiet. He had lowered the glasses and looked about overhead, tracking the dark shadows in the trees. Something exploded in the bush next to him—some four or five birds, bending the branches as they landed, steadying themselves with their outstretched wings. They were perched mere inches from Alistair. One of them walked gingerly to the end of its branch, its waxy toes curling, and regarded him with bright black eyes.

There was a long pause as Alistair and the bird regarded each other. "Perhaps we've seen all we can here," said Alistair softly at last.

Matthew picked up the camera and tripod. I picked up the case. We made no sound, as if in mutual agreement.

Alistair looked at the bird on the branch next to him again. He bent toward it a little, gazing into its face. I wanted to scream.

"Hello," he said softly.

The bird stretched out both its wings, raised them above its dark black head. It opened its beak as far as it could and emitted a long, low, growling rasp, a sound I heard down the back of my spine and in the pit of my stomach.

Then Matthew's hand came down on Alistair's shoulder. "Time to go. Now."

We walked back to the inn. The birds did not follow us. But they watched us go, dark and silent in the trees.

Chapter Fifteen

I went back to my room and put on my ridiculous white night-gown and lay on the bed. Sleep eluded me as I stared at the ceiling. My mind swept in circles, flying from thought to thought, never settling. I was restless.

I rolled to my side and drew my knees up. The bed was cold, but still I lay on top of the coverlet, with no blanket on top of me. My pulse raced warm under my skin and hot in my temples. I wanted to run and shout. I closed my eyes, felt the delicate beat of my eyelids. This long day was over, and yet it wasn't. I knew it wasn't, and I waited for it.

How different I was, I thought, from the girl who had left London. I had been terrified, of course. I was terrified still. But the girl in London had been asleep. She had been sleeping for years. Now I was awake, for better or for worse, and I would never sleep again. I did not want to sleep again.

Eventually, I dozed. And dreamed about crows.

I'm not sure what awakened me, whether it was a sound—the

soft click of the door, I imagine—or whether I sensed a change in the air of my bedroom. I pulled slowly out of my doze, languorous, my limbs heavy. There was a quiet step on the floor next to the bed. I opened my eyes slowly. I was lying on my back now, my body warm. I smelled a familiar scent. A lazy thrill went through my body, and it never occurred to me to be afraid.

I watched the dark, shadowed outline of Matthew Ryder as he sank onto the edge of the mattress, his weight making the bed creak and sag. He leaned over me, bracing himself on one arm. He knew I was awake.

I looked up at him. He was dressed as he had been earlier in the evening, his white shirt glowing softly in the gloom. We did not need to speak. I was surprised, I suppose; but part of me simply throbbed in expectant anticipation, as if I had known he was coming, and why. And perhaps I had.

He did not look in my eyes, but in the dim light I saw his gaze travel my face, my neck, and down farther. He touched my cheek with his fingers, tracing them down to the sensitive skin beneath my ear. If he was unsure of his welcome, he gave no sign.

He bent his head, put his face close to my neck, as if breathing me in. *Screaming nightmares every night,* he had said earlier. I wondered if tonight was one of those nights, if he had come to me to get out of the nightmares. I pressed my cheek lightly to his.

His fingers were slightly rough, and they rasped against my skin. I closed my eyes and drank in the sensation. I was beginning to breathe hard. His hand traced down my neck, my collarbone. My skin was feverish under his touch. I thought perhaps I could hear his breathing, coming heavier as well, or perhaps I was only hearing my own.

He undid one of the cloth buttons at the neck of my nightgown, then another. With a tug—slightly harsh, and I knew now his control was slipping—he pulled the fabric from one shoulder. Then he slid his dark hand into the gaping opening and cupped my breast.

It was an electric shock going through me. I made a strangled sound and arched under him, pressing my breast tighter into his hand. Then I reached up, tangled my hands into his soft hair, and pulled his mouth down to mine.

He growled. He bit me, ran his teeth over my lip, and I opened my mouth. He kissed me hard, his tongue rough, one of his palms now bracing my jaw, the other still kneading my breast none too gently. Clumsy, perhaps. I did not care.

He had no patience; I gave him permission to have none. He was in the grip of something raw, and I received it gladly, meeting him blow for blow. I was not patient either. I kissed him just as hard as he kissed me in the unreal darkness. I was aflame.

He pushed me down into the mattress, swung himself on top of me in one smooth motion, pinned me down. I squirmed under him. He broke the kiss and his mouth traveled down my neck, my shoulder, his stubble stinging like sandpaper. He drew my skin between his teeth, tasted it. I gasped, kept my fingers tangled in his hair.

He kissed my mouth again, deeply, shifting his body over me. He pressed his legs between mine, pushing my thighs apart. I could not tell you what possessed me. Never, never had I imagined I could act like this; but now I reached down and pulled frantically at my nightgown, pulling up fold after fold of fabric, rucking the hem up to my waist. He made a deep groaning sound, almost angry. He fumbled at his trousers, frantic himself now. He pushed my knees apart and thrust inside me.

I bit down a cry. I held on to him, my arms about his shoulders, fistfuls of his shirt in my hands, my face pressed against his neck. He withdrew, then thrust into me again, hard. A choking sound came from his throat. He was big and heavy inside me. I was all sensation, burning with every movement he made. I whimpered into his neck and pushed my heels into the mattress, bringing my hips up to brace more tightly against him. He began a ragged rhythm, our bodies locked together in something that felt almost like an argument.

The muscles of his shoulders bunched like stone under my hands. He threw his head back, slid out of me, and pulsed onto my stomach as I tasted the sweat on his throat. The sound he made was almost like a sob. Finally we were still, both of us panting. I pulled my face from his neck and looked up at him. His eyes were closed. Sweat was running down his temples.

It had taken only minutes, minutes without words. Minutes in the dark.

He pulled away from me, righted himself, and swung his legs over the edge of the bed. Without a word he stood, took a towel from the basin, and handed it to me. He sat on the edge of the bed, his elbows on his knees, his back to me, as I cleaned myself. I pushed down the hem of my nightgown and rolled to my side, facing him. My body was humming as if touched by an electric wire. I watched the tense line of his shoulder blades under his shirt, the motion of his sides as his breathing slowed. Finally he put his head in his hands.

"I'm sorry," he said hoarsely, and I could hear the self-loathing in his voice. "Not—" The words seemed to choke in his throat. "Since before the war," he finished.

It wasn't a complete thought, but it didn't matter. I could complete it for him. I lay quiet, watching him.

"I shouldn't have," he said to the floor.

"I'm glad you did," I said softly.

This didn't seem to comfort him. His shoulders sagged. He rubbed his forehead. Finally he lifted his head again and straightened. Still he did not look at me.

"I won't be back," he said.

I was silent.

He stood and walked to the door. I heard it click softly shut behind him.

I lay staring into the dark, trying to untangle my emotions. I ached, and part of me—a physical part, an emotional part—was unfulfilled. He was hardly a kind, tender lover. But then, what did I want of him? What had I asked of him? And what did he ask of me?

Wound up in it was a fierce euphoria. A man seeking a simple physical release can always find it—with a willing girl, perhaps, or even with a woman who takes money. Matthew had not done these things. Something had stopped him. Perhaps he was indifferent to me, but in the end it was me he had chosen, me he had not been able to resist.

I could still feel the sting of his beard on my neck, his hands on me. I could still feel him inside me. I closed my eyes, and after a long time, I slept.

Chapter Sixteen

I slept late the next morning. When I finally awoke, the sun was already coming through the dingy window of my room.

I washed and dressed and looked in the mirror. I appeared no different than I had yesterday. I was still myself, dressed in skirt and blouse and cardigan. A foolish rush of questions came over me. I had always thought myself plain, unremarkable. Was I truly? Did Matthew think so? Did he think I was in the least bit attractive? One would think, since he had visited me last night, that he had seen something in me. And yet, I knew that men were perfectly capable of intimacy with a woman who interested them not in the least. They were susceptible to the physical closeness of a woman, any woman, if mixed with boredom and desperation. Last night I had felt powerful, but that power dissipated in the pitiless sunlight.

I looked down at myself. I knew I was slim. I knew my legs were well shaped, my ankles pleasing. I knew my arms were slender, complemented by the narrow watch I always wore. Yet I also knew my breasts and hips were awkward, and that I tended to slouch my shoulders down, as if hiding, and that my face, with its dark slashes of brows, brown eyes, and narrow nose, was not the kind that made men look twice. Perhaps he had simply been using me. In fact, it was likely. The confidence of last night had vanished, and I wanted to hide in my room.

I won't be back.

I took a breath and turned from the mirror. Well, if he had used me, so be it; life would go on. I went downstairs to the private room and found Matthew and Alistair there already. Alistair was at the table, his chair pushed away, one ankle crossed rakishly over the other knee. Matthew stood at the sideboard, pouring himself a glass of water from a jug, his back to me.

"Ah, there you are, noddyhead," said Alistair, and his grin was enough to set any normal girl rocking back on her heels. He was freshly shaven, his light brown hair combed back from his forehead, lean and fit and strong. In that moment he looked like the ideal of English manhood, perfect and unscarred and whole, and only someone who knew him would suspect anything otherwise. "We have been wondering when you'd bother to arise."

"Hello," I said softly. My heart was hammering in my chest. I could not help glancing at Matthew, watching his arm hold steady as he poured the water, the back of his neck as he bent his head. I now noticed his silhouette, strong and lithe, the way the waist of his trousers sat perfectly just above his hips, where his clean white shirt narrowed from his broad back. I forced my gaze away and maneuvered carefully around him at the sideboard, taking a little toast and some tea. Matthew did not look at me.

"We have been discussing today's plan," Alistair said jovially. Something had made him very happy this morning, and I wondered what it was. "Matthew thinks we should make another call on Roderick Nesbit. What do you think?"

While Alistair and I had been shopping for new clothes for me yesterday, Matthew had in fact found a lead regarding Maddy Clare. He had spent yesterday morning taking a tactic he called "the shortest route to the real truth." That was to say, instead of questioning the villagers, he had questioned the servants.

The servants were willing to talk, but their knowledge was scanty. They had not known Maddy, who had never left the Clare house during her tenure there. Most of what they could tell Matthew was rumor, conjecture, or outright lies. The Barrys had been mentioned often in these conversations; despite their money, they were despised by even the servant class as employers no one of any quality would want to work for—an attitude that followed Mrs. Clare's. Tom Barry's claim to be Waringstoke's leader of opinions, it seemed, was not founded in truth.

However, the morning had truly paid off when a groom told Matthew of walking a horse past the graveyard during Maddy's small funeral service. Attending the service had been only the vicar, Mrs. Clare, and Mrs. Macready; but the groom had seen someone else far back, hidden in the trees, who had quickly disappeared. He recognized the man as Roderick Nesbit, an odd-job man who lived in the village.

Matthew had promptly found direction to Roderick Nesbit's house and gone there to interview the man. He had found the place on the edge of the village, isolated and run-down. No one had answered the door, or any of Matthew's shouts, but Matthew was certain someone had been home.

It was yet another piece of the puzzle unsolved. Why had Roderick Nesbit gone to Maddy's funeral, unseen?

I sat at the table and forced a small bite of toast down my throat. I looked at Alistair, but my awareness of Matthew just out of my line of vision was distracting.

"I think that's a good idea," I said, hoping I sounded normal.

Alistair smiled at me and tipped his chair by flexing one long leg. "It is a good idea," he said. "An excellent idea. However, I have a better one."

"And what is that?"

"We're going back to the Clare barn."

I set down my cup of tea as a chill went through my body. Behind me, I heard Matthew go still. "I beg your pardon?" I said.

"We're going to the barn," Alistair said with absolute confidence. "We'll go as a team this time. Matthew will bring the sound recorder. I'll operate the camera myself. Sarah, I would like you to take notes."

"You mustn't," I managed to say, though it felt as if my throat had closed.

Alistair tipped his chair back down to the ground and leaned forward. "And why is that? Because you sensed some sort of danger to me when you were there last? I appreciate that, Sarah— truly I do. But I am not afraid."

I looked at him and knew that he told the truth. He wasn't afraid in the least of Maddy Clare, whom he saw as an echo, a vibration of sorts, a cobweb. He would go into that barn as fearlessly as if he were in his own home. Part of me knew that he should be afraid—that there was something terrible waiting to happen if he did this. But I knew Alistair well enough already to know that he would not be swayed. After he'd fought in the trenches, it would be a rare thing indeed that would give Alistair any fear.

I turned my head and looked at Matthew, who was standing at the sideboard, leaning his hip against it, watching us. "What is your opinion?" I asked him.

Matthew frowned pensively at the floor. I wondered if he was even considering the danger, but when he looked up, I knew he wasn't. He looked as fearless as Alistair. "The recorder is fixed, as far as I know."

"Excellent!" said Alistair.

I kept my gaze on Matthew. "You didn't answer my question."

He turned to me. In the late-morning light he looked beautiful to me: not a golden beauty like Alistair's, but large, looming, solid, and male. I remembered how his strong shoulders had felt under my palms last night, and pushed the thought away. I knew what his answer would be before he opened his mouth.

"I'd like to see this ghost for myself," he said. "I'm in."

I turned away in helpless frustration. Why had I been saddled with two pigheaded men so completely unafraid? I tried another tactic. "Mrs. Clare hasn't given permission. You'll be trespassing."

Alistair nodded. "I knew you'd say that. But as you so sagely pointed out yesterday, Sarah, Mrs. Clare wants us to rid her of this ghost. I've decided I can't do that unless I experience it. It will just have to do."

"You'll break the padlock on the door in daylight?"

It was Matthew who answered. "Padlocks aren't a problem."

I stood up and paced the room, unable to stay still. "You saw those crows last night. They were uncanny."

"It was quite fascinating. I wonder if there are any bird experts in the area who can help us."

"Alistair!" I could have screamed in frustration.

"They are *birds*, Sarah."

I stared at him helplessly and he leaned toward me, his elbows on his knees. "This brings me to something else," he said.

"What is it?"

"Sarah, I hired you to replace Matthew. Now Matthew has returned, and it seems to me I've not given you the option of going back to London if you wish. Do you wish it?"

I opened my mouth, dumbfounded. "Are you—?" I stuttered. "Do you wish me gone?"

"No, no, of course not. But this assignment has been upsetting for you. The encounters with Maddy, having your room ransacked—I just thought you might have a wish to put all of it at the back of you for good. Perhaps you don't want to say it, so I should offer you the opportunity. Matthew and I can make do now that he's back, if we have to. What do you think?"

I looked at Matthew. Had this been his idea? Did he still hold a grudge against me, even after last night? But Matthew's dark eyes gave nothing away.

I thought of going back to London, of my damp flat and the oppressive heat and the noise of the city, and most of all my lonely, routine life. I could not go back to that, not now, perhaps not ever. And there was no chance on this earth that these men were going to encounter Maddy without me along to help.

"I would like to stay," I said.

Alistair blinked, as if that was not the answer he was expecting. Then a grin broke across his face, so handsome and so genuine it gave my heart a squeeze.

"Well, that's good, then!" he said. "Don't you think so, Matthew?"

Behind me, Matthew only gave a low grunt.

Alistair rolled his eyes at me. "Such manners on a gentleman. Let's get the equipment together and we'll go."

"Alistair," I tried again, "I have to say I don't think this is a good idea."

"You must stop worrying so, Sarah," he said to me. "Everything will be fine."

❧

We left the inn and crossed the narrow road, taking the now-familiar path across the fields and through the small cluster of trees. Alistair strode ahead, confident and eager. Matthew, to my surprise, let himself drop back to walk level with me.

As soon as I saw what he was doing, I felt myself blushing, and I hated myself for it. Could I think of nothing else but what had happened last night?

But Matthew made no mention of it. Instead, he said in a low voice that Alistair would not hear: "I think you should know something. When I came down this morning, I found Alistair outside, talking to Evangeline. She was walking her dog."

I took this in and said nothing.

"I don't know how long they had been talking," he continued, "but I believe it was a long conversation. It's affected his mood all morning."

"I take it it was not an interview about Maddy," I said.

"No. No, I don't think so."

So, they had spoken to each other, and had perhaps even come to an agreement—an agreement that suited Alistair very well. I should have been shocked that Alistair would have a tête-à-tête with a married woman, for all to see and gossip about, for a long length of time. But I could not find it in myself to be shocked anymore. And if he'd found some happiness in having a conversation that was years overdue, I couldn't find it in my heart to begrudge him it.

It made depressing sense. Ahead of us, Alistair was still walking as if his feet were not quite touching ground. And it explained why he had made the offer to send me back to London, for that had almost certainly been Evangeline Barry's idea. Likely couched in terms of concern, wondering if perhaps I were secretly yearning to leave and unable to ask. Alistair had taken the suggestion at face value, of course, as a man infatuated will do. But Evangeline had been making her move. She had been trying to get rid of me.

It even explained this sudden resolve to go to the barn. Alistair wanted to wrap up this business, perhaps to look better in Evangeline's eyes. And so he plunged ahead, the valiant knight who will fix all. And all for a woman already married. I thought of her calm obedience to her husband the day before, and the languid, condescending wave she had given me, and I hoped he was not on the road to disaster—though I very much thought he might be.

"Oh, Alistair," I sighed.

I turned to see Matthew looking at me, and I would have given anything, all I owned or would ever own, to read what I saw in his eyes. But as always, Matthew remained a mystery to me.

I turned away as we crested the small rise, approaching the place we had been the night before, photographing the barn.

"I thought you had a torch for him," Matthew said softly, next to me. "For Alistair."

Ahead of us, Alistair stopped and turned. "Hurry, slowpokes!" he shouted. I saw the barn become visible over his shoulder as we drew closer. Before I could answer Matthew, the words dried in my throat with fear.

The barn was covered in crows, just like last night. They nestled everywhere, along the roof, in the eaves, the sills of the windows. A low gabbling reached us, the sound of their bird chatter. There was motion as they flitted through the surrounding trees. In daylight, the scene looked different—less terrifying perhaps, but somehow sickening. It did not make it any better, to see the weak morning sunlight glancing off their oily wings.

Alistair had turned again and was approaching the building. I made myself put one foot before the other, following him, following Matthew, who had set out ahead of me at a brisk pace, despite the heavy suitcase he carried.

"It looks like the padlock won't be a problem," said Alistair as we got close. I could see the lock lying on the ground. It had not been opened and dropped, or even forced. It was in pieces, the body in one place, the heavy arm twisted and lying nearly a foot away. As if it had exploded.

"I see we're welcome," said Matthew.

"Wonderful," said Alistair. "In we go."

Chapter Seventeen

Once inside the barn, both men went to work. Alistair set up his camera, and Matthew righted a dusty, overturned crate to use as a table for the wire recorder. It was something I had not thought of, having put the recorder on the packed-earth floor of the barn when I had used it earlier.

All was quiet, at first. A few early-summer flies buzzed, and the morning sunlight, already filtered by the gray clouds outside, came weakly through the streaked windows. Alistair looked at the chaos of the barn—ropes and rotted blankets strewn about, dry and dirty straw in the corners, large pieces of equipment and old boxes smashed as if flung against the walls—and gave a low whistle. "Interesting," he said, bending to his camera, now mounted on a tripod, and taking a few photographs of the scene. "Unless Mrs. Clare is harboring a circus strong man at Falmouth House, it looks like classic poltergeist activity to me."

"This is no poltergeist," said Matthew from behind me.

Alistair's brow creased as he took another photograph. "It's certainly stronger than any poltergeist I've ever seen. I'll grant that."

"What is a poltergeist?" I asked, feeling stupid.

"It's a ghost of sorts," said Matthew. He turned the knobs on the recording machine and watched in satisfaction as the reels turned, then shut them off again. "Yet without a personality. Not exactly a ghost."

"I don't follow," I said.

Alistair snorted. "What my learned assistant is trying to express is that a poltergeist is a spirit, but it manifests itself in uncanny bursts of energy. Often they're mischievous—breaking crockery, slamming doors, that sort of thing. There is a theory about poltergeists that is rather fascinating—that unlike ghosts, they actually manifest through the energies of the living. So say, perhaps, if you are under great stress, Sarah—then the poltergeist in your house will be more active than if you are calm."

I tucked my hair behind my ears. I did not know where to look; I felt that Maddy would appear at any moment, and I did not know from what direction. My skin was prickling with sweat. "That sounds horrible," I said.

"Yet fascinating." Alistair grinned at me. *He's having fun*, I thought. "Don't you think, Matthew?"

I turned to see that Matthew had stilled, the recorder apparently forgotten. He was looking upward to the rafters, a strange look on his face, as if a memory or a thought had come over him suddenly, taking him deep inside himself. He raised a hand, wiped it over his forehead as if he was in some sort of pain. "I fucking hate barns," he growled.

The grin left Alistair's face and he turned back to his camera.

I was wondering what had just passed between them when I heard the sound.

It was the light sound of bare feet, behind me—the brush of the heel against the dirt floor, the slap-slap of the base of the toes. Someone running, toward me from behind and, before I could turn, past me and into the gloom. A cold chill brushed my neck. I saw nothing move.

I turned on my heel, staring, and turned again. "Did you hear that?"

"Hear what?" said Alistair, suddenly alert.

And there it was again, the quick brush of footsteps, from another direction this time, toward me and past. Again I felt the cold breath of icy air on my neck. I turned, realizing my throat was closing and it was becoming hard to breathe.

"There," I said. "Did you hear it?"

"I heard nothing," said Alistair.

"There was something." This from Matthew. "I saw it."

Alistair turned to him, his hand on the camera. "What did you see? Where?"

"I'm not certain," said Matthew. "It was—"

A long, low creak came from overhead, a groaning coming from the rafters. The sound was centered above where Alistair stood. I was covered in sweat now; I felt trickles run between my shoulder blades, felt my dress begin to stick to my skin. I struggled to breathe. The groan came again, like something heavy dragging on the wooden beams overhead.

I looked up and saw nothing. But Matthew was staring, too, and the look on his face was truly horrible, shocked and pale. "Jesus God," he said, his voice nearly breathless.

"For God's sake!" Alistair cried. "What is it! I can't see it! Is she here?"

Cold breath on my neck, the low gurgle. Right behind me. My head pounded. There was no mistaking it. "She's here," I managed. Maddy, playing games.

Alistair was staring wild-eyed, his gaze darting everywhere, trying to catch what we were seeing. Matthew was still staring upward, transfixed in horror. I heard the footsteps again, *flap-flap-flap*, this time running past me, toward Alistair himself.

Matthew looked away from the ceiling, followed something across the room. "Alistair, look out!"

"I don't—" Alistair stopped, and a queer look came across his face, distracted, unfocused. He cocked his head. "Wait. . . . Do you hear that?"

Despite the sweat running down my skin, I felt a chill in my spine. For the footsteps had stopped, and so had the creaking. The barn was silent.

I exchanged a glance with Matthew, shook my head. I heard nothing. I could tell from his expression that he did not either.

"Alistair?" he said.

Alistair raised an impatient hand, as when telling someone to be quiet for a moment. "There," he said, his voice trailing and vague. "There. Do you hear it? Music. Where— Matthew, start the recorder."

Matthew turned to the recorder and twisted the dials. "Damn it." He plugged in his headphones and put them on, reluctantly. "I don't know, Alistair. All I hear is—" He ripped the headphones off again, pain on his face. "Feedback."

"Feedback? No. No, not at all." A strange look was settling

over Alistair, as if he were hearing something far away, an expression that frightened me. "It's music," he said.

Something broke through my terror, through the difficulty I felt moving, thinking. I ran to Alistair and grabbed his arm. "Alistair, come with me. Let's go."

He tried to shake me off. "No, no. Sarah, don't you hear it?"

"No!" I cried. "And neither does Matthew! She's somehow haunting us separately—don't you see?" Sounds for me that the others did not hear, visions for Matthew that we could not see— Maddy somehow had the power to do it.

But it was what she was doing to Alistair, only to Alistair, that made me sick with fear. Because it was Alistair she wanted.

Alistair looked at me, and his eyes were growing vague, as if he remembered me from long ago. "Separately? That's unheard of. What a find. I should document it."

"No!" I pulled at him, willing to drag him bodily to the door. "Please!"

But he shook me off, though I gripped as hard as I could. I staggered back and nearly lost my balance. Matthew came forward, but he stopped, a grimace on his face, and clapped his hands to his ears. He swore furiously. "Feedback!" he shouted, as if trying to be heard over a deafening noise. He turned to see his headphones, dropped on the old crate next to the recorder, several feet away. He gripped his head harder, ground his palms into his ears. "It isn't bloody possible!"

I stepped back, and then I was watching all of this as from a distance. The room was swirling away from me, as if it were a play, and I was lost in a susurrous, scratching sound, nearly physical in the air; I realized with the slow stupidity of terror that it was the sound of the crows on the roof overhead, moving.

Time seemed to telescope. Sounds came eerily loud or from far away. I have always wondered since, what was real in what followed and what was not; how long, exactly, passed between the moment when Matthew put his hands to his ears and the moment when Mrs. Clare came into the barn, screaming. It felt like hours upon hours, eerily still hours, as if I were in the eye of the storm, in the strange silence and red-yellow light as the destruction went on all about me.

And yet it could not have lasted more than a few moments. Despite the madness of all that was going on, Matthew would not have lagged for long.

I saw him put his hands to his ears, and then I closed my eyes. Because Maddy had come into my head; she was speaking in that sickening way of hers, somewhere inside my mind.

Well-done, little girl, she said.

I groaned, helpless. I knew what she meant. She had set me to bring Alistair to her, and somehow, against my will, I had.

"No," I tried to say, not knowing if I was saying it aloud or only in the terrified confines of my mind.

Yes, said Maddy. There was a long pause, a sickening sound of dead breath, almost like a sigh. Then she said something else, though it was lost in the gurgle of her voice—something that sounded like *Beautiful, beautiful.* And something else that sounded like *Mine.*

"No!" I said.

You smell like the other one now, Maddy said. *This one I will take.*

"You cannot have him!" I screamed.

I gagged; something cold had been shoved down my throat. A wave of insane, wild rage came over me. My heart bloomed in my chest. It was as overpowering as the blast of heat from a white-hot fire that bends and bubbles the air; I opened my eyes to see the very walls of the barn bowing with it, the force of Maddy's rage. I tried to weep. *This is what a lunatic feels like,* I thought. *This is what it is like.*

I do not take orders, Maddy hissed, her voice a pain and an itch in my head. *Not ever again.*

I choked, tried to speak. "Yes."

Do you understand, little girl?

"Yes!"

The icy mass withdrew from my throat and I gasped for breath. I was on my knees now, though I had no recollection of falling.

The rage subsided, but only faintly. I could feel myself breathing it in. It made my blood pound wildly in my veins. I began to truly feel it—anger, outrage. Part of me wanted to growl, to hit something. I wanted to scream, though not in terror this time. I tried to breathe and stay calm. *Talk to her,* I told myself.

"Please," I said, and I still had no idea whether I spoke aloud or not. "Please don't take him. You'll kill him. Please."

I like the beautiful one, said Maddy, a note of petulance in her voice.

"Please."

A long pause. Then her voice again, sly and pleased with herself: *You can do something for me, I think. And then we'll see.*

Everything in me revolted against making a promise to Maddy. She was terrifying, childish, and certainly devious. But what choice did I have? "Anything," I said.

I smelled like man once, too, she said. The rage still pulsed around me. *No beautiful ones, not for Maddy. Three of them on me.*

"I don't understand," I said, my mind whirling. What was she asking me to do?

I screamed, but I tasted their blood, she said, as if I had not spoken. *Each of the three. They each tasted different. I took orders, but I knew I would taste it again. Every one of them. I will do it, little girl. I will have my revenge.*

I listened, no longer speaking. Horror hit my stomach like a fist.

Poor little dead girl, staring at the sky, Maddy said in my head. She was nearly singing it. A false cheer that pulsed with hatred, that gurgled with rage.

What sky is she looking at, little girl? So dark and so green? You've seen it, haven't you? I showed it to you. You'll see it in your dreams, like I see it in mine. Poor little dead girl opens her eyes and it's all gone, all of it, until that day she came from the barn.

Poor little dead girl. Find them. Find her, and I will give you back your beautiful one. Refuse me, and the beautiful one is mine. I can see you, little girl. I can follow you. Refuse me and I will kiss your children. They will taste so sweet.

"Oh, God," I whispered. I felt wet tears on my face.

No gods here, she gurgled.

There was a loud crash; I turned to see the barn door burst open, and Mrs. Clare came flying in, wild-eyed, an oil lamp held high in one hand. She whirled around, took all of us in. I saw Alistair, limp on the floor, Matthew bent over him. I saw the recorder on the crate, juddering to a start of its own accord. I saw Alistair's camera, lifeless and broken on the ground.

Mrs. Clare saw the recorder. Her gaze flew to the corners of the barn, the ceiling, looking, looking.

"Where are you!" she screamed.

Deep in my head, Maddy moaned.

"Where are you!" Mrs. Clare screamed again, her voice breaking. "Get out! For God's sake, Maddy. Go!"

Maddy screamed a laugh, but it was faint; the sound flew to the roof of the barn, echoing off the wooden rafters.

Mrs. Clare stumbled forward, and in that brief moment, as my mind became my own again and time came back into focus, I thought she looked utterly out of her wits. I wondered with a chill why she carried an oil lamp in daylight. And then I knew.

"No!" I cried, my voice back now. "Matthew! Alistair! Look out!"

Matthew looked up, saw Mrs. Clare with the lamp, and stood. "Mrs. Clare!"

She took a step back. "I can't have her here anymore," she said.

I thought of my first visit to this barn, of the vision of fire Maddy had sent me. I thought of Mrs. Clare's calm voice as we interviewed her: *I do hope Maddy does not plan to burn down the barn.*

It seemed Maddy would not burn down the barn after all.

Matthew and I both ran. But before we could reach her, Mrs. Clare smashed the burning oil lamp to the floor.

Chapter Eighteen

The fire caught quickly in the dry, dusty barn, spreading through the desiccated remnants of old straw on the floor. As it climbed the walls, Matthew and I hauled Alistair upright—his eyes were rolled back in his head, though he was awake and breathing, as if he was in some sort of trance—and carried him outside onto the grass.

We set him down and Matthew turned toward the barn again. "Where is Mrs. Clare?"

I watched as the flames appeared through the streaked windows, aware that people had started to gather. Mrs. Macready came sprinting down the path. "My lady!"

Matthew ran back to the barn. I followed, but I got only a few steps before my knees buckled under me and I fell to the ground. My legs shook uncontrollably, and the world grayed around me. I found myself shaking, nauseated, short of breath. Matthew disappeared through the door and I watched that small space of burning light for him to reappear.

Mrs. Macready ran as close to the barn as she dared, pacing like a mother cat. "My lady!" she cried again. A woman I didn't recognize—one of the neighbors, perhaps—approached her and tried to soothe her. A clump of other strangers stood a few feet away from me, watching. I heard murmurs of "fire brigade" and "constable," but not one of them approached me, even as I sat shaking in the grass.

I turned and crawled back over the damp ground, returning to Alistair. He lay on his back, pale and unmoving. He moaned as I gently took his head and placed it in my lap.

I looked up at the small knot of people who stood staring at me. I recognized none of them. "Will no one send for a doctor?" I cried.

A girl of about sixteen broke away from the group and came forward. "I'm next door, mum. I'll ring Dr. Cheswick on the telephone. Is he hurt?"

"I don't know," I said, truthfully. "He seems swooned. Please—hurry."

The girl ran away. I brushed Alistair's fair hair from his forehead and soothed him. He seemed to be struggling to awaken. "Shh," I said to him, as I turned my eyes to the barn again.

Matthew reappeared at the door, one arm about Mrs. Clare's waist. She sagged against him as if weak, but she walked on her own powers. In Matthew's other hand, incredibly, was the suitcase containing the sound recorder. He staggered toward Alistair and me. Mrs. Macready cut him off, taking Mrs. Clare from him, clucking in her employer's ear. Matthew came the rest of the way to Alistair and me, stumbling, and sat in the grass.

"Someone is phoning a doctor," I said.

He said nothing and stared down into Alistair's face. "How is he?"

"I don't know. Are you all right?"

"Jesus God." Matthew pulled up his knees and ran his hands

through his hair. His face was ashen. I opened my mouth to say something else to him—I knew not what—when the firemen arrived.

The barn was burning brightly now, the walls and eaves on fire. The Waringstoke villagers were all gathered to watch, though it was becoming too hot to venture close. There was a shrill cackling, a loud flurry of wings—and we all watched as the crows on the barn roof rose up as one, in a blue-black cloud arching into the sky. Higher and higher they stretched, like the column of an army, crying their hoarse cries, until they flew away as one toward the dense, green woods.

There was a quiet hush over the small crowd as we watched the eerie sight. I felt Alistair move on my lap. He raised his head. I looked down to see he had opened his eyes and was watching the birds with feverish intensity.

"Do you hear that?" he said softly.

Matthew looked down at him. "Gellis. Are you all right?"

"Do you hear that?" Alistair said again. His eyes were unfocused, like those of a man in the grip of an illness. With uncanny speed he grabbed Matthew's arm and held it so tight I could see Alistair's knuckles whiten. "Planes," he said, his eyes following the birds as they disappeared. "An air strike. We should warn the sergeant."

A chill went down my spine. I looked at Matthew. He gazed down at Alistair in surprise; his brow lowered, and he opened his mouth as if to say something. He seemed to change his mind, and slowly a sad knowledge came into his eyes.

"I hear it," said Matthew, softly.

"I knew it," said Alistair. "It's been too damned quiet. They always come back sooner or later. We need to raise the alarm."

Matthew shook his head, and I marveled at the calm in his

deep voice. "It's too dark, Gellis. We're under cover here. There's no point. They can't see a thing."

"You're right." Alistair stared up at the bright blue midmorning sky. "Hasn't stopped them before, though. I hear it. I know I do. God, I'd have a cigarette, but you can't light a match in this damned place—"

"No matter," said Matthew, his voice rough. "Get some sleep."

"You'll wake me for my turn at sentry duty?"

"Yes."

"You'd better." Alistair closed his eyes.

Matthew raised his eyes to mine. He looked haggard, as if that little exchange had taken the last ounce of energy he had. "What in God's name is happening to him?"

I bit my lip. "Maddy . . . wants him. I told you that. She's done something to him."

"That *thing*." Matthew's eyes blazed. "I saw it. Plain as day. But I saw you. You didn't see her, did you?"

"No." My stomach turned and I realized I was suffering from some sort of shock. I touched Alistair with my icy hand. "I didn't see her. I only heard her, when she talked to me." I took a breath and looked into Matthew's eyes. "I understand it now. Maddy told me everything."

As the fire dwindled, the doctor the neighbor girl had phoned for arrived. He was thickset, in his sixties, his breath wheezing from the haste with which he'd traveled. There was still no sign of any police—I heard several people say there was no bobby in Waringstoke, and someone had had to make a call to a nearby village.

I wondered if the poor, faraway bobby had a motorcar, or if he would have to ride a bicycle all the way here.

The doctor saw to Mrs. Clare first. She was lying on the grass by the path to the house, in a near swoon, Mrs. Macready tending to her. The doctor examined her, then rounded up a few of the tallest, strongest gawkers to help carry her into the house. With that in motion, he came to us. He took one look at us and bade a few more villagers to help Matthew carry Alistair into the house as well. I followed on shaky legs that would barely obey me.

He had Alistair installed in one of the upstairs rooms, and bade Matthew and me wait in the parlor as he examined his patient. Matthew and I sat in silence for only a few minutes before Matthew excused himself and left the room without another word.

The doctor came down twenty minutes later, as Matthew returned. "Well," the doctor sighed as he sat heavily on one of Mrs. Clare's fussy flowered sofas, his stout bulk making the wooden frame creak. "He seems healthy enough, in body anyway. I can't say exactly what's wrong with him." He looked from Matthew to me. "It's possible he's had some sort of shock to the mind."

"What should we do?" I asked him.

"I gave him a mild sedative to help him sleep," said the doctor. "Leave him be for now. He's comfortable enough, I daresay. I'll check on him later to see if he's improved. Maybe a rest will do him some good." He lowered his gaze on me. "How are you, young lady? Were you hurt?"

I shook my head, but the doctor heaved himself out of his seat and came to me anyway, checking my pulse and pulling up my eyelids to look at my pupils. "Mild shock," he declared a moment later. He stood straight, pressed his hands into the small of his back. "I'd worry about you, dear, but you're strong as a horse next to your companion here." To my surprise, he turned to Matthew. "Are you injured, young man?"

Matthew's face was ashen, his features slack. "No," he said, his voice, normally hoarse, made more so by the smoke he had inhaled in the barn.

"No burns? No shortness of breath? They say you went into the barn to bring out Mrs. Clare."

"I'm fine," said Matthew.

"Oh, I'm sure you are," said the doctor, shrugging his shoulders. "And yet, unless I'm much mistaken, you've just spent the past half hour throwing up in the privy."

Matthew turned an angry glare on the man, but the doctor seemed unfazed. "It's battle fatigue, son," he said with rough gentleness. "I can always tell. You may as well have a sign about your neck. I've been treating it for years. Nothing to be ashamed of."

I watched, surprised. Matthew did look stricken, like a man who has been dealt a serious blow. And yet his eyes were defiant, as if he were fighting it with everything he had. He glared steadily at the doctor, his gaze never wavering, though he was canted to the side, gripping the edge of his chair with one hand as if he was about to fall over. Had the fire brought back memories of when he had been so badly burned? I remembered him looking up into the rafters of the barn, his expression unreadable. *I fucking hate barns,* he had said, and Alistair had gone quiet.

The doctor sighed. "There's nothing more I can do here, and I have other patients to see. I'll check back this afternoon, as I said. I have no idea what's gone on here, and Mrs. Clare refuses to say anything. I don't suppose either of you would like to fill me in?"

We said nothing.

The doctor grunted. "I thought so. Well, it's no matter to me—I'll let the police sort it out when they show up. Dear," he said to me, not unkindly, "make sure you get some rest. Don't strain yourself. And eat something—you'll need it, though you won't feel like eating. As for you"—he turned to Matthew again—"I have my hypodermics in my bag. I can give you an injection if you like."

"Fuck off," rasped Matthew.

The doctor turned to me again. "Soldiers are the worst to treat," he confided, as if Matthew were not sitting three feet away. "Surly and usually ungrateful, but I can't bring myself to blame them. It's a right mess we put them in, if you ask me." He snapped his bag shut, picked it up, and headed for the door.

After he left, Matthew and I sat in a long moment of silence. My head was spinning, my stomach still nauseated. The house was quiet around us, but for the murmurs of voices from outside, down the path to the barn. I pressed my palms together, then squeezed my hands between my knees, trying to regain my composure. I watched Matthew run a shaking hand through his hair.

"You're not all right," I said, worried.

I thought perhaps he would swear at me, but he didn't. He only stood and paced to the window. "What a bloody mess this is," he said hoarsely. "A bloody mess. I need to think. I didn't know it would hit me like that. It's been five years. I didn't know it would—" He trailed off, pressed his palms to his eyes.

I waited. It was none of my business, I knew, and yet I couldn't pull away. I couldn't give him privacy. I sat there with my hands between my knees and watched him.

"All right," he said after a moment. He dropped his hands and looked out the window at nothing. "All right. Listen. We were in

France. We had dug in. I was positioned near the back of the line. I'd had six weeks at the front and they were giving me a breather before sending me forward again."

I listened, my breath stilled.

"There was a sniper nest," Matthew went on. "Somehow they'd got into position. They were picking us off. The air strikes kept missing them; we could hardly show our heads. We knew well enough where they were, but they had too much cover. I was sent in a detachment with three other men to reconnoiter and, if possible, to take care of the problem."

The voices outside had died down. I wondered if the crowd had dispersed. I prayed no one would come in the room before I had heard the end of this. I did not think Matthew would ever tell me this again.

"We hiked all day," he said, "and found them. We took care of it, like we'd been ordered, and started back. But night was falling, and one of the men had a fever. We found an abandoned barn and bunked down to sleep for a few hours.

"I woke up to an explosion. Fire everywhere. We'd been bombed; or the barn had, though no one knew we were in it. God knows why. Target practice, maybe, or a pilot letting off the last of his shot. We had just enough time to hear it coming—ten seconds, maybe less. I flew four feet when it hit. The place was on fire and all of the others were dead. I ran out of there and kept running.

"I was twenty feet into the woods before I realized the back of my uniform was on fire. I dropped, tried to put it out. I couldn't get the flames out. I lucked into some mud, still wet, only about an inch or two deep. Still, I rolled in it. That's the last thing I remember."

He turned and looked at me. I was thinking of him, running

back into the burning barn to get Mrs. Clare. What that had taken of him.

His gaze darkened. "Don't feel sorry for me, Sarah," he said. "Don't. I don't feel one bit bad about it. I was in the hospital for six months, and every time I felt sorry for myself, I remembered that not three hours before it happened, I blew out a German sniper's brains as he looked me in the eyes and begged me for mercy."

"That isn't fair," I cried. "It was war. What were you supposed to do?"

He crossed his arms. "I don't know if you're naive, or just hopelessly foolish. There is no *fair*, Sarah."

"There is," I insisted, dashing the tears from my eyes. "Everyone just lost sight of it. We all lost sight of it for years. But the doctor was right—we put everyone in that situation. It was impossible. The sniper was killing people, too. He was doing it because he was under orders; so were you. You can't blame yourself when every aspect of it was madness. And now you're so angry with me, just because I saw your scars! As if they're shameful. I don't give a—a *damn* about them."

I broke off, too embarrassed to go on. Perhaps he was right, and I was just a fool. It wouldn't do me any good to confess how I felt about him, how badly I wanted him, that he seemed a hero to me. Matthew didn't believe in heroes, and he wouldn't want a naive girl who saw something in him he didn't believe existed.

But he was frowning, as if I'd said something to confuse him. "I'm not angry at you," he said.

"You're furious with me," I answered. I knew as I said it that it was the truth. "You can hardly stand to look at me. You think I'm naive, that I have a *soft shell*—yes, I heard you say it." I ignored his look of shock as he realized I'd overheard him say that about me to Alistair. "You hardly spare me a glance and then at night you come to my room and—and—"

He looked stricken. "Sarah . . ."

"No." I jumped to my feet. Perhaps with the shock I was a little hysterical, but the words tumbled out of me nonetheless. "If you say you're sorry, I'll never forgive you. *Never*. I'm not sorry. If you have regrets, please just keep them to yourself and don't insult me with them. I'd rather be deluded and think that you spent at least a few moments with me without wishing you were somewhere else. That's all I want. I don't care if it makes me stupid. And now I don't want to talk about this anymore. We need to talk about Alistair—and Maddy."

Matthew looked at the floor for a long moment. His arms were still crossed. He was still, thinking, as impenetrable as ever. "You're right," he said at last. "We need to be rational. Because it seems we have a very large problem."

"You certainly do," said a voice from the doorway. A tall man with a drooping mustache stood there, one hand on the frame. He wore a dark wool uniform. The police had finally arrived.

Chapter Nineteen

✿

"**I**t's a downright mess." The big policeman moved into the room, his hat under his arm, and looked at us from his deep-set eyes. "And I'm puzzled over it, I don't mind saying. But you two look relatively sane. Perhaps you can help me make heads or tails of this."

My heart tripped in my chest. What were we to tell the police? We had a story about ghosts of maidservants attacking the living from beyond the grave. We'd sound like madmen. Matthew and I had been so busy arguing we'd had no time to discuss it. And now time had run out.

I shot a glance at Matthew, but he was not looking at me. He was standing unmoved, his arms still crossed. He looked the policeman steadily in the eye. "*Sane* is a relative term, sir," he said in his voice of deep gravel. "But we'll help you if we can."

The policeman chuckled and held out his hand to Matthew. "Constable Moores, sir. A bit tardy, as I had to come from Spireschurch."

Matthew shook his hand blandly. "Matthew Ryder."

"Ah, yes." Constable Moores turned to me. "You must be Miss Piper, then."

"Yes, sir," I said, wondering how he knew my name.

The big man's eyes twinkled, though the keen intelligence there could not be missed. He did not look dusty, so I guessed my surmise about the bicycle had been incorrect. "According to Mrs. Clare, you're the ghost hunters, then."

At that, Matthew and I did trade a glance—his inscrutable, mine undoubtedly nervous. So we did not have to explain ourselves to him, but how must the situation sound to a policeman's ears?

The constable eased himself onto one of the fussy flowered chairs and set down his hat. "Now, then. Please start from the beginning. And please, I beg you—make some sense."

I couldn't think of a thing to say, but Matthew covered the gap. He put his hands in his pockets and looked down at the constable. "All right, then. You know that Mrs. Clare charged us with getting rid of her ghost."

Moores nodded. "She said as much. The less said about that, the better."

Matthew reddened. "We are not charlatans, sir. We don't take any pay. And Falmouth House does indeed have a ghost."

"Yes, I know of it." Moores looked uneasy. "I knew Mr. Clare when he was alive. He was the magistrate in these parts. I remember he wrote me, asking if I had any girls gone missing. Said one of them had turned up on his doorstep, unable to speak. Described her." He shrugged. "I had no answers for him. Then the girl died, and Mrs. Clare thinks she haunts the place."

"She does," I said.

Constable Moores blinked at me, as if he had forgotten my existence. Then he waved a hand. "Go on, then. Tell me about the barn. It's the fire I'm concerned about."

"We were in the barn," Matthew said smoothly, "attempting to make contact with the manifestation. Mrs. Clare came into the barn while we were there. She was very upset, agitated. She said she'd had enough, she wanted the ghost to be gone. Then she broke an oil lamp and set the barn on fire."

"Hmm," said the constable. "Well, she said as much to me. Admitted she burned her own barn down. Right convenient for you, I daresay."

"Is she in trouble?" I asked.

Moores shrugged. "We'll see. Hard to charge someone for destroying their own property, you know. I could fine her for mischief, perhaps—public endangerment. If any sparks had caught on the neighboring buildings, we'd have a serious mess on our hands. However, the Clares are a respected family in these parts. And it didn't happen." He rubbed a hand on his forehead. "It's the rest I can't make sense of. I'm hearing stories of birds on the roof—crows, to be exact. You see those?"

"Yes," said Matthew. His former shock had disappeared, and under the constable's gaze he was strong, confident, and perfectly clear. I marveled at the strength it took. "There were birds on the roof, nesting, it seems. They flew away when the fire got going."

"A large number of them?"

"Yes, sir."

"You ever recollect seeing crows in such large numbers before?"

"No, sir."

"Is it true you went back into the barn to rescue Mrs. Clare?"

"Yes, sir."

"You staying at the inn across the way?"

"Yes, sir."

"Planning to leave town soon?"

"No, sir."

"Your friend up there." Constable Moores jerked his chin vaguely toward the stairs. "I hear he's had a bit of a breakdown. Is that so?"

Matthew crossed his arms again. "I suppose," he said.

"Ever happen to him before?"

A muscle twitched in Matthew's jaw. "Not that I've seen."

"Know him well, do you?"

"Yes, sir."

"You'd call him stable—overall?"

"*Yes*. Sir."

"Ah, well." The constable rubbed his head again and stood. "I hear he was rambling about attack formations. My own son was sick for a year after he came home. We had to send him away for a time. Your friend had a bit of a shock, then?"

The questions were so subtle, so quick, it was impossible to see how the constable was leading the conversation. "A bit of a shock, yes, I suppose," Matthew said.

"So, it was there, then."

"Pardon?"

"The 'manifestation,'" the constable quoted. "The ghost. You said you were trying to contact it. Looks like you succeeded, or at least your friend thinks you did."

Matthew was quiet. "Does it matter?" I asked.

Again the constable looked at me as if I'd just come in the room. "I'm just trying to piece the story together, young lady." His voice was flat, but his sharp eyes took me in. "Did you see this ghost, then?"

"No," I said, truthfully.

"Ah." Constable Moores turned back to Matthew. "What about you, son?"

The two men looked at each other, a challenge between them. Something dark passed over Matthew's eyes. "I didn't see it," he said at last.

The constable looked at Matthew for another long moment. "So—perhaps your friend was deluded, then?"

"I don't know," said Matthew.

"All right, then." Constable Moores stood, his shoulders drooping as if admitting defeat. He picked up his round hat. "Don't leave town, son. You either, young lady. I may need to talk to you again."

◦♋

As we ascended the stairs to Alistair's room, I grasped Matthew's elbow. "The policeman," I said. "Perhaps he could help us."

He paused and looked at me. "I don't see how."

"He knows these parts," I said. "He knows all the people. He may be able to fill in the gaps—find out what happened to Maddy."

He shook his head. "He won't help us. He's more likely to have us locked in a madhouse or a jail before helping us with anything. As far as anyone knows, Maddy simply killed herself. There was no crime."

"What about the attack before she came to the Clares'? That was certainly a crime."

"Which they tried to investigate at the time. But when the victim won't speak, there isn't much to go on." He saw my expression. "Sarah, whatever she may have told you in that barn, we can't go to the police with it."

"All right," I said. "We're on our own. Let's see if Alistair is awake and I'll tell you what I know."

Alistair was awake, propped up against his pillows. He looked groggy and tired, but when he turned his eyes to us, they were his eyes—Alistair's eyes—we saw. I let out a deep breath of relief. He had come back from his world of delusions.

"Jove," he said. "My head hurts."

I sat on the edge of his bed. Matthew pulled a chair near and sat on it, leaning forward. "You all right, old man? It was rather rough back there."

"I think so." Alistair rubbed his forehead absently with his fingertips. "I remember the barn—the fire. Was there a fire? Things got all jumbled at that point."

"There was," I said. "Everyone is fine."

"The barn is gone, though," said Alistair to me. It was not a question.

"Yes," I said.

His eyes brightened with the old obsession. "Fascinating. If the barn is gone, then where is Maddy?"

I exchanged a look with Matthew. Where, indeed? "I don't know," I admitted.

Alistair looked at the ceiling, his eyes calculating, as if he could find answers there. "A dilemma. If the place haunted is destroyed, what happens to the manifestation? Is it tied to the place, or independent of it? Does she leave, or haunt a pile of charred wood?"

"Alistair," I said, touching his wrist. "We must think quickly. Maddy spoke to me in the barn. She told me things."

Alistair's eyes were focused on me now, bright and interested. "What did she say?"

I took a breath, and tried to paraphrase what Maddy had said in her dark, disturbing language. "We know that when she came to the Clare house she was—injured," I said.

"Yes, yes."

"She told me she had been"—I reddened, for I had never spoken of such things before, but I pushed the words out—"violated. By—by three men." *Three of them on me,* she had said.

Alistair and Matthew were silent now, both staring at me. "Did she name them?" Matthew breathed.

"I don't think she knows," I said. *Find them,* I heard Maddy say. "She told me to find them. Did you not feel it? The anger? I thought it would choke me."

Alistair looked bemused, but Matthew looked shocked. "Yes. I felt it. That was her?"

"Yes. She told me to find the men. As for the rest of it, I think—" I bit my lip. "She kept saying, *Poor little dead girl, staring at the sky.* I think it means to find—where she is buried."

Again they both looked at me in surprise. "She's not in the churchyard?" said Alistair.

I shook my head. "I don't think so. She's given me glimpses—visions of it. Very brief." I looked from one to the other, watched them realize I had been keeping this from them. "It is only a snapshot—a place in the woods from which I can see a redbrick chimney over the tops of the trees."

Alistair and Matthew exchanged glances. Matthew shook his head, once. Alistair turned back to me. "It doesn't sound familiar. You say she's buried in this place? How do you know?"

"How do I know anything?" I answered. "I don't—not truly. I can't prove anything in a court of law. But she showed me this place, and she asked me to find it. She's furious that she has been buried somewhere. She wants us to right what is wrong."

"And if we don't?" Alistair asked, softly.

I looked steadily into his eyes. "She wants you. She told me she'll—take you, unless I do as she asks."

"You mean she'll kill him?" said Matthew.

"I don't know. I'm afraid it will end up that way, whether she intends it or not. But, Alistair, she seems to be able to—affect your mind. You said things were jumbled. Do you remember anything after the fire?"

"I hardly remember the fire at all," he admitted. "Everything was mixed up. It was like in dreams, you know, where time has no meaning, and nothing makes sense." He blinked, remembering, and I saw a look of fear cross his eyes. "She can do that to me, then? Why? Why, in God's name?"

"She . . ." I was embarrassed again. "She, ah, likes you."

"Likes me? I thought she hated men!"

"Not you," I said. "She finds you . . . beautiful."

He stared at me in bewilderment, as did Matthew, and I realized I would not be able to explain. It was the girls who locked themselves away, who had never felt the loving touch of a man, who, when they loved, loved the fiercest. Maddy and I were different in every way, but this much I understood.

Maddy wanted Alistair, and she was determined to have him. And if I did not find the men who had attacked her, if I did not find her grave, she would take Alistair over completely, and she would never think it wrong. He would end up in a madhouse, or, yes, likely dead, perhaps by his own hand. And what would happen to Alistair after death?

I shook away these frightening thoughts and came back to the present. "We need to do something," I said. "The constable was just downstairs. I thought perhaps he could help."

"No, no." Alistair flung back the blanket. He was fully dressed in the bed, and he sat up, scanning the floor for his shoes. "We can't have the police in this. It's too crazy. We'll start with Mrs. Clare—interview her again. Mrs. Macready, too. There may be something they remember that we've missed. Then we'll go back to the inn. Matthew—the recorder?"

"I saved it," said Matthew. "But not the camera. I'm sorry."

"Ah. Well, I believe I may have dropped it, right before—right before. It was broken anyway. But the recorder may have picked something up. I'd like to know."

"And then what?" I asked.

"And then we'll pay a visit to the sexton, Jarvis," said Alistair. "He told us he buried Maddy himself. Either he lied, or someone has fooled him. I intend to find out which."

Mrs. Clare was sedated, and unable to talk to anyone, and Mrs. Macready sent us away. She refused to be interviewed herself. "There's been too much today," she said—and, indeed, her reddened face looked tired. "I'll not have any more. Not for myself, not for my lady. I'll not be talking to you unless she tells me to, and that's final." She looked at us. "You need a rest yourself—all of you do. Maddy is gone. I can feel it, the quiet. We can all rest now."

I thought of Alistair's question—where was Maddy with the barn gone? But Alistair simply asked Mrs. Macready, in his sweet, charming manner, if she would relay the message to Mrs. Clare when she woke that he wished to speak with her. We left Falmouth House and walked to the inn.

In the second blow to our plan, we had not even reached the main path before Alistair's mind began to wander again. He complained of a headache first. Then he cocked his head, as if listening. "Do you hear that? That music?" By the time we got to the

SIMONE ST. JAMES

inn, his eyes had started to cloud over, and he was stumbling. He had been given back to us only briefly, and now he was gone again.

I hid my dismay as we helped him to his room, as we laid him on his bed, as Matthew removed his shoes. I hid my panic as he again started to talk of the war. He had come out of his fog once; perhaps he could do it again. But what if he could not?

What would we do without Alistair?

Matthew shut the door behind us as we stepped back out into the hall, and a choked sob escaped my throat. I felt hot tears of despair flow down my cheeks.

Matthew put his hands on my shoulders and looked at me. "Jesus, Sarah." I could hardly see him through the tears in my eyes. I couldn't seem to stop crying.

Matthew gripped me harder. "Sarah. Don't cry. Do you hear me? Don't cry." There was a note of desperation in his voice, as if he was near the breaking point himself. "Just don't, all right? Just don't."

I shook my head so vigorously I felt my hair fly against my cheeks, but it was foolish. I was already crying and I could not promise to stop. He let me go and somehow, in that darkened hallway, we swayed toward each other, as if unable to help it. All I knew was that I was closer to him, feeling the warmth coming off him, and it was impossible not to touch him. I slid my arms around his neck and pressed my cheek into his shirt.

He didn't resist. He stood there, hot against me, and then his hands came up, his palms tentatively pressing my waist. He smelled like smoke and sweat. I closed my eyes. His hands traveled to the small of my back, pressing me closer to him, my belly to his, our bodies flush together. One of his hands rubbed up my back, the palm along my spine. I felt my tears drying on the rough fabric of his shirt beneath my cheek.

With the pressure of his hands, he backed me up. I felt the wall of the dim hallway at my back. He pushed me against it, slow and sure, pressing his body into mine. I raised my head from his shoulder. He tilted my chin and kissed me.

He was insistent, though not rough. He ran his thumb along my jaw and opened my mouth, taking no argument, sliding his tongue into me. I was like hot wax, burning from the ache deep in my belly, my body molding effortlessly to his. I opened my mouth when he bade me, and kissed him back. He was strong beneath my hands, the muscles bunching and flexing along his arms and his back, and I felt him again and again, unable to get enough. One of his hands dropped to my hip and he pressed against me, the two of us fitting together perfectly, and he kissed me harder. My body remembered his, remembered the feel of him inside me. I wanted him again.

He broke the kiss but did not let me go. I felt his warm breath on my lips. In a daze I felt his hand slide up my body, my waist, my rib cage, a touch that felt possessive. He had me pinned to the wall. He looked into my eyes, his own dark with lust and with his uncanny intelligence.

At first I didn't understand his words, so lost was I in the sound of his voice. But when I put the words together, he surprised me.

"It occurs to me," he growled, "that I have told you my little tragedy. But you have not told me yours."

"I don't have one," I said helplessly.

He shook his head, just the barest motion. "Yes, you do. I can see it in you. I saw it on your face at the churchyard. I can practically taste it on you, Sarah."

I had never spoken of it to anyone, and I could not form the words. "No," I said.

He brushed his lips against mine, just the purest heat against my skin. "I think I will have it out of you."

He was torturing me, and suddenly I was bold. "I will tell you," I breathed, "if you come to me tonight."

He pulled back a little, though he still did not let me go. "No."

"Then you won't hear it," I said. I wouldn't give up a piece of myself if he was not willing to do the same.

He pushed his body away from mine, though he braced his arms against the wall, one hand pressing above each of my shoulders. "You don't understand."

"Then make me understand."

He looked steadily at me, his dark eyes piercing into mine. "I told you. I won't come back."

I thought I detected the faintest waver in his voice. "Then why are you kissing me?"

He looked away, but not before I saw a spasm of self-loathing cross his features. "Because I can't seem to help it."

I felt his words like a blow to my stomach. That was what I was to him, then—a willing girl, available. Easy to throw away. The kind of girl who makes a man disgusted with himself. I could have cried, and I could have slapped him. I did neither.

He pushed away from the wall and stood straight again, his face blank. "I'm going to wash up. Meet me in the private room in an hour. I'd like to check the recorder. Alistair is sick; there's nothing we can do about that. We have to carry on with the plan."

I turned my gaze away. I kept my voice level. "All right."

He turned and left without a word. I heard his steps retreating down the hallway, the door to his room open and close. I let out a breath and went to my own room, my face still hot, my eyes still stinging from the tears I'd shed for Alistair.

Well, then. So much for the bold, sophisticated Sarah Piper. I had offered him carte blanche and he had not been interested. Of course. Why would he be interested? A kiss, perhaps; a quick nighttime visit on a whim. But to repeat the experience, or to have more—no, he was not interested.

I splashed cool water on my embarrassed face and changed out of my smoky clothes. After I stepped out of my blouse and skirt, I brushed them carefully and dabbed at the dirt smudges with a wet handkerchief—they were the new clothes Alistair had just bought me, after all, and I did not want them damaged. I stood in front of the mirror in my slip—also new—and regarded myself. I was thin, flushed, my dark bob stark against my pale and splotched cheeks and forehead. My hair was tousled, the short, straight locks twisted one over another. No one would ever call me beautiful. I got out the pretty silver-backed brush that had survived the attack on my things and slowly brushed my hair straight again.

As I watched myself in the mirror, my gaze fell to the white bandages on my arms. The places Maddy had grabbed me still ached, but I had not checked the wounds as I had promised Matthew I would. Frankly, I was too frightened. The sight of those chalk white marks on my own body had unnerved me.

But right now I needed to prove something to myself: that I was brave, perhaps, or that I did not need Matthew's help. I put down the brush, and using my right hand, I unwound the bandage from my left arm.

The wound was still there, but the shape of it had changed. It was a long, gray band around my arm as before, but it had narrowed. I took in the shape of it with detached horror, as if I were looking at someone else's body through a window. I lifted my left hand and unwound the bandage from my right arm. It was the same. The shape of both was opposite, but the same.

Handprints.

They were too narrow to be fully human, the palms and the fingers far too long. But with the bruising and blotchiness disappeared, I could clearly see the oval shapes of the palms, the tapering fingers, the deeper gray where the tips of the fingers had dug into my skin. I could see, flexed away from the palm in an elegant V shape, the dull shadow of a preternaturally long thumb. The skin in the center of the palms was the same chalky white as before.

My breath came short as I looked. I felt my blood pound in my ears. Maddy's handprints were on my body, the imprint of her dead flesh on mine. Perhaps forever. *I will kiss your children. . . .*

I stood there looking for a long time. Then I took a deep breath, crossed my arms, and gripped the bruises with my own hands.

Instantly, the room disappeared. I was looking at familiar treetops and a redbrick chimney. A familiar feeling of near panic came over me, and I wanted to drop my arms, but I forced myself to stay still. This was important. *I showed it to you,* Maddy had said. She had shown me this vision for a reason. I needed to stay calm, to look carefully.

It was the angle that struck me this time. I was looking at treetops, but not at their level; I was seeing them from a vantage on the ground. I was looking, I estimated, at the edge of a stand of trees some hundred feet away, able to see the tops and the chimney visible behind them. But I was on the ground. Low on the ground.

Too low. I was not standing. I was lying down.

And something was very wrong. I struggled to breathe. I was suffocated, pressed down. I shouldn't be lying here. The panic rose in my breast. If only I could raise my head and see—

A knock on the door sliced through the vision; I jumped, let out a gasp. My hands dropped their grip. A voice came through the thick wood, muffled. Matthew's.

"Sarah, are you all right?"

I glanced at the clock on the mantel, and a sick feeling came over me. I had passed nearly thirty minutes standing there, my hands on my upper arms, lost in Maddy's vision. It had felt like seconds.

"Sarah?"

I looked down at myself. I was still wearing my slip. How could time simply disappear like that? "Yes," I said shakily, so that Matthew wouldn't open the door. He had no desire to see me in my slip, anyway. "I'm just dressing. I'll be down in a moment."

"Good," came Matthew's rough growl. "There's something I want you to hear."

Chapter Twenty

He had the wire recorder set up in the private room, the headphones attached as before. There was a plate of food on the table, a thick stew, bread, cheese, some warm sandwiches. An empty plate indicated Matthew had already eaten his share while he waited for me.

He stood by the sideboard, pouring a glass of water from a pitcher. He had changed his clothes, was now wearing a fresh shirt under a worn jacket that had once been forest green. It had faded, over apparent years of wear, to a soft, deep green that contrasted with his dark hair and dark eyes. "You should eat something," he said.

"I'm not hungry."

"Eat anyway."

I sat down before the plate of food. It seemed we were going to pretend the little scene in the upstairs hallway had never happened. I was angry and hurt, but Matthew was right. It was only past noon, though this day seemed as long as a year, and we had work to do this afternoon. We could not rest. Maddy would not.

I ate some of the soup and started on a sandwich. "Did you listen to the recorder?" I asked.

"Yes." Matthew sipped his water, his gaze on me. I could not read his expression.

"What is on it?"

"Finish eating. It can wait."

I put down my sandwich, alarmed. "What is it?"

He sighed. "You never do anything you're told, do you?"

"I work for Alistair, not you."

"I just thought you need a little food in you, that's all."

"I've eaten," I said. "Play it for me."

He put down his water glass and handed me the headphones. Moving to the recorder and turning the dials, he said, "I recorded while we were in the barn, but all I could hear was—"

"Feedback," I said, remembering him throwing down the headphones, pressing his hands to his ears. It had all been so jumbled, the entire scene like an illogical dream. "You heard feedback, and Alistair heard music."

"And you heard Maddy." He wound the reels. "I thought all I'd hear would be feedback, but our recorder got its own little performance."

At first I heard nothing; it seemed the recorder had picked up only a hiss of silence. Then the hiss changed its tone, and I realized I was hearing something after all. It was the sound wind makes in the trees.

I closed my eyes and listened, concentrating. The breeze rose and fell. A bird sang somewhere in the distance. I pictured the scene I'd just seen upstairs in my room, the waving trees and the sky. Maddy was returning to the scene yet again, this time in sound. There was no way to know that, of course. And yet, I knew.

A harsh rasp broke the peace, and I jumped in my chair. It was breath, taken painfully, through a ruined throat. Another followed, and another. The last was exhaled on half a sob, a hitch of panicked despair.

Where am I? came Maddy's voice.

It was she, and yet it sounded different; on the recorder, she sounded less inside my skull, more like a living girl. The mocking tone, the furious teasing, the petulance, had gone from her voice. She sounded alone, and not a little afraid.

Where am I? she said again.

The rasp again, then the voice: *No. No. No . . .* There was such despair in it I put my hand to my forehead, forcing myself to listen. *No, no . . . What has happened to me?*

I shook my head. What was this? Did Maddy not know she was dead? Did she somehow forget she had hanged herself? What did it mean?

The rasp came again. *Run,* Maddy said. *Run.*

And with a sharp sound, the recording stopped.

I put down the headphones and sat for a long moment. Matthew was standing by the window, looking out. We were silent for a while.

"It makes no sense," Matthew said finally. "I turned the recorder on, then off again, then on again. It turned itself off at some point— I don't remember when. And then it turned itself on again."

"Yes." I remembered seeing the recorder coming to life, right before Mrs. Clare had smashed her lamp in the barn. "And yet it's one unbroken recording."

Matthew shrugged, still looking out the window. "I've given up trying to explain it. I've given up trying to explain anything."

"It was her burial place," I said. "The place by the trees, by the redbrick chimney. She's telling us that she doesn't know where it is. And she seems . . . confused, as if she doesn't know she's dead."

Matthew turned from the window at last and looked at me. "*Poor little dead girl.* Isn't that what she said to you?"

"Yes."

"And what does *run* mean?"

I felt a spurt of fear in my chest. "I don't know." I looked at his haunted expression and asked something I had wanted to ask since we'd come out of the barn. "You saw her, didn't you?"

His gaze turned inward, as if he were seeing it again. "Yes."

"What did she look like?"

His brows drew together as he remembered. "All I saw was a figure. White. Long black hair down its back. Big, dark eyes in the face. It moved so *fast*." He paused, went on. "She was wearing a dress perhaps, or a nightgown—something long. She was indistinct, but there was something off about her—the proportions. . . ."

"Yes." I thought of the impossibly shaped hand marks on my arms.

He looked at me in surprise, and I explained. He shook his head. "Those marks worry me."

But I changed the subject. "You looked up at one point. I heard a creaking. Was she—was she—"

"Hanging." Matthew's expression shuttered. "She showed herself to me, hanging from the rafters. She must know she's dead, Sarah."

And why only Matthew? Why had Alistair and I not seen her? Matthew was right—we could drive ourselves mad with wonder. And in the meantime Alistair sat in his room, sent back to a war he was starting to lose.

Mr. Jarvis, the sexton, was not in the churchyard at Waringstoke when we returned to find him. He was not in the church either, but the vicar himself was there, dressed in shirtsleeves and tan trousers, quietly tidying the place after service. I realized with a start that it was Sunday.

It was Mr. Jarvis' day off, but the vicar directed us to his house, just a short distance over the rise. Matthew and I set out at a walk through the cool spring sunshine.

We didn't speak. Matthew was troubled, far away in his own dark thoughts. I felt much the same, though I would have liked to talk to someone. There was no time to try to open Matthew up, however, as in moments we were in view of a shabby little cottage that apparently housed Mr. Jarvis.

The man was home, though he seemed reluctant to let us in, and would gladly have left us standing there in the overgrown crabgrass and weeds. He reserved an especially hostile glare for me, and set it on me from his dark, deep-set eyes. He was dressed in shirtsleeves, like the vicar had been, over an undershirt that could be clearly seen. His trousers were held up with braces, and I was surprised to notice that, though over sixty, he possessed still-powerful shoulders and oxlike arms. Perhaps a man who dug graves for a living would be so strong, but I still found the physical verve of the man unexpected.

He turned his glare from me to Matthew. He greeted us with, "The ghost people."

"Yes." Matthew held his gaze for a long moment.

Finally Mr. Jarvis shrugged. "All right, then. For God's sake. But don't be long. It's my day off." He turned from the door.

We followed him into a small, dingy front room. An old floral sofa, sagging and shabby, sat against one wall, its matching chair in another corner. A radio took up much of the narrow end of the room, next to it a small table covered in dishes and empty bottles of beer. The fireplace was cold and unlit, and over it jutted a short mantel with an ornate, dusty, and intricately carved wooden clock, painted with inexpert tree branches and songbirds.

"I won't offer you tea," Mr. Jarvis said roughly. "Just get on with it. Like I said, I haven't got all afternoon."

I took a seat on the sofa. Matthew strolled directly to the radio and looked closely at it. "This is nice," he said.

Mr. Jarvis, who stood in the doorway, dropped his fists into his trouser pockets and grunted.

"I know a bit about radios," said Matthew. He bent, looked carefully at the radio, then straightened again.

"My Sunday shows come on in fifteen minutes," said Mr. Jarvis pointedly. "I never miss them."

"Right, right." Matthew glanced at me, then turned his gaze back to Mr. Jarvis. "We're here about the servant girl, Maddy Clare."

Mr. Jarvis shrugged, but his eyes gleamed. "You convinced Mrs. Clare you been talking to ghosts—is that it? Sounds like a bunch of bunk to me."

Matthew let this glide by. "Mr. Jarvis, I'll get to the point. Is there any way that Maddy Clare is not buried in that coffin in the churchyard?"

Mr. Jarvis went still. "Is this your story, then? That you're getting messages from the other side? Stirring things up, are you?" He looked from Matthew to me. "There's no ghost, and we all know it. Who's been talking to you, then?"

Matthew shrugged. "We're just investigators, Mr. Jarvis."

"You're shams, the lot of you." He turned to me. "Especially you." I reddened, remembering Mrs. Barry's theory that I was Alistair's specially imported "ghost expert." Apparently the rumor had made its way all over town.

"Are you married, Mr. Jarvis?" I asked.

That stopped him. He looked at me long and hard. It was a cheap blow, perhaps, but it made me feel a little better.

After a long pause, he said, "She's long gone, missy. Took herself off in 'twelve, God knows where. I never heard from her again. Maybe she's dead. I wouldn't mind that."

My stomach turned, but I nodded. I had guessed as much. A woman had furnished this room, once—the flowered furniture, the badly painted clock—but she had not been here in a long, long time. This was now a man's room, in which he listened to the radio and drank beer and did not clean up his dishes.

"We've had a lead," Matthew said, bringing our attention back to him. "I'm not disclosing the source. We've been told Maddy may not be buried where we think she is. We're following up on it."

His coolness was impressive. A lead! Not half an hour ago we had listened to that eerie recording, one that simply couldn't exist. Now he was talking to Mr. Jarvis as if he'd heard someone mention at a cocktail party that Maddy Clare was not buried in her coffin but somewhere in a shallow grave in the woods, and he simply felt idle curiosity to wonder why.

Mr. Jarvis' deep-set gaze took in Matthew, up and down, where he stood in front of the radio. "You play rugby?" he said.

Matthew shrugged, surprising me. "When I have time."

Jarvis nodded. "I can tell. I played, myself. It's in the shoulders, rugby is. You'd be a good player."

"I'm not bad." I recalled the feel of Matthew's shoulders, the muscles that bulged from his arms and back, and felt a small piece of my curiosity fall into place. "Your show starts in five minutes, Mr. Jarvis. Are you going to answer the question?"

Jarvis' eyes narrowed. "You think you're so smart, don't you? Both of you. Well, fine, then, I'll answer your bloody important question. That girl is in her grave in the churchyard, right where she belongs. I buried her myself. I vouch for it. You don't believe me? You ask the constable, Moores. He cut her down that day, and he saw me lay her out. Or just try to get Mrs. Clare to agree to dig that coffin up, why don't you? Fool that lady again, just like you've been doing. You'll go through all of that just to find the girl's dead body rotting in there, right where it should be. I buried Maddy Clare, Mr. Ghost Man. And now we're done talking."

There was a silence after this unexpected speech. I caught Matthew's eye and saw my own thoughts reflected there. Constable Moores had never told us about cutting Maddy down in the barn.

"All right, then," Matthew said as I stood. "You know where to find us."

"Aye, I know you're staying at the inn. Everyone in town knows it, Mr. Ghost Man. You and your blond-haired friend and your *special researcher* here." He sneered at me. "You and your source are chasing the wrong game, you know. There's no mystery about that servant girl. She's just another girl who killed herself. She was no better than she should be."

"You knew her?" I said, surprised.

He turned to me. "I didn't have to," he said. "I've known enough girls like her, missy." His eyes glinted. "Girls a little like you, come to think of it."

A chill of fear went down my spine. Suddenly Mr. Jarvis and

his bulky strength no longer seemed curious, or pitiful. If a man like this wanted to hurt me, I would have no chance; he knew it, and he watched as I realized it.

Matthew grabbed Mr. Jarvis by the shirtfront, slowly, almost gently, with one powerful hand, and flexed his arm to bring the man closer. "That's it," he said, his voice stony. "You're finished now."

Surprise flicked across the man's face; then he covered it with a nasty laugh. "So that's how it is, is it? I suspected as much."

Matthew was silent. His fist tightened on the man's shirt, his knuckles whitening; for one stark moment, I thought he would give in to the anger pulsing from him in waves.

Mr. Jarvis stared from Matthew to me and back again, beadily uncertain, until Matthew let him go. I let out a breath I had not realized I had been holding.

I followed Matthew from the house, cold sweat on my back. My heart beat in my throat. I felt Mr. Jarvis watch us go, though I knew without turning that we would not see him from any of the dark windows of his tiny house. He watched us, and he watched from the shadows.

Matthew waited until we were out of sight of the house, and then he stopped and took my shoulders. He turned me to face him, his eyes on mine. "Are you all right?"

I gave him a small smile as I felt the warmth of his hands. "Yes. A little shaken, perhaps. But yes."

His hands released some of their tension, but they did not move from my shoulders. He looked troubled. "Alistair would have handled that better."

I raised one of my hands and put it over his. "You did just fine, and I thank you."

My hand touched the scarring on the back of his wrist, and he pulled away. His gaze traveled over my shoulder, fixed on something there. "We should go."

I turned and looked. Two large black crows sat in a nearby tree, perched on its lower branches, their beady eyes on us. As we watched, a third arrived and perched with them.

I suppressed a shudder and followed Matthew back into town.

Chapter Twenty-one

❧

By the time dark fell, I was sick and exhausted. It wasn't a sickness of the body that afflicted me, though I was more tired than if I had been awake a week. It was a depression of the mind, a feeling of hopelessness, that dogged me to my bed that night.

The doctor had just been and gone again. Alistair had not improved. Indeed, far from improving, he had grown worse, unable to recognize the doctor, hardly able to respond. He had not eaten any of the food we'd had brought to him, nor taken any water. "That man," the doctor declared, "needs to go home."

Matthew had said little to this. But after the doctor left, Matthew slumped in his chair, his head in his hands, the sight of him confirming my own hopeless thoughts.

"He can't go home, can he?" I said softly.

"No." Matthew rubbed his forehead and did not look up. "He has no one there—no one but a skeleton staff of servants."

And he will only get worse. The words hung there, unspoken, between us. There was no way to fool ourselves that Alistair would simply recover on his own. This was no ordinary illness, after all.

Alistair was already unable to care for himself; a few maids and a butler would be of no help. When the doctor found out that Alistair had no family—and he would, sooner or later—the only option would be commitment to a hospital.

I made a small sound as I followed this thought to its logical conclusion. "He'll be locked away," I said. "He'll be—"

"Don't say it," said Matthew. "We had enough of hospitals in the war. I won't see him go back to one, and a madhouse as well."

"Perhaps we can delay things a little," I said. "Doesn't one need family authorization to be committed? He may have distant relatives we need to track down. Perhaps we could consult a lawyer. We could say we have to wait for—"

"Sarah, if he keeps refusing to eat, we won't have any time. He either goes into a hospital or he dies of starvation."

"We could hire him a private nurse," I said.

"With what money?"

"Alistair has plenty of money."

"If Alistair is mad, who will let us spend it? There's no one, Sarah."

I looked down at my hands. "I won't let him go without a fight, any more than you will."

"There is only one way out of this. Maddy has to let him go. And she has to do it soon, before he starts to starve to death."

Maddy has to let him go. I felt the frustration come over me as I climbed the steps to my room, the hopelessness of it. Someone in this town knew something—Mr. Jarvis, or Mrs. Barry, or Constable Moores, or the man who had trashed my room. Or the man I had seen watching us. Was it the same man each time, or a different one? Was Mr. Jarvis the one who had searched my things? Did Mrs. Clare or Mrs. Macready know something they were not telling?

The answer was so close—I could feel it, sense it just from the corner of my eye, flickering into my consciousness and out again. Something small was missing. Something that would fall into place if only I could see it . . . or if only someone would tell the truth.

I changed into my voluminous white nightdress and sat on the edge of my bed. The maid had been through, and the bed's white sheets were clean and starched, stretched and folded with military precision over the corners of the mattress. Though clean, the bed was cold, and I ran my hand over the knit wool comforter for warmth. A draft played its way along the floor and chilled my feet. I'd had no idea the nights were so cold this time of year, but I supposed a late-season frost was possible.

I rubbed the sole of one foot over the top of the other for warmth. Alistair had been unresponsive when we'd checked on him. He'd only stared at the wall, oblivious to everything we said. I hated to leave him, but I could hardly move. I felt as if a cold, heavy blanket had come down on me. Pulling the comforter over me, I swung my feet up from the floor and lay on the bed.

There was most definitely a draft. The end of my nose was cold. I snuggled all my extremities under the comforter and stared up at the gloom of the ceiling. As my drowsy gaze focused and unfocused, I imagined I saw movement in the shadows of the beams, like tendrils of smoke.

Outside in the hall, a door slammed.

That roused me for a moment. Matthew's door was to the right of mine in the hallway, Alistair's to the left. The sound had come from the left. Who could be slamming a door? Not Alistair, certainly, and we were the inn's only guests. A maid, perhaps? I had not seen one when I came upstairs, nor had I heard one, but perhaps one had come up a servants' stair since I entered my room.

Yes, it must certainly be so, for now I could hear a low shuffling in the hall. A soft sound, padded, though not furtive; she was, perhaps, taking care to be quiet. A muddied thump against a hallway wall. Perhaps she carried linens, and they had made the sound when she stumbled.

I should ask her for another blanket, for I was still cold. But I must have been more tired even than I had thought, for my body was in a heavy languor, and I was unable to move. Threads of alarm wound their way through my weary thoughts, and I wondered if there was something wrong with me. Certainly, I would never sleep. It was my last thought as I closed my eyes.

And then I dreamed.

How to describe the dream I had? Even now, when I think of it, I am filled with unnameable horror, a fear that seems primal, dredged from the depths of my brain like a long-dead body from a deep lake. It was cold, very cold. I was outside, still in my nightdress, my feet soaked in the dewy grass. I was crossing the short clearing to the edge of the woods, heading for the place where I had seen the man watching. The place I had dreamed of before, when I had dreamed of Mrs. Barry. I was drawn to that place, but all the same I did not want to go.

My feet kept moving. They were losing sensation in the chill, a sharp sting along the soles at first and then an icy numbness. I felt the soil sticking to them as the grass gave way to the dark, foggy woods.

I did not want to cross into the woods. I knew I didn't want to go in there, in the darkness. But I had to move because suddenly the pins of awareness between my shoulder blades told me someone was behind me.

Run, Maddy said. *Run.*

I ran. The ground here was uneven and harder to travel, and I had to dig my toes into the ground to keep balance. My breath was ragged. Branches came from nowhere and stung me, on my cheeks, my neck, my arms. Behind me, something breathed. I ran faster.

I didn't know where I was going, or even what direction I had taken now; there was no path. I pushed myself, my knees pumping, to the gaps in the trees as I saw them, trying to avoid the obstacles that rose in the darkness. A fallen log, a malevolent spray of undergrowth. Overhead, night birds scrabbled in the trees.

There was the sound of water, a stream somewhere, and I abruptly changed course to avoid it; I wanted nothing to do with the stream, and what might be hidden there. I tracked the sound to my left and continued to run, taking care not to cross the water. The woods seemed endless. My throat burned. My follower dropped back for only the shortest moment, then found me again. Its footsteps were steady, unrelenting. I tried not to sob in panic. *Quiet, I must be quiet, to get away.*

My feet hit clearer ground, and I found myself on a path of sorts, a rough-worn valley through the trees. I stepped onto it and nearly stopped, keeled over in fear. There was something on the path—something entirely different from the attacker behind me. A pure malevolence that beckoned me. *Take the path. Take the path.* I put my hands on my knees and gasped, bent over, trying not to retch. Something waited on the path, and if I turned and ran toward it now, it would grab me, and my God, it would—

The underbrush shook behind me, spurring me into motion again. I sprinted across the path—I hardly even wanted to touch it with my feet, and indeed, as I left it, I imagined icy fingers tracing my ankles—and raced on. The attacker behind me had gained precious time; I could hear it closer now, and gaining. A sob broke in my chest. Hopeless, it was hopeless. I was lost in the woods like a hunted rabbit and I would never go home again, never be safe again. I would run until it killed me and no one would ever know—

I broke through a thick stand of prickly brush and stopped. In my terror I had lost track of the water, and here it was, the short slope to the muddy bank of a river, cold and swift, before me. I was hemmed in by a high stand of rock on my left and more prickly bushes on my right; I could not go back into the arms of whatever chased me. I stood frozen for a moment, unable to bear to go forward, because the river—there was something in the river.

And in that second I knew what it was, and that nothing could be worse.

I fell to my knees. So I would die, then; I no longer cared. I could see a white shape on the riverbank, tangled in the weeds. An arm, a bloated hand, with a woman's wedding ring. The old nightmare, coming into this one. I would never escape it. The sight pulled a sound out of me, a screaming moan, a sound of pure grief.

The thing came through the bushes behind me, and grabbed me.

I kicked; I thrashed; nothing worked. It gripped me with hot, strong hands that burned my skin like fire, pinning my arms. It threw me to the ground, wrestled its way onto my back as I lay there, talking to me in a voice that sliced terror through my body like knives. I sobbed into the mud.

The thing on my back stilled, as if something had caught its attention. I raised my head and saw, farther down the bank, a shadow retreat into the trees. So we weren't alone, then. The thing from the path had come as well.

Then the monster on my back leaned over me, and I felt its breath on my cheek. And I closed my eyes and knew nothing more.

Chapter Twenty-two

*W*hen my eyes opened, I no longer saw the river, the trees, the mud. I was in my bed at the inn.

I rolled onto my back and looked up at the ceiling. So it had all been a dream, then—a horrible, terrifying dream.

"You're awake," said a soft voice.

I turned my head. It was Alistair, standing near the foot of my bed in the blue dark, his arms crossed over his chest. He was looking at me with perfect comprehension, a twinkle of humor in his tired eyes. I stared at him in amazement, wondering if I was still dreaming.

He took a step closer. "She left for a while," he said, as if answering my question. "It's me."

The world was still falling into place, after swirling apart in my nightmare. "What are you doing here?"

"We thought someone should stay with you until you woke."

I shook my head, confused. "Did I wake you? I'm sorry. I may have made some noise. I was having a dream."

Alistair's expression fell into seriousness. "Sarah," he said softly.

I saw how he looked at me, with meaning and sadness, and I did not want to contemplate what he meant. "No," I said. "It was a dream."

"Sarah," he said. "Look down."

I did not want to do it. I wanted to close my eyes, disappear into nothingness again. I pushed myself up on my elbows and looked down to see I was covered in mud, down the front of my nightdress. My bare feet were crusted in it. I touched my cheek and felt the thin film of dried mud crumble away. I thought of my dream, of the thing on my back, pressing me into the mud by the river.

A sob escaped my throat. Real. It had been real. If Maddy had left Alistair for a while, she had come to me instead. She had come to my dream.

"I was in the woods," I said to Alistair. "Something was chasing me. Something was—"

"Hush. I know."

I looked up at him. "How?"

"Matthew told me." He frowned as I stared at him in incomprehension. "You didn't see him, then?"

There came a soft creak, and the door opened, letting in a thin, pale crack of light. Matthew came into my room carrying a mug of hot tea. He stopped when he saw I was awake.

The breath left me. In one terrified sweep I took him in, the mud dried on him like it was dried on me, on his knees, on his elbows and forearms—where he had pinned me to the ground.

"You," I breathed, pulling myself upright, remembering the thing chasing me, its burning hands on me, its breath on me. "It was you."

He didn't move. "Are you all right?"

I stared in horror, remembering how I had fled the thing in the woods, how I had run from it with all the strength in me. Had I been running from Matthew, or from something else?

"I hope I didn't hurt you," he said. "You must be cold." He came forward and set the mug of tea on the bedside table. I couldn't speak. My knees came up and I wrapped my arms around them. He moved away again, back to the foot of the bed, into the shadows.

"Sarah," said Alistair, "you were sleepwalking. You were outside, heading for the woods, when Matthew saw you. He followed you and brought you back. How did you think you got back here?"

"I don't know," I said. "I don't remember." Everything had gone dark when the thing—when Matthew—had grabbed me. Had he carried me all the way back to the inn? "It's all so confusing."

"Was it Maddy?"

"Yes," I said softly. She had been there. I had, in the strange way of dreams, been her. "She was telling me to run."

"From what?"

I looked up to see Alistair leaning forward, looking at me avidly. "I don't know," I said. "Does she—does she talk to you?"

"Yes," he said, and for a moment the exhaustion left him and he was the old Alistair, sparked by the pursuit of his passion. "She talks to me, but I can never remember. It always leaves me. I can't remember it. It makes no sense. It's almost hallucinatory." He sagged a little in frustration. "If only I could remember."

"You must be hungry," I told him, remembering that we had not been able to get him to eat.

Alistair frowned. "I might have a bite in a moment or two. I just need to think for a minute."

Behind him, Matthew moved. "She's right," came his low voice from the shadows. "You should eat."

But Alistair had dropped his gaze and was looking, of all places, at my feet. "Wait," he said. "Wait."

I looked at my feet—bare, caked with mud—and back to him. "What is it?"

"Wait." Alistair frowned again, rubbed his forehead. "Your feet. There's something—something important. . . ." He rubbed his forehead again as he trailed off.

Matthew came forward. "They look fine to me."

"Yes." Alistair closed his eyes, pressed them shut as if in frustration, took a breath. His features started to sag, though he fought it. "They're fine. Her feet. They're fine. . . ."

"Alistair?" I said.

But Alistair stood quiet now, still rubbing his forehead slowly back and forth. His eyes were still closed. I felt tears lump in my throat.

Matthew came forward, put his hand gently on Alistair's shoulder. "You should eat something," he tried again.

Alistair shook his head. "The tack's gone moldy," he said hoarsely. "I don't want to eat it. It's only a short march. I'll go without."

I looked at Matthew. Half-hidden in the shadows, his face looked haggard with sadness. "All right," he said after a moment, as if his throat was choked like mine. "Just a short march, then."

The tears came down my face then, washing away the mud, as he led Alistair from the room.

※

I was still sitting on the bed, hugging my knees to my chest, when Matthew returned a few moments later.

There was no chair, so he sat on a side table. "We need to talk," he said.

I looked at my dirty toes and said nothing.

"I want to clear this up."

"There's nothing to clear up," I said, though my voice sounded weak in my own throat.

"Yes, there is," he insisted, his voice familiar and yet unfamiliar. I tried not to shudder. "Because we still have to work together, and now you're afraid of me."

I didn't deny it. Just his presence in the room made me remember the dream, the spurt of fear that made me run. "I can't help it. The dream was so real."

"Some of it was real," he said. "Not all of it."

I looked up at him. He was in shadow again. Part of me knew he was staying far from the bed in deference to my fear, but part of me thought perhaps he preferred not to be seen. What did I know of Matthew, after all? "How did you find me?" I asked. "Why weren't you asleep in your room?"

"I told you. I don't sleep." Even in the shadows, I felt his gaze move away. "I doze, for short times, until I wake up again. I do it all night. When I sleep, I go back, so I don't sleep. Sometimes I think I've forgotten how."

I ignored the pang of sympathy in my stomach. He had chased me through the woods, after all. "Your room faces the back of the building. You wouldn't have seen the woods from your window."

"I was wandering." I felt that dark gaze move to me again. "I heard noises. Didn't you?"

I thought of the door slamming I had heard right before I dropped to sleep, the shuffling in the hall. "I heard a maid."

Matthew shook his head. "There was no maid."

"How do you know? She had linens, I thought. I wanted to ask her for a blanket."

"Because it was cold."

"Yes."

He nodded. "In my room, too. Cold, like a sudden draft had blown in. A door slammed, and I thought it was you. I thought—" He broke off, his voice bitter. "No matter. Like an idiot, I went to my door and opened it."

I raised my head and stared at him. For the first time, the tatters of the nightmare began to fall away. He'd thought it was me, coming to his room. I wished for more light in my room, so I could see him. My mind began to spin. "Maddy," I said.

Matthew said nothing.

It came together now. "You saw her," I said. "She was in the hall." I swallowed my fear, thinking of the sounds I had heard, the soft shuffles and thumps, of how I had thought it was a maid. "You opened your door and saw her there."

Still, he said nothing.

"Why you?" I asked. "Why only you?"

He grunted. "I don't know." The bitterness was stronger now, tempered with anger. "I don't bloody know. It isn't something I want, believe me."

My heart tripped in my chest. "What—what was she doing?"

"What does it matter?"

I frowned. "Matthew—tell me."

He had stiffened, and even from where I sat, I could hear the reluctance in his voice. "She was standing in the hall."

"Yes." He didn't want to tell me, and I could guess why. But I would have it out of him. "Go on."

Matthew sighed. "She was—outside your door. At your door.

God, she's so—strange-looking. I can't describe it. I could hardly see her in the shadows. But she reached out both her hands—I saw that, clearly. Those long hands of hers. She reached them both out and put them to your door, like she was feeling the door with her palms. I didn't think. I just reacted."

Pieces of the dream fell away again, and I remembered how quickly I had fallen asleep. I must have gone under just about then. "What did you do?"

"I stepped out of my room. Into the hall. And just like that, she was gone."

"Did you see—where she—" I could hardly say it. Had she disappeared? Or had she gone through the door, into my room?

"I didn't see," he said. "I walked down the hall, up and down. The cold was still there, in places, but I didn't see her. I went downstairs and looked. The cold wasn't as bad there, and I didn't see anything, so I came back upstairs. I thought then she must have gone to your room, so I went to your door and opened it." He shook his head. "You were gone. You must have been fast, and quiet; I wasn't downstairs long, and I was listening all the time. I went back out to the hallway and I noticed something out the window, the one at the top of the stairs. It was you, in your white nightdress, heading for the trees."

"And so you followed me," I whispered.

"You were damned fast," he said. "Once you got into the woods, you were harder to keep up with. I kept calling your name. If it weren't for the white nightdress, I'd likely have lost you."

"I was so afraid," I said. "I thought—Maddy thought—you were going to kill me. She told me to run. I can't tell you how terrified I was." I shook my head. "I didn't hear you calling me. I swear it."

"I know," he said.

I thought of what had happened when I crossed the path. "It felt as if there was something else—another presence there. Did you feel that, too?"

"No," he said. "I didn't feel anything except certainty that you didn't know what you were doing. I didn't notice anything until I found you by the riverbank. Then I saw there was someone in the trees."

My gaze flew up to him. "What?"

He shifted uncomfortably. "I'm sure it was there. It was clear, just for a second. Watching us on the riverbank. Then it disappeared." He looked at my shocked face. "A person, I'd swear it. A man, unless I miss my guess."

My mind raced. So there had been something—someone—on the path. There had been someone else in the woods, someone besides Matthew, watching me. Waiting. For what?

I held back a shiver. I had the sudden idea that I had come very, very close to something much more dangerous than Matthew. Someone had been warned off only by his presence. If I had been alone . . .

"What was in the river?" Matthew asked me.

"Didn't you see it?" I rasped, thinking of that pale arm floating in the water.

"No. There was nothing, Sarah. It was just a muddy bank. Nothing in the reeds. I checked. But you were screaming. You nearly kicked me to death. You saw something in your dream. What the hell was it?"

I pressed my hands to my face. "I'm too tired," I said. "I don't want to think of it now. I can't. I'll tell you in the morning."

I heard him move, felt his presence come closer to the bed. He took my hands from my eyes and I looked up as he leaned over me. For the first time that night I saw him clearly, the exhausted lines around his eyes, their dark pain and uncertainty. He looked ragged and run-down, his skin leached of color. I pictured him striding the halls, looking fearlessly for Maddy, and I wanted to put my hands on his face and feel the rough stubble of his skin.

"You need to say it," he said, his gaze never leaving mine. "It's tearing you apart."

I swallowed. Something was coming loose in me; perhaps it was exhaustion, or the aftereffects of the nightmare terror. "It wasn't real, what I saw," I told him haltingly. "But it felt real."

He said nothing and waited.

I could not fight anymore, and I realized I did not want to. Tears began to course down my face before I even began. "I lived with my parents. The three of us," I said.

Matthew waited.

"My parents—I suppose they got along all right. We all got along all right. What child notices how her parents get along?" My throat was rasping and dry, but I kept speaking. "My father got the influenza in 'nineteen. It was sudden. We took him to the country-side, to a house that belonged to a friend of my mother's. She'd gone to America on a trip. We thought it might make my father get better. Mother and I nursed him. Neither of us slept. We were exhausted."

"Yes," said Matthew softly.

The words were coming out of me now of their own accord, as if I could not have stopped them. "On the fourth morning, I went to the market. It was June, and the strawberries were just coming into season. Mother and I had worked so hard. I thought to buy us some strawberries and cream, the first of the year, as a treat." I thought of that morning—the bright golden sunlight, the crisp air that was not yet warm yet promised to be—and something stabbed me on the inside, hard. I felt my features crumple as new, hot tears came down my face. "I thought we could cheer ourselves up—oh, God."

I looked down, but Matthew put his fingers gently under my chin. "What happened?" he asked.

I took a breath. "When I got home, the house was quiet. I didn't want to call out, in case Father was sleeping. I went upstairs and I didn't see anyone. I got to Father's room and—" I bit my lip. "He was in bed, and he had—passed away. He was lying quietly, as if he'd just gone to sleep. I couldn't find Mother anywhere."

His hand still on my chin, Matthew waited.

"I looked all over the house—the cellar, the attic. Mother was gone. I called for the doctor to come for Father. I didn't—I didn't think to call for the police. I was so distraught. Finally it occurred to me to ask the neighbors. The woman next door said she had seen Mother behind the house, walking toward the ravine."

Matthew's dark eyes blinked in understanding. "Ah," he said. "Sarah."

A sob heaved from my chest. I bit down on it, but still it came. "They found her two days later," I said. "In the river. She had been dead all that time; they could tell. Father had died and she had simply stood up and walked into the river. *Just like that.*" Another sob came, but I choked it back. "I was—I was gone less than an hour. I still can't stand to think of it. She could have waited fifteen minutes for me, Matthew." I looked into his eyes. "*Fifteen minutes. I would have been home. I could have comforted her. We could have comforted each other, stood it together. But she just left." I blinked as tears washed down my face. "I think that's the worst thing about it. It tears me apart, and at the same time it makes me so horribly angry. How can I be angry at my mother?"

Matthew lowered his hand. It had been only the slightest touch, but I missed it. "Sarah," he said again, on a sigh of such sorrow that I knew he, of all people, somehow understood in a way I could not fathom. The bed creaked as he sat beside me. He rifled in a pocket. "Do you know, I think I will never cease being ashamed of my first thoughts of you?"

I dashed tears from my face. "What do you mean?"

He produced a handkerchief—white and spotless, vintage Matthew—and handed it to me. "I thought you timid and soft. I thought you wouldn't be able to stand hardship."

I thought of the life I had been living in London, the life that was not really a life. "Yes," I said softly. "I thought so, too." I took his handkerchief, and I dried my tears.

Chapter Twenty-three

*Evangeline Barry was unmistakable, even in the foggy mist of early morning. I watched her tall figure emerge, lithe and careless, from the gloom. Her fashionable hat was pulled low over her forehead in a stylish rakishness, and her little dog's leash was looped over one slim, cashmere-covered arm.

She approached me where I stood waiting for her in front of the inn and stopped. As before, I found I could not read her features. Was it concern I saw there? If so, was it for someone else, or only for herself?

"I've come every morning," she said after a moment, when I did not speak. "I'm glad to see you here."

I said nothing. I could not make myself look away from her: the way a dark lock of marcelled hair wisped under the corner of her jaw like a line drawn in ink, the flawless tone of her skin that I could not detect as powder. It was rude, but I couldn't help it. I shrugged deeper into my nondescript wool sweater against the early-morning chill and looked at her.

She looked away with a sigh, as if it were a normal thing for people to stare at her without speaking. Her profile was perfect in the gray light. "How is he?" she said.

"What have you heard?" I said.

"That he's ill," she replied. "A mental breakdown of some kind. That he went into the barn at Falmouth House and came out . . ."

"Mad," I supplied.

"I'm not sure I believe it," she said. "It isn't like him. And you were there." She looked briefly at me, then away again. "And his assistant. And neither of you were affected."

I coughed a humorless laugh, thinking of last night's nightmare. "Sometimes I think I might be mad after all. That I just don't know it yet."

"What is the truth?" Mrs. Barry looked at me, and for a second I saw an avid look in her eyes. "Will Alistair be all right? Did you see—her?"

Her gaze held mine. I tucked a lock of hair behind my ear, unsure of how to answer. "No, Alistair will not be all right," I said. "And it isn't just about seeing Maddy. You—experience her."

Uneasiness flickered behind her eyes, and something else that looked a little like fear. "She talks to you?"

I tilted my head, thinking. I realized suddenly that despite how inferior I always seemed to feel around Mrs. Barry, I was in control of this conversation. She was hoping for something from me—I did not know what, but I sensed her waiting, willing to follow my direction.

I didn't want to talk about what Maddy had said to me.

"Do you know Mr. Jarvis?" I asked.

She blinked in surprise, her manicured brows rising a fraction. "The sexton?"

"Yes."

She shrugged and looked away again, disappointed. "Of course." She reached in her pocket for her cigarettes. "Everyone knows everyone in a town as small as Waringstoke."

"What do you know about him?"

She placed a cigarette between her lips and lit it. "He lives near the churchyard. His wife left—oh, years ago now. She said he had a temper, and she couldn't stand it anymore. The last I heard, she moved to Scotland with another man."

I thought of the empty house I had seen, its bachelor's mess and frilly furniture, and nodded.

"It doesn't surprise me, really," Mrs. Barry went on. "Helen was always flighty—completely unsuited to him. How they got on as long as they did I'll never know. Is that what you want to know about? The sexton?"

"You can talk about Alistair if you prefer."

She blinked down at me from under her dark lashes. "Well, then." Her voice was lower. "Are you in love with him?"

I sighed. "Everyone is a little in love with Alistair."

She drew on her cigarette. "Yes. I suppose so."

"It isn't what you think. I knew when I saw him with you."

She looked at me for a long moment in the silence. Nothing moved around us; though we stood by the narrow courtyard, and the country road beyond, no one moved. At the moment, we were alone, unheard, as if we stood on a deserted theater set.

"I met Alistair before the war," said Evangeline. "Did he tell you that?"

I stayed noncommittal. "He told me something of it, yes."

She turned away and drew on her cigarette again. "It was in London. New Year's. I was at a club with girlfriends. It was late;

God, we'd been drinking. I went to the bar for more drinks, and Alistair just appeared." The corner of her mouth quirked in a smile. "He approached me like a torpedo. Just walked right up and started talking." She laughed a little. "He was so confident, you know? Some would say cocky, perhaps—I don't think so. Just gloriously confident and sincere. He told me I was the most beautiful woman in the room and he had to dance with me."

"What did you say?"

She looked down, the cigarette burning forgotten between her fingers. "I danced with him, of course. It was—well, I can't really describe it. We talked and things just fell into place. Before I knew it, we were dancing a second time. He was so open, so honest about his heart. He was wonderful. I wasn't used to men like that. I'd never met anyone like Alistair."

She tossed the cigarette away. "Well. I couldn't do more than two dances. My girlfriends were watching, and I never knew what would get back to Tom, or how. I was lucky Tom had let me go out without him at all. I didn't feel like explaining that nothing had happened, that Alistair was a stranger I'd just met, all of that. I should have, of course. But I didn't. I've regretted it every day since, you know. Regretted that I didn't take the chance and dance with Alistair all night. But I'm just not that woman."

I noted that she'd left out Alistair's proposal of marriage; perhaps she didn't like to think of it, or perhaps it was a memory kept only to herself, like a secret photograph. She looked up at me. "I suppose I'm an awful wife, aren't I, to think of another man like that? But Tom and I had been married two years by the time I met Alistair, and I knew what I was dealing with."

"What do you mean?"

Mrs. Barry shrugged sadly. "Tom isn't much of a husband. I

shouldn't say so, but it's the truth. He couldn't enlist in the war—he had a riding accident as a child and his knees are ruined. He'll be crippled with arthritis before he's fifty. But I don't think he was unhappy to be refused. Deep down, he didn't want to go."

"Some of them didn't."

"No, I suppose not. So Tom traded stocks during the war, and he made a lot of money. Sometimes I lie awake at night and think that makes us terrible people. It simply does. He already owned this place. It was empty until he inherited it, and we lived here when we were first married, before we went to London in 1914. I never thought I'd see it again, but we came back from London after the war—he wanted to retire, he said, like a lord. Everyone here loathes us; we don't fit in, our money is too new, and Tom thinks it makes him better than everyone. I don't blame them. I hate it here, too, but it doesn't matter to Tom. He doesn't notice me much anymore. He's too busy hunting."

"Hunting?"

"Yes. The woods hereabouts are famous for it, didn't you know? Tom can't get enough of it. That's how I know Jarvis."

"He hunts with your husband?"

She nodded, and a wry smile touched the corners of her mouth. "You wouldn't think it, would you? Tom, the richest man in Waring-stoke, slumming with the town sexton. But Jarvis is a snob. He treats Tom as if he really were a lord, and Tom loves it. Roderick Nesbit is the same, though he doesn't hunt much with them anymore."

I frowned. Nesbit—the man who had been seen at Maddy's funeral. The man Matthew had not been able to rouse from his home. "Your husband knows Mr. Nesbit?"

"I told you—everyone knows everyone in this hellish place." She grabbed the loop of her dog's leash between her gloved fingertips. "I must be walking. Tom is waiting. If his condition changes—please tell me. I'd like to know."

❧

It all spun in my mind. Jarvis knew something about Maddy, and Jarvis knew Tom Barry. He even knew Nesbit. I wanted to tell Matthew everything, lay the burden of it on him, let him tell me what we should do. But I didn't have the chance to talk to him before Mrs. Clare came to see us at the inn.

She arrived in the private room, where Matthew was writing notes, his tired forehead propped in the palm of his hand, and I was pouring tea and beginning to speak. We both turned and looked at her as she came in the room so prim and gaunt, Mrs. Macready in tow.

"They said I'd find you here," she said. "We need to speak."

Matthew stood and wordlessly closed the door behind them.

I took more teacups and continued to pour. "Are you well, Mrs. Clare?"

"Well enough," she said, taking a seat. She turned her arrow gaze on Matthew. "I believe I owe you thanks, young man."

Matthew returned to his chair and shrugged. "You're welcome."

"I heard that Mr. Gellis has suffered some ill effects."

She tilted her head, as Mrs. Macready handed her a cup of the tea I had poured. "It's too bad. I had hoped to thank him as well."

"For what?" I asked.

She looked at me. She looked aged even further than the last time I had seen her—frail and bony, her eyes sunken in her face. "Why, for doing what he said he would do. I can't tell you what a relief it is now that Maddy is gone."

Matthew rubbed the back of his neck slowly with one large hand. "Mrs. Clare, I hate to be the one to tell you so, but Maddy is not gone."

"She is," Mrs. Macready put in. "The house is so quiet now, you have no idea."

I exchanged a glance with Matthew. Mrs. Clare was so frail. It crossed my mind not to tell her, to let her go home to her quiet house and her burned-down barn. The woman had suffered for a long time.

But Alistair hung in the balance. And Mrs. Clare had at least some of the answers.

"Mrs. Clare," I said as gently as I could, "we need to tell you what's been happening since the barn at Falmouth House burned."

When we finished—Matthew doing most of the talking, as she seemed to believe him more than she believed me—there was a long silence.

Mrs. Clare sat pale and straight. Her breathing was shallow. We had told her of Alistair, of my nightmare, of Maddy in the halls of the inn last night. Of Maddy wanting to know her burial place.

"It isn't true," said Mrs. Clare softly, looking at no one. "It isn't true."

"Now, there." Mrs. Macready stood and took her teacup from her. "You need to stay calm. We all need to stay calm." She looked at us pointedly. "Don't we?"

"Maddy was never like this," said Mrs. Clare. "She was— mischievous. She liked to play pranks. All right—she was unsettled. Angry, even. But never like this . . . tormenting people, chasing them through the woods . . . In all the years I've known her, she's never gone further than the barn!"

It was true. Alive, Maddy had stayed in the house. Dead, she had never strayed from the house or the barn.

"What could have set her off, then?" said Mrs. Macready.

Mrs. Clare looked at me, and her gaze was flat. "This started with you."

Perhaps they expected me to deny it, but I did not. "Yes."

"Miss Piper is extraordinarily receptive," said Matthew. "Even Alistair knew it. Perhaps it was the appearance of someone Maddy could finally talk to."

"I'll tell you something," said Mrs. Clare. "That girl is buried in the churchyard. I'll vouch for that with my life. I saw her laid in there—in that coffin. I don't know what she's thinking. I don't. She's where that gravestone says she is, and nowhere else."

"Hush, now," said Mrs. Macready, handing her a fresh cup of tea. "It's all right."

"She is, Meredith."

"Yes," Mrs. Macready agreed. "She is."

So, Jarvis had been telling the truth, then. Still, something was wrong.

I pulled up a chair and sat close to Mrs. Clare. "Please, let's go back. I have a feeling the answer is buried somewhere. Can we start at the beginning?"

"What do you mean?"

"Well, the night Maddy appeared. Let's start with that. You've described the basics of it to us. I would like to hear more."

Mrs. Macready took her own seat, next to her mistress. We sat in a circle now, the three of us women, with Matthew somewhere in the room behind us. He stayed quiet, but I knew he was listening.

"She just appeared at the back door," said Mrs. Clare. Her eyes started to take on a faraway cast. "It was dark, and pouring rain. She was drenched. She was hardly dressed—just her underthings, really. Her hair was matted. Her hands were filthy, her fingernails caked. All of that was bad enough—but she couldn't speak. She tried, and tried. No sound came from her, but it was more than that. It was like she didn't even know how. She had no words."

"You said her hair was matted," I said. "What with?"

"Dirt," Mrs. Macready chimed in. "That I remember clear. Her hair was long, no sign of pins in it. It had mud in it, caked from the ends to her scalp. It took three or four baths to get it out, it did."

I resisted the urge to look at Matthew. How had Maddy had so much mud in her hair? "What else do you remember?" I asked Mrs. Macready now.

Mrs. Macready appeared thoughtful. "Well, I already told you how badly she was injured. It was fearsome. We wanted to send for a doctor, but when we did, she started to scream. Not loud—she had near no voice, as Mrs. Clare says—but as loud as she could manage. It sounded like a broken whistle. She screamed and screamed. . . . God, I still remember it. That was how we knew she understood what we were saying, even if she couldn't speak herself."

I was remembering Alistair's words from last night. *Her feet.* Maddy's feet? "What else do you recall? About her condition?"

"Well." Mrs. Macready was warming up now. "We tried to figure out so bad who she could be. She wasn't skinny—well, she was, but not strangely so. She'd been fed at some point, some-where. Her hands were a little rough, but not too much. Not a lot of muscle on her, like a lower servant would have. Still, not lady's hands. Do you know what I mean? Not soft." She shook her head.

"Her underthings were plain cotton and linen, no monograms. Nothing fancy. I'm no policeman, but she was a servant girl if I've ever seen one. A little higher than a lower servant, perhaps. A serving maid, or a seamstress." She bit her lip. "It just makes no sense. We asked everywhere. A servant girl like that would be missed, and no mistake. She would have had training, come with references. No one was missing a servant girl."

Mrs. Clare was still. Her jaw hung open the slightest inch, as if she had wanted to speak at some point and had forgotten long ago. She looked stricken, as if she had just seen someone she recognized and hoped never to see again. I continued with Mrs. Macready.

"Where was she most injured?" I asked.

"Her neck," was the answer. "It was red and bruised. And—well." She glanced at Matthew and blushed. "In female places. You know."

"Not her feet?"

She frowned. "Her feet? No, there was nothing wrong with her feet. They were muddy, of course, but they were fine. Why would you ask about her feet?"

"No cuts?" I asked. "Did she limp?"

"No, not at all." Mrs. Macready looked from me to Matthew. "Why is she asking me about Maddy's feet?"

I did not bother to let him answer. What was formulating in my mind was so horrible I wondered if it was even possible. "She had no shoes?"

Mrs. Macready was getting annoyed now. "No, nor stockings neither. I told you, she was hardly clothed. I've told you all I know."

From his place at the table behind us, Matthew stood. "I think what Miss Piper is getting at is that if she had been running through the woods for miles, it's strange her feet were not damaged. Don't you think?"

Mrs. Macready looked at him. Mrs. Clare had gone utterly still, ignored by all of us, still stricken with horror. I thought perhaps what had occurred to me had occurred to her as well. As a matter of fact, it had—but not in the way I thought.

Mrs. Macready, for once, was not noticing her mistress. Her eyes were narrowed in concentration as she looked at Matthew. "You're right. She hadn't run miles at all, had she?"

"No," said Matthew.

"She hadn't run from a neighboring town at all. What happened to her happened here—in Waringstoke somewhere. In our woods."

"Who in Waringstoke has servants?" I asked.

"There are a few left. But I told you, no one was missing anyone." Mrs. Macready looked at her employer and her features fell. "My lady—are you all right?"

Mrs. Clare's gaze stared straight ahead, unwavering, as if she were seeing something we could not see. "My God," she said. "Edward was right. My husband was right. All these years—"

"My lady?" Mrs. Macready rose from her chair in alarm. She took the teacup from Mrs. Clare's hand before it fell to the floor. "You look ill."

Mrs. Clare looked up at her. "She came from the woods, Meredith. Our woods. But no one knew who she was. You remember?" Her gaze searched the other woman's face. "You remember what Edward said about her?"

"No. You mustn't think it." Mrs. Macready put the cold teacup down. "You just forget about that."

"What did he say, Mrs. Clare?" Matthew came forward.

She looked at him. "My husband—you have to understand. Maddy hated men, but she tolerated my husband. It took me some time to understand why. He never went near her, never spoke to her. It was the way she liked it, but that wasn't the reason. He was afraid of her, you see."

"Afraid of her?" Matthew frowned.

"Nonsense," Mrs. Macready broke in. "It was nonsense, I always said."

"Mrs. Clare." I spoke gently, and she turned her fragile attention to me. "Please tell me. Why was your husband afraid of Maddy?"

Tears began to course down her cheeks. She seemed hardly aware of them. "He always said—he always said that night she came, she looked like she'd been buried. She looked like she'd come from a grave. My husband believed Maddy was dead before she even came to Falmouth House."

CR

There was a long silence. I knew my mouth hung open; I tried to think what to say, but my mind was white. I had no words.

I looked at Matthew, hoping he would scoff, would make things sensible again, but he was only frowning. The thought was insanity, but wasn't our entire situation insanity? With Alistair upstairs in a dreamworld, and me exhausted from a running nightmare in the woods? For a dark, spinning moment, anything seemed possible.

Mrs. Macready broke the silence. "Nonsense," she said, with such force I turned to her and saw a dark red flush coloring her neck and cheeks. "It's nonsense. That girl was no such thing."

"She wasn't right, Meredith," said Mrs. Clare. "You know she wasn't. The way she looked at us—the way she behaved. She was never right. She came from somewhere in the woods with dirt in her hair. That girl was never right."

"She was a girl!" Mrs. Macready looked at us, pleading and disgust on her face. "Was it a dead girl who got those terrible ear infections the first few years? Was it? A dead girl I nursed with those fevers, who sweated and cried out in her bed? Was it a dead girl who liked to eat plums and hated the taste of my Christmas cake? A dead girl whose hands chapped from the lye soap, whose hair I cut every six weeks, who got her first courses the spring she came to us?" She glared at all of us, forgetting even to be embarrassed to mention such things in front of Matthew. "I gave her her first linens and taught her how to use them. That was no ghost. I'll lay my life on it."

Mrs. Clare wiped her face. "I loved her, too, Meredith. But even I knew she was inhuman somehow. She was a monster."

"She was broken." Mrs. Macready stood firm. "There were times—she'd look around her, and I could swear she had no idea where she was. Her memory came and went. Most of the time she knew me; but sometimes—even after years—sometimes she looked at me so strange, like she had never seen me before. Those were the times she went quiet, wouldn't speak. Yes, she had rages. I didn't understand them either. There were times it felt like—oh, like getting near her was getting near a shark, or a deadly snake. Something that would kill you if you let it. But sometimes, when she was calm, when she was half-asleep or sitting quiet peeling apples, you could see the girl she'd once been. Before someone broke her."

"All right, then." Matthew spoke gently—or as gently as he could. He sat in the chair Mrs. Macready had vacated, next to

Mrs. Clare. "Maddy wasn't dead when she came to you. We can establish that. But still, you may be on to something."

We looked at him. The glint of excitement had come into his eyes—the one I'd seen before. "What do you mean?" I said.

"She may not have been dead." He looked around at us. "But you do not have to be dead to be buried."

Chapter Twenty-four

He was right. Even as I recoiled, I knew it. The implications were so horrible, it took a moment to even imagine them.

Pretty little dead girl, Maddy had said. *Staring at the sky.*

"It can't be," said Mrs. Clare.

"It can," said Matthew. "Someone molested Maddy. Then that person strangled her. And then that person buried her, believing she was dead."

"But she wasn't," I said, feeling it, believing it, my voice hoarse in my own ears. "She woke up, and then she ran."

Run. Run.

I closed my eyes.

"My dear girl," Mrs. Macready breathed.

"If it happened the way you say," said Mrs. Clare, "then some-one is guilty of murder."

Behind my closed eyelids, it all came together. Maddy. What she had said. "More than one person," I said. *Three of them on me.* "There were three of them, at least for the original attack."

Run. Run. "I think perhaps," I went on, "Mrs. Macready is right. I think when Maddy woke, she had little or no memory of what had happened—at least for a time."

"It would be why she couldn't speak, at least at first," said Matthew. "If she had been strangled."

My gaze met his. "And it's why she wants to know where she's buried," I said. *Pretty little dead girl, staring at the sky.* "She wants to know where she was buried the first time."

"Can we find it for her?" asked Matthew.

"I think we can," I said. "I know what it looks like—she has shown me her memory of it. I think we can find it, if we look for it."

"What does it look like?" said Mrs. Clare.

"A redbrick chimney," I replied, "visible in the treetops. Do you know of any house that looks like that?"

She thought about it, then shook her head. "No, I don't. But if the roof is visible so high, the house must be large. We don't have many buildings that big in Waringstoke." She shrugged, and I had a terrible feeling I knew what she was about to say. "And the largest house in town, of course, is the Barrys'."

꧁

We checked in on Alistair, who was sleeping uneasily, cold sweat on his forehead, his chest rising and falling. In the corridor outside his room, Matthew and I made a plan.

"This isn't good," I said under my breath. "If Evangeline Barry is involved in this . . ."

"I know," he replied, scrubbing a hand over his face. I heard the scrape of bristles against his palm. "I don't even want to think about it. But we have to look into the possibility, and go to the Barry house."

"Do we pick a pretext?"

"I don't know," Matthew said. "I've never done anything like this."

"Neither have I."

Matthew's jaw was set in pain. "Alistair would know what to do. I sit thinking about it—wondering what his next move would be. He was never out of ideas. I'm not him. I just don't bloody know what to do."

I bit my lip. "I think that Tom Barry will be suspicious if we turn up, no matter what we say. And if it's the right place . . ."

"I don't suppose you'd let me go without you?"

"No. You need me to identify the spot."

"All right, then. But we'll go after dark and have a quick look, that's all. In and out. I won't have you in danger. If we do it now, everyone will see."

I looked longingly at Alistair's door. He had not eaten or drunk again today. Time was running out for him. "What do we do in the meantime?"

"I'm open to ideas."

"Let's go into town. I want to see Mr. Nesbit."

Matthew stared at me. "What?"

I explained to him what I'd had no time to say before—about my conversation with Mrs. Barry. "I'd forgotten about Mr. Nesbit," I said, "but he was seen at the funeral. And he was avoiding you. Perhaps he knows something."

Matthew looked down, thinking. He put his hands in his pockets, and in that moment I could see him in uniform, somewhere on a damp green field, slouching in the early-morning fog, a tailor's son of hardly twenty, suddenly trying to live to see another day.

He looked back up at me. The boy disappeared, and there was a man in his place, dark-jawed and battered, whose deep-eyed gaze took me in with a long, slow burn.

"All right, then," he said in the voice that stayed with me always. "We'll do it your way."

We walked to town. It wasn't right to take Alistair's motorcar; in any case, I had no idea how to drive, and Matthew drove only a motorcycle. His cycle was housed in the inn's old stables, in a stall under a blanket, as if it were a steed. It seated only one.

The sun had come from the clouds and burned off the fog. It looked to be a warm day, hot even, the first cloying air of late June pressing down. Only a faint breeze brushed us as we ascended the hill.

Matthew's gait was leisurely, and I did not know whether this was on purpose, or whether his injuries pained him somehow. Perhaps he was simply exhausted, like me; I was so very tired I had passed into free-flying giddiness, as if I were weightless, my head buzzing. The world looked very bright. I fell in step next to him and we walked side by side, Matthew's boots crushing the weeds by the side of the road.

"Maddy is quiet right now," I said. "I can't sense her. It should be a relief, but I don't like it."

"It's day," said Matthew.

"It makes no difference to Maddy. I saw her in the barn during the day. Now that she's left the barn . . ." I looked off into the trees, which waved their dark green tops only a little in the breeze. "We don't know where she is. It seems she could be anywhere. I didn't sense her in Alistair's room, but I've missed her before."

"You have extraordinary sensitivity," said Matthew. "Have you ever seen ghosts before?"

I considered the question, surprised. "No. Never. Just Maddy." Just Maddy. She had chosen me, for reasons of her own. I shuddered.

"Interesting," said Matthew.

I thought of my house that June day years ago, the hot, sunny, oppressive quiet when I came home. The silence that seemed like torture to my ears. It had been horrible, but I had seen nothing, been given no sign. In all the years since, I had seen nothing of the only people I wanted to see. They had simply gone over the edge, without looking back. "Have you seen many?"

"No." I thought that would be all, but he continued. "I've seen lots of evidence, I suppose. But evidence that could not be faked, or mistaken—no. Only a few times. And Maddy."

I shook my head. "I know nothing about any of this. I don't know what can be falsified, what to look for. I don't know the first thing about ghosts. Honestly, I have no idea why Alistair even hired me."

"Don't you?" said Matthew.

"Well, he needed someone quickly, of course. And I was available. And I suppose it isn't a very popular specialty. I heard him say something about knowing how sensitive I am, but I'm not sure I believe it."

Matthew grunted. "Alistair has always liked beautiful women."

I felt myself blushing hotly in the warm sun. I could not look at him. No one had ever called me beautiful before, but for Matthew to say it—and yet it wasn't much of a compliment, in its way. To keep the tone light, I risked a glance at him from the corner of my eye and said, "Are you saying I have no other attributes, Mr. Ryder?"

"You have other attributes," he said.

"Like what?" I kept my tone teasing.

"Long legs," he said with deadly seriousness. "Big, dark eyes. An interesting mouth. Nice breasts."

If I was blushing before, now I felt I was truly on fire. I turned and found him regarding me steadily as he walked, from those amazing eyes of his. There was a glint of humor there, but he was not making fun. "Well," I said unsteadily. "That is . . . certainly . . . an interesting list. But I don't think Alistair hired me for that. I'm not much next to Mrs. Barry."

"Evangeline?" Now he sounded surprised. "She's pretty enough, I suppose. I don't really know why Alistair is so hung up on her."

"Are you blind?" I said. "She looks like Norma Shearer."

"Hmm." He seemed to ponder this. We crested the hill and entered the beginnings of Waringstoke. "Perhaps."

"Trust me—she does." I had seen all of Norma Shearer's films, so I should certainly know.

"Well. It could be." Matthew put his hands in his pockets. "I'll tell you something, though. Even when I was in the trenches with the army, when we hadn't seen a woman in what felt like years— not one of us fantasized about undressing Norma Shearer."

At my look, he laughed, the sound coming rusty from his throat. I tried to look stern, but the smile came to my lips anyway. After all, I had never heard him laugh before.

Chapter Twenty-five

Roderick Nesbit's house was still run-down and silent. It sat on a large, weedy clearing on the edge of town, backing onto the woods. The windows were grimy and the house stared at us from behind its peeling paint with blind eyes. There was a damp wood-pile in the back, and next to it a small rotting shed with its roof caving in.

Matthew knocked on the door and waited. Though the house was quiet, there was a feeling of presence, as if someone was home. Matthew knocked again.

To our surprise, the door opened and a tall, thin man stood there, wearing a well-worn tweed coat and old leather slippers. He had a beard of brown hair and appeared about forty-five.

"Yes?" His eyes took us in from beneath an impressive ridge of forehead.

"Roderick Nesbit?" Matthew asked.

Something entered the man's eyes that looked, for a moment, like abject fear. "Who is asking?"

As Matthew introduced us, his features changed again, the fear replaced with a rigid jaw of annoyance. "I have nothing to say to you."

"Please," I said. "We want to ask you about Maddy Clare."

He turned to me and his expressive gaze took me in, from my everyday hat to my flowered sundress and my summer shoes. His voice was arch and dismissive. "I'm sure I don't know who you're talking about."

"You should," I said boldly. "You attended her funeral."

He paused for a long moment, his gaze still on me. Then: "Come in, then."

His was a bachelor's house, like Jarvis'. But if Jarvis had lived in an obvious bit of masculine mess, Roderick Nesbit lived in near squalor. The wallpaper in his front hall was peeling, the baseboards thick with old grime. He led us to a small sitting room, furnished with a filthy stuffed chair next to an unlit fireplace and a dusty, opaque mirror in a gaudy gilt frame.

"You're wasting your time," said Mr. Nesbit. "I hardly knew the girl."

"Then why did you attend her funeral?" Matthew asked.

Mr. Nesbit sat in the stuffed chair. He did not offer us a seat; indeed he could not, as he occupied the only chair in the room. He plucked absently at the chair's grimy arms and looked away.

As my eyes adjusted to the gloom, more details came to me. Mr. Nesbit was not only thin; he was gaunt—his clothes hung loosely, and under his beard his cheeks were hollow. He also had the bloodshot eyes and ruddy veins of a perpetual drinker.

"I just felt sorry for her, that's all," he said, and his defensive posture seemed to fall away, as if it tired him too much to maintain it. "I heard she killed herself. She was just a maid. But servants are people, too, don't you think?"

"How did you hear about it?" said Matthew quietly.

One thin shoulder rose in an affected, careless shrug. "Everyone in town heard about it. I'm an odd-job man, so I'm at people's houses, hearing lots of things. That constable, Moores, he wanted it kept quiet. But nothing is ever quiet in a town like Waringstoke."

"Had you met Maddy while she was alive?"

Nesbit blinked his bloodshot eyes. He looked miserable. "No. Of course not. She was a maid, wasn't she, and doesn't everyone say she was mad and kept to the house?"

"But you're an odd-job man," said Matthew, and his voice was gentle and unrelenting. "Did you ever do any odd jobs at the Clare house?"

It was clear Nesbit was weighing the odds of lying against the easy possibility that Matthew could ask Mrs. Clare for the answer. "Maybe here and there," he decided. "I don't exactly recall."

"Think about it," said Matthew. "We can wait."

Again, the expressions on Nesbit's face told everything. If this man ever thought to enter a poker game, he would lose every penny he had. "Now, see here," he said, shifting in his chair and manufacturing anger. "You're not police. I don't need to answer you. So what if I worked for Mrs. Clare once or twice? I never met that maid of hers. I just felt sorry for her. That's—that's the end of it."

Matthew stood silent for a long moment, watching the man squirm in his seat. "All right," he said at last. "We'll go, then. I have one more question for you."

The man's misery was acute; likely he was thinking of his bottle, wherever it was, and how quickly he could get to it the minute we left. "Just say it," he snapped.

Matthew nodded toward the fireplace, over which hung a long, dusty rifle. "You like to hunt?" he asked.

Nesbit followed his gaze and again the fear crossed his face, but this time he tamped it under control. "I've hunted from time to time, yes."

"But not lately," said Matthew. "That gun hasn't been cleaned."

"I've been busy," said Mr. Nesbit. "Trying to get some work here and there. It hasn't been easy since the war. Some of us don't have endless time all day to go hunting and whatever else. Some of us don't live a life of leisure."

"Like Tom Barry," said Matthew.

Nesbit stilled. He raised his gaze to Matthew and said nothing.

"I hear you don't hunt anymore," said Matthew.

"I do." Mr. Nesbit's voice was hoarse and his words were automatic. "I do. Just not lately, that's all."

"That's a shame," said Matthew. "It's a nice pastime."

"You have to leave," said Roderick Nesbit. "Now. Or I might dust off my rifle right now."

"All right," said Matthew.

"Now," said Nesbit. "Now."

As we left, I heard sounds. Perhaps I dreamed it. It sounded like wings, like scrabbling birds' feet on the roof. But when I looked behind me, there was nothing there.

❧

We walked to the pub for lunch, but we had hardly taken a seat at a small table in the corner when a large shadow came over us. It was Constable Moores.

"Oh God," Matthew muttered. "Now what?"

"I'm glad to find you here," said the constable, helping himself to a seat. "I've just been to the inn, looking for you. The innkeeper said you'd gone to town." He lowered his heavy gaze at us. "I took a little time to visit your friend Mr. Gellis before I came. He's not doing so well, or didn't you notice?"

The barmaid arrived and served us a beer; there was a short silence until she left, and then Matthew spoke, staring calmly at Constable Moores over the rim of his glass. "What are you implying?"

"Nothing much," said Moores. "Just that you seem happy to let a man sit alone in a room, losing his mind. The innkeeper is none too pleased, by the way. He's about to send your friend out into the cold, and you with him."

Matthew sighed. "I've been making arrangements to take care of him."

I stared at Matthew, surprised. I hadn't known. What arrangements could he mean? Constable Moores was not impressed.

"Your friend needs to go to a hospital," he said.

"Perhaps," said Matthew. "Without his solicitors, I have no power to send him anywhere."

"Damn it, boy, the man is sick!"

Matthew's glass banged on the table. "And I said I would handle it." His voice was low and cold. "Constable, if you think I'm going to send my colleague off to some asylum just because he makes the innkeeper uncomfortable, you need to think again. Alistair is going to be cared for. Properly. I do not need your advice, or anyone else's."

"Please," I said to them both, trying to keep my voice soothing.

"You are pushing things, my boy," said Constable Moores, his voice leveled at Matthew in a growl. "This is a small town, with good people. And there has been nothing but trouble since you and your friends arrived."

"I don't know what you're talking about," Matthew growled back.

"Please," I said again. Something about the animosity in Constable Moores' stare made the back of my neck prickle. "What did you want to see us about, Constable?"

He cut a glance at me. "I'll tell you what," he said. "In fact, I'll ask a question. Where were you last night?"

For a second I was so shocked I couldn't speak. My face must have shown it, but luckily the constable had looked away and was glaring at Matthew again. How could he know about the woods? "What are you talking about?" I managed.

"It's very simple," said Moores. "Last night. Where were you?"

"At the inn," I stumbled, a semblance of my composure returning. "In bed." No one at the inn could have seen anything—there had been no servants about in the middle of the night. Had someone been out there? Or had someone seen me from a window?

"All night?" the constable shot at me. "Alone?" He glanced at Matthew. "Both of you?"

"Now, look here," said Matthew. "What the hell kind of question is that?"

"An honest one that deserves an honest answer. Can anyone vouch for either of you all night?"

"But why?" I asked.

"Because Bill Jarvis didn't show up for work this morning," the constable snapped, "and now we find he's gone missing. And then I hear you were at his house none other than yesterday, both of you. That's why."

There was a long silence. Finally Matthew spoke. "Missing?"

"Missing," said Moores. "Sometime in the night, I think. His bed was rumpled. Hard to tell if any clothes were gone, but I don't think so. His wallet and money are still sitting on his bedside table, and his front door is unlocked." He looked back and forth between Matthew and me. "What did you talk to him about, when you paid him that little visit yesterday?"

Matthew glowered into his beer, so I spoke. There seemed no reason not to tell the truth.

"We talked about Maddy Clare," I said.

Constable Moores' complexion darkened. "That ghost stuff of yours."

"It's why we're here, isn't it?" I said. I kept my voice light, but I raised my gaze and looked him in the eye. "You may not believe in any of it, Constable, but Maddy's ghost is real. We had information that we wanted to ask Mr. Jarvis about."

He let my statements pass. "What information?"

"We had heard—that perhaps Maddy was not in the grave Mr. Jarvis dug in the churchyard. That she may have been buried somewhere else."

He seemed to pale. "That's balderdash."

I pressed my advantage. "I suppose we could have just asked you."

"I don't see why," Moores grunted. "I'll just bet Bill was happy to have a visit from you on a Sunday, accusing him of burying an empty coffin."

"In fact," said Matthew with tight calm, "he told us to ask you."

The constable sighed in frustration and looked away.

"Is it true?" I asked softly. "Did you cut Maddy down the day she hanged herself?"

Constable Moores was quiet for a long moment. The fight seemed to seep slowly out of him. "We don't get many suicides around here. It was a horrible day."

"You didn't mention it," said Matthew.

"No."

"Did you know her?"

Moores shook his head. "No, of course not. No one did, from what I hear."

"But you know she's buried in the churchyard, don't you? You saw her in that coffin."

"Yes. I suppose I did." He turned back to us and glared at us again, though this time the glare was weary. "It was a sad case, and I don't deny I don't like to think about it. I don't deny I wonder what happened and where that girl came from. But that doesn't mean I think she came back from the dead, or that she haunted the Falmouth House barn. I don't believe in ghosts, or devils, or whatever it is you're looking for."

His voice had risen, and I looked around. We were getting stares from the other patrons of the inn. It truly hit me that we were outsiders—seen by all these people as crazy, and likely charlatans. Aside from Mrs. Clare, everyone in Waringstoke saw us as more than slightly sinister. The public disagreement with Tom Barry had not helped. Even Evangeline Barry had never said she truly believed in Maddy's ghost; she had only worried about the possibility, and what it might mean to her, for reasons I had yet to discern. We had no allies here. We were on our own.

"Constable," said Matthew, rubbing a hand through his hair, "you might not believe as we do, but that doesn't mean we've come to Waringstoke to abduct the inhabitants. You said yourself you can't be certain whether any of his clothing is missing or not. What makes you think he didn't just go for a walk and injure himself in the woods?"

"Because he took his shotgun with him," said Moores. "We found it loaded and primed, in a thicket of weeds less than half a mile from the house, near the edge of the woods." He leaned back and looked from Matthew to me, gauging our reactions. "I cannot tell you," he said slowly, "how much that shotgun bothers me. Bill Jarvis kept that gun in prime condition. He used it only for hunting. I am deeply disturbed to think of what would make him take it out of its cabinet and prime it, ready to shoot. Even worse, I cannot imagine what would make Bill drop that prized gun in a damp pile of weeds and walk away. It eats at me. Something made him prime it—and something made him drop it."

I felt cold. Suddenly I remembered the crows we'd seen in the trees when we'd left the house.

It was too easy to picture. Maddy, outside Bill Jarvis' door, as she had been outside mine; the chill of her, the scuffling sound. Had he seen her, or only heard her? Had the birds covered his roof, as they'd covered the barn? Had he chased her outside, thinking her an intruder? If so, what had made him drop the gun? And where was he now?

Or was it nothing to do with Maddy, and something else entirely? Something perpetrated by one of the living people of Waringstoke?

"So we're suspects," said Matthew, "though you have yet to find proof of a crime." If he was thinking along the same lines I was, he was hiding it admirably.

Constable Moores would not rise to the bait. "At this point, you are the last people who saw Bill Jarvis alive. Until he walks back through his front door and declares it all a misunderstanding, he is a person missing under suspicious circumstances. And yes, you two are suspects. I ask that you don't leave town for a few days."

"You already asked us that," said Matthew. "After the Clare barn burned down."

"Then I rest my case." Constable Moores pushed back his chair and stood. "Trouble seems to follow you two wherever you go, and don't think I don't notice it. I suggest you go back to the inn and sit quietly with your friend until we have everything sorted out. If anything else happens, I can't answer for the consequences. I may have to take you in."

Cold sweat prickled the back of my neck. "We understand," I said.

"Enjoy your luncheon." He turned and left.

"Well," I said quietly after a long moment, as Matthew took a deep, angry drink from his beer. "Are we going to reconsider our plans for tonight?"

He set down his glass with a soft click. "I don't know. Are we?"

We looked at each other for a long moment. His dark eyes were unafraid. "We can't help Alistair if we're arrested," I said.

"Then let's finish this without getting arrested," he replied.

I took a breath. He was right. We needed to find Maddy's burial place, constable or no constable. We just needed to be careful.

"Are you in?" he asked softly.

"Yes," I breathed.

"Good," he said. "We start after dark."

Chapter Twenty-six

A̶t nearly midnight that night, I stood on the edge of a rise, the woods behind me, disheartened and swaying with exhaustion.

"So, that's it, then," said Matthew beside me, putting his hands in his pockets.

Before us, across the manicured green and placed with care on the curve of the slope, stood a tall, elegant gray house. The Barry home was an old structure, expertly built over, expanded, and painted; no doubt all modern conveniences had been installed inside, the old barn and outhouses taken down and carted away. The building that stood now was admirable in every way, and it was most certainly high enough to be seen through the tops of the trees.

The chimney, now cold, was of dark slate gray.

"I suppose we should be grateful," said Matthew.

Relief mingled with disappointment in my tired brain. Maddy had not been buried here; Evangeline had not been involved. Wherever the place Maddy insisted on showing me was located, it had nothing to do with Evangeline.

But we were back to the beginning. We were wandering in the dark, no closer to finding out what had happened to Maddy, how to give her what she wanted. Another day would come in which she took Alistair deeper and deeper.

The thought of Alistair had me turning away, walking back to the woods. There were no lights in the windows, but there was no way of knowing if anyone was inside. "We should go before they see us."

"Still angry with me?" said Matthew, as he followed me.

I only shook my head, unable to think of what to say.

"Sarah," he said. "You have to see it's the only way."

I kept walking. We had taken a roundabout route to the Barry house, so we would not be seen by anyone in Waringstoke. The path took us along the edge of the woods, and I tried not to think of my dream. I wiped my damp palms on my skirt and watched the ground.

Matthew had contacted a former colonel he'd known in the army, who now helped at a charitable veterans' association. They ran a small hospital for the poorest shell-shocked patients. They had agreed to arrange a room for Alistair. He would be taken the next day.

I was furious at the idea of it, and we had argued for the entire journey, revolving the problem around and around, until we had arrived at the Barry house and reluctantly dropped it.

"A charity case," I said now.

Matthew knew I was taking up the argument where we'd left off. "Until I can figure out a legal way to use his funds, he is a charity case. At least for now."

"I'm a charity case. Alistair isn't. He should have more than a charity hospital. What can they do for him? They'll leave him alone in a room and hope he gets better, with no one to care for him. How will we see him? How will we know what sort of care he's getting? How will we know if they're mistreating him? How can we—how can we solve this problem, if Alistair is not even in Waringstoke? Maddy is tied to him—she comes and goes. . . ."

"Sarah, the innkeeper was going to call the constable and have him turned out. He said he can't have a madman at the inn. What would you have me do?"

"He isn't mad!" I said, forcing back tears. "He isn't shell-shocked either. He's haunted, and the only ones who can help him are you and I."

"If we don't get any food or water into him, he'll die before we can. We need help, Sarah."

We said no more until we reached the inn. It was nearly one o'clock now, and we entered the sleeping building silently, not wanting to alert anyone that we had been out. We padded in stealthy single file up the stairs to the door of Alistair's room. There was a small, muffled sound from inside. Matthew glanced at me and opened the door.

Alistair lay on his narrow bed, unshaven, his eyes open, staring at the ceiling. Sweat covered him and soaked his clothes. As we watched, he moaned softly, the low sound of a man in the grip of unendurable pain.

Matthew moved to the bed, talking gently. Alistair shook his head. Matthew poured some water from the basin and tried to get Alistair to take some; but Alistair lay rigid, his jaw clenched, his hands shaking at his sides, until he tried to smash the cup to the floor. "Don't touch me," he moaned at someone we couldn't see, as Matthew tried to quiet him. "I killed you. Don't touch me. Don't *touch* me—"

When he had done all he could, Matthew turned and looked at me where I stood in the doorway. "Sarah," he said. "You're crying."

I nodded. I knew I was; I could feel the moisture on my cheeks. I looked away before I could detect the contempt for my weakness in Matthew's eyes. "If only we had more time," I said. "One more day. If only I had more time." I rubbed the back of my hand over my tears. "I'm going to bed."

I was sitting on the edge of my bed, in my robe, wondering if I could stop weeping, contemplating the nightdress I had muddied the night before and wondering what to wear to sleep, when a soft knock came to my door. "It's me," came his voice.

I dropped the nightdress on the bed and crossed to the door. He was standing there, looking at me with those dark eyes. I did not see contempt there, but I saw something else I recognized.

"No," I said, and made to push the door closed.

He stopped it with one hand. "Sarah."

"No," I said.

"I just want to talk to you." His voice was gentle.

I hesitated, then took a step back, cursing myself for a fool. I could not resist Matthew when he gentled his voice like that. "Then talk," I said, trying to sound harsh.

He sighed and closed the door behind him. "He wouldn't want the hospital. Do you think I don't know that?"

I tried not to feel any sympathy, any understanding of what Matthew's position must be like. "You said it yourself—he's had too much of hospitals."

"I can't consider what he wants. I have to consider how to keep him alive."

I had stopped crying. I was tired of arguing. "We were supposed to find it tonight. We've failed him, Matthew. We've failed."

"We haven't failed," he said quietly, taking a step toward me. "There is still time."

"There isn't."

"I'll make time," he said. "I'll tell you what I'll do. I'll call the colonel and tell him to wait another day before coming." He touched my chin. "It's all we can afford. Will that be better?"

I sighed. "Stop it. I can't take it when you're gentle."

He gave a soft laugh. "That's what I'm hoping."

I looked up at him. The cynicism was gone from his eyes, the aloof twist gone from his mouth. He was looking at me with naked hunger that made my blood burn in my veins.

"And as for the other . . . ," he said.

I took a breath.

He didn't finish his sentence. Instead his hands came to my shoulders, slid up my neck, cupped my jaw. I leaned forward, into his grip. I wanted to rub my cheek against his hand like a cat. His thumbs brushed my cheekbones as his eyes darkened. I laid my hands against his chest. Still he hovered; still he wouldn't kiss me. I wanted to scream with frustration, with the agony of looking at him for the last two days, watching him, the way he moved and sounded, the way he sometimes ignored and dismissed me.

But other times . . .

He kissed me then. I thought it would be rough and thoughtless, like the other night, but it was not; it was urgent, but it was soft and warm. His tongue met mine, and I opened my mouth. He gently slid my lower lip between his teeth, and just like that, I was melted against him, hot and feverish, sliding my arms around his neck, trying to get him closer. His hands moved down my back, squeezed the curve of my waist and my hips. His mouth traveled down my neck, his breath husky on my skin. I closed my eyes and gasped.

Something pressed against the backs of my knees, and I dimly realized we had moved and I was pressed back against the bed. I braced myself on Matthew's shoulders and bent one leg, then the other, until I was kneeling on the edge of the bed, kissing him as he was still standing. I was level with his height now. I tangled my hands in his hair and kissed him again.

When he pulled away, his eyes were alight with dark fire. He pulled at my robe. I pulled the shirt from his waist and tugged it upward, but he pushed my hands away.

"No," he said.

"Yes," I said, tugging his shirt again. God, did he think I cared about a few burn scars? I was mad to touch him. But he pushed my hands away again.

"Jesus. No. Don't do that."

I nipped his neck, tasting his skin with my tongue, and he groaned. "I want to," I said.

He was distracted and he let me get the shirt halfway up his abdomen—which was as tightly muscled as I had imagined—before he pushed my hands again. "I don't want my shirt off."

"I do," I said, but when he pushed my hands yet again, I pulled away. Even when we were mad with desire for each other, we couldn't seem to stop arguing. I took a breath, knowing my face was flushed and my lips red from kissing him. "Fine, then. You can leave your shirt on, but I won't undo this robe."

He had managed to untie the robe's sash, but it stayed closed, the two sides hanging loosely together. Even through the narrow gap he would be able to tell I wore nothing underneath. I saw his eyes travel down. "Sarah," he said.

"No." I pulled the two halves of the robe together as he watched, crossed them one over the other, made as if to retie the sash.

"Sarah." He turned his glare on me. He was breathing heavily, like a bull. *"Take off the goddamned robe."*

I stared him down. "Only if you remove your shirt."

He closed his eyes. He seemed to be having an argument with himself, deep down, over something I could not hear. "It's disgusting," he said at last, self-loathing in his voice.

"You forget I've already seen it," I replied. And because I could not stand to hear that loathing, I slid my palms up under his shirt, over his stomach, over the wiry hairs of his chest. "Take it off," I whispered in his ear. I nipped his earlobe, unable to stop myself from tasting him. "Please."

He did not do it, but he let me do it this time, his body tense, his jaw flexed in an unyielding line. I undid the buttons at his collar and pulled the shirt off over his head. He was strong and thickly muscled, his chest defined, the muscles sliding like ropes in his arms, just as I remembered from my glimpse all those days ago. But now I could not only see him; I could feel him, the silken heat of his skin, and I could smell the lust radiating off him, the tang of our exertions earlier tonight. From the front, I could see only a lick of scar tissue on the soft section of his shoulder, another under his chest, and I glimpsed the tight skin on the backs of his arms.

But he was in no mood to be observed. His part of the bargain done, he grabbed my robe and nearly tore it off me, throwing it to the floor. I was completely exposed; I moved backward on the bed, away from him, by reflex, but he followed me. He knelt on the bed, too, now, and grabbed me to him none too gently, my bare body flush against him. I felt my breasts tickle against his chest and then all thoughts fled my mind as he kissed me more ravenously even than before.

Still, this would be different from our first encounter. I could feel the difference in him, less harsh, his hands more caressing on my back and the backs of my thighs, even as he pulled my knees apart. He devoured my mouth but his tongue was gentle, imploring me over and over. He wanted to please me this time. I rubbed my body against him, felt the electric shock of his skin against my nipples. I wanted to be pleased.

He pushed me farther back and again something pressed against me from behind. It was the bed's headboard, and when Matthew felt it, he pressed my hips upward until I rested precariously against it, bracing my weight on it. His mouth traveled down my neck again as he slid his hand between my legs.

I made an involuntary sound, halfway between a sigh and a moan, a sound he must have found erotic, for I heard him draw his breath between clenched teeth. I closed my eyes and lost myself. His hand was slightly rough, and his caresses were not practiced perfection, but I cared nothing for that; I pressed myself shamelessly against him, and he responded, as he nipped my neck, my ear. Never had I felt anything so incredible in my life, and it seemed to get better, better, more intense. I felt my head drift back to rest against the wall. I could not catch my breath.

Dimly I was aware of how wanton I must look, pressed against the headboard, Matthew kneeling between my legs. I was too tired to think of it, too tired to do anything but feel. I gripped my hands on his shoulders and felt the hard, knotted muscles underneath.

Somewhere I found breath. "Matthew," I gasped. "Matthew—"

Something overtook me, a great pulse of energy. I cried out as the pleasure came, my body clenching itself against him, my knees gripping him, my fingers digging into his shoulders. I pressed my face into his neck and gasped against his tangy skin.

"Jesus God," he said hoarsely, and then he was jerking clumsily at the buttons on his pants. I helped him push at the waistband, nearly as frantic as he, our hands overlapping, and he gripped me with his big strong hands, raised his hips without preamble, and thrust into me.

Pleasure had made me boneless. I melted against him, sated but wanting more. I was pressed hard, Matthew plunging into me and the headboard behind me, and the sensation was exquisite. I raised my legs and wrapped them around his hips, feeling his muscles clenching under the backs of my knees. He nearly shouted something unintelligible and thrust harder.

I ran my hands over him as he worked, feeling the play of muscles under my palms, his back, his shoulders, the scarred skin on the back of his neck. My fingers grasped up into his dark hair. And then he stilled, deep inside me, pulled free of me, and I felt him pulsing as a painful, ragged groan tore from his chest. After that, we were still, panting against each other.

My muscles were trembling and the headboard bit into my skin, but I didn't care. After a moment Matthew slid his hands up to my waist and lifted me gently from my awkward position. He turned me and laid me flat on the bed, bracing himself over me on his elbows. I slowly unlocked my legs from around his hips.

He looked down at me, his hair falling over his forehead. He was out of breath. His eyes devoured me, looking for I knew not what. "Are you all right?" he said.

I ran my index finger gently across his bottom lip. He was so truly beautiful. I wondered, dimly, if he would leave. "Yes."

He looked surprised at the gentle caress; it seemed he might pull away, but he didn't. Instead, he leaned down and kissed me, his lips warm on mine. "You look ravished," he said when he pulled away.

I couldn't help but smile up at him, what felt like a siren's smile. "I am."

He pushed off me and sat up. He handed me a towel, as he had done before. Then I watched in dismay as he picked his shirt up from the floor and untangled it, preparing to put it on.

There was my answer, then; he was leaving. I sat up, pulled up my knees. I could have screamed at him like a fishwife; I could have begged him in tears. I didn't know what to do. I pulled the covers over myself to hide my nakedness.

Before I could speak, he turned back to me, wearing only his shirt, threw back a corner of the covers, and came into the bed next to me. When he saw what must have been shock on my face, he suddenly looked very tired. "Sarah," he said. "Just leave it be."

"You're not leaving," I said.

"What?" He frowned at me. I wondered if, no matter how many times we were intimate, we would always be talking at cross-purposes. He looked down at his shirt and comprehension slowly lit in his eyes. He took my wrists and in a single smooth motion pressed me back onto the bed. As he slid on top of me, he nibbled hungrily along the nape of my neck. The fabric of his shirt was soft against my nipples. I lost my breath.

"I'm not leaving," he said.

I bit my lip as tears stung the backs of my eyes. He had put on his shirt—that was all. He had taken it off because I insisted, but he was deeply uncomfortable without it. He had put it back on to come back to bed with me.

He pulled the covers over us and the darkened room disappeared. There were only the two of us, alone together, all the terrible fears and insoluble problems banished. I was safe beneath him. There was only the warmth of him, the weight of him, the rasp of his chin, the press of his large strong hands on my wrists. I inhaled him. I thought I was beyond exhaustion, but he made love to me again until I climaxed helplessly beneath him, my body hardly my own, as inevitable as water tumbling down the rocks of a waterfall.

Afterward, we slept. And when I woke, he was gone, and Maddy Clare was in the room with me.

Chapter Twenty-seven

It was the metallic smell I noticed first, as I surfaced slowly from a deep slumber. A familiar rush of cool air, perhaps, over my face and neck, though I could not be sure. I opened my eyes and discovered that I lay on my back, still naked, barely covered by the bed's blankets, staring at the ceiling, and I could not move. With a jolt of awareness I knew that Maddy had me in thrall.

I tried to force my jaw to move. "Maddy."

There was a movement in the dark corner of the room, a scrape against the wall. I rolled my eyes in my head, trying to see her.

"Maddy." Again, I was not sure if I was speaking aloud. It was dreamlike, but I knew it was no dream. I could hear my own voice, but I could not feel my jaw move, could not lift my tongue. My heart started to beat with terror. Her malevolence filled the room like a miasma, choking like a bad smell. Something was wrong.

It's difficult to describe the particular fear she inspired, the knowledge of frozen helplessness. She could have done anything to me, and I would have been powerless to prevent it. Worse was the knowledge that she *would* do anything to me, that a misstep on my part, the wrong word, and I knew not what would happen. And still, I couldn't see her. What did she want? Did she want anything I could give her? My mind raced in its helpless trap as I counted the seconds and wondered if they were the last seconds of my life.

The sound came again, the scrape against the wall, and then she moved closer. I could hear her breathe. The cold came over my chest and neck again. I tried to see her but could see only the faintest of shadows from the corner of my eye.

"Maddy, please."

Weight leaning on the foot of the bed. On one side of my ankles, then on the other. She had climbed on the bed. Still she did not speak. Tears ran helplessly down my face, into my pillow.

"Please."

A rustle, a whisper of cloth; I could picture her, crouching down. I did not feel the depression of her knees hitting the mattress. So she squatted over me then, on the bed, staring at me as I stared at the ceiling.

She paused a long time. I nearly choked on my own terror. I prayed to a God I had long forgotten about; I begged him. Still Maddy crouched over me as the cold seeped into the bones of my feet, breathing and breathing. She was in one of her terrible moods. I thought she contemplated killing me in those long, endless moments.

Finally, she spoke.

I'm hungry, she said in my head.

I gasped, but all I could do was plead with her incoherently.

Always hungry, she said, as if she heard none of my pleas. *Ever since the first days. Hungry with the rest of them, never enough. Oh, yes. If you want enough, Maddy, you must learn it. You must go. You must do as they say. Eyes down always. And I did it, until they bade me go. Little girls don't matter. Little maids don't matter. Poor little dead girls don't matter. And now I'm hungry again.*

"What do you want from me?" I asked her.

She breathed for another long moment, a tortured whistle from her ruined throat. *I saw you with the other one,* she said at last. *You are a good little girl, sometimes. You find things. But you haven't found the place. Not yet.*

"Please," I begged her, and I knew now I was begging for my life. "Please. I'm trying." What did she mean by *the other one*? Had she set her sights on Matthew? "Just leave him alone. Please!"

She laughed, and the sound was more terrible than her rage. *I don't want your rough one,* she said at last. *I like mine. I want to keep mine. But the other one will come with me. Yes, he will.* Her voice turned singsong, a mad sound in my head. *Yes, he will. . . . Yes, he will. . . .*

"What are you going to do?" I cried.

Stupid girl, she said almost pityingly, *I have already done it. But the hunger eats at me. So you will help me do it again.*

My God, what was she talking about? I needed to find Matthew. I needed to warn him. He had been right. We had to get Alistair out of here—could we get him away from her? She breathed heavily from her post over me on the bed, and I could only speak one question, a question that had been burning at me for days. "Why me?"

She took a long time yet again, and I thought she would not answer. She was finished with me for now; she had decided not to kill me—that much I gathered from her words—and as such I was of no interest to her anymore. I already sensed she was going to leave. When she did, I planned to jump out of bed as fast as I could and find Matthew.

But she surprised me by speaking one last time. *Everything was dark until you came,* she said. *Memory is like a fist. But now I know. Now I remember what their blood tastes like.*

She was quiet again as the moments ticked past, and I felt the rage subside by the smallest degree, replaced by a pulse of thoughtful sadness.

Find it and you'll have him back, she said, and then she was gone.

I opened my eyes to yellow sunlight coming through my window.

Groggy, I lifted my head. I was still in my room, in bed. It came back to me in a rush—Maddy, crouched over me. What had happened?

I flung the covers back and put my feet on the floor. Sunlight in the window—what time was it? I picked up my watch from the bedside table and a sound of sickened alarm came from my throat. It was nearly eleven o'clock in the morning, and I had been sleeping like the dead.

I ran a hand through my hair. It wasn't possible that I had slept. I had been too terrified. I remembered my panicked urge to find Matthew. There was simply no way I had fallen asleep after that unspeakable episode.

I pressed my hands to my face, realizing. Oh, God. Maddy had somehow put me to sleep. Why? What had she wanted to do without me?

I washed and dressed in a fumbling rush, then hurried to Matthew's room. When he didn't answer my knock, I pressed lightly on the door. It was unlocked.

Matthew lay on the bed, facedown, one arm sprawled across the pillows. He was deeply asleep. It took minutes to rouse him; he seemed drugged, the way I had felt, the groggy sensation only falling away from me now through sheer panic. I shook him and shook him until he reluctantly rolled over and looked at me.

"Please, Matthew," I said. "It's Maddy. She put us to sleep. She came to me last night. She's doing something."

He blinked his dark lashes and his brow creased. "What are you talking about?"

"Get up," I said. "Come on, Matthew, get up. Maddy put us to sleep. It's eleven o'clock in the morning!"

I watched comprehension thread its way through his consciousness. He pushed himself upright and swore.

"Get dressed," I said.

"The private room," he said, awake now. "I'll meet you there in five minutes."

I hurried back into the hall, and stopped. A woman was coming out of Alistair's room. She was in her midthirties, with heavy arms and wide hips, her hair pulled back in a bun, her dress of serviceable serge. She closed the door quietly behind her.

"Excuse me," I said as I approached her. "Who are you?"

If she noted my rudeness, she did not show it. "I'm the nurse, miss," she said, as she looked me discreetly up and down. "I started this morning."

I stared at her in shock. "Nurse?"

"Yes." She motioned to the door behind her with a nod of her head. "The fellow in there has taken ill. Mighty ill, if I can say so, but I'll see to it."

"I—I know," I said. "I am his employee. I know he's ill." This could not be Matthew's doing, as we had argued about sending Alistair to the hospital just last night. "I beg your pardon, but I had no idea anyone had hired a nurse. Who sent for you?"

"Why, my employer did, miss. I work for an agency. As to who wrote my employer, I don't know, as I'm not normally told. Usually it's the patient's family, though this poor boy"—she nodded at the door again—"seems to have taken sick while traveling on holiday. It wasn't you that sent for an agency, then?"

"No," I said stupidly.

She shrugged. "It must be the family, then. Probably they're worried about him. It's terribly trying to be sick on holiday—I've done cases like it before, though never quite as bad as this one." She put out her hand to me, like a man. "Nan Chambers, miss, though you can just call me Nan."

I shook her hand and told her my name. As a fellow employee, she had decided we were on the same level, so I saw her relax a little and she became confidential. "I was just about to get him some tea." She shook her head. "I've seen some terrible illnesses— and not all of them of the physical kind, if you know what I mean." She raised her eyebrows meaningfully. "You see a lot of things in my line of work. But this one is particularly bad. The poor boy thinks he's still fighting the war. The things he says!"

I ran a hand through my hair. Nan's tone was concerned, but she didn't sound nearly as hopeless as I felt. "Do you think you can do anything for him?"

She shook her head, though more in pity than in negation. "He needs tea, and broth if I can get it into him, for certain, and a proper change of sheets. He doesn't want any of it, but you'd be surprised how strong I am. I've dealt with some brutes in my day. He needs a good rest and a bit of care. It helps some of them, to know there's someone there. Some of them . . ." A flicker of doubt crossed her expression. "I'll do the best I can—that I can say."

I sighed. "Nan, you sound very competent, and I'm sure whoever sent you had the best of intentions, but I think I should warn you—you may not be here long. The landlord here at the inn wants Mr. Gellis removed."

"Bless you, dear, no, he doesn't. I just talked to him not a minute ago. He's told me that as long as I keep the patient quiet, I'm welcome to whatever I like."

"I don't understand it," said Matthew ten minutes later, as we sat in the common room and I explained what had happened. "Alistair simply has no family. And who talked to the landlord? I don't even know how we're going to pay the bill here."

"Matthew, the bill is paid—though I don't know how. Does Alistair have a solicitor?" I asked. "Some sort of a man of business?"

"If he does, I don't know anything about it. Which begs the question, who does know? And who wrote him?"

He dropped his forehead into his hand and rubbed it. Though he had washed and dressed in a rush, as I had, he had still managed to put on a clean white shirt, even if the button at his throat was undone. I could still see drops of water in his hair. Despite the problems that surrounded us, I took a brief moment just to look at him, to take him in when he didn't know it. I felt as if I could look at him for years.

"I don't know who did this," I said finally, "but I'm grateful for it. I feel better knowing Nan is here. We have other problems to solve." I told him about Maddy's visit to me, the terrible details coming back as I spoke. I finished and stared numbly at my cold cup of tea.

Matthew thought it over, though he looked nearly as ill as I felt. "Jarvis," he said. "That's what she was talking about. *I've already done it.* She's done something to him. Killed him somehow."

I closed my eyes. "That means—that means he was one of the men who attacked her."

"Or so she believes."

I shook my head. "Do you honestly think she could be mistaken in that?"

"I don't know anything," he replied. "She's not even supposed to exist."

My stomach turned. I had stood in that musty living room with Jarvis, looked him in the eye, listened to him lie—a man who had abused a helpless girl and left her for dead. But had I led Maddy to him, caused his death? "She's so vague," I said, trying not to believe. "Perhaps she wasn't talking of Jarvis at all."

"It all fits together." Matthew raised his head and looked at me. "She's been following you, ever since the barn burned down. She said she's been watching you."

"The birds," I said.

"Yes. And last night she said, *I saw you with the other one.*"

I felt myself heat. "I thought she meant you."

A slow beat of silence, as we both remembered our lovemaking the night before.

Matthew spoke softly. "I think we would have noticed if she was watching. Don't you?"

I bit my lip and said nothing.

"She didn't mean me."

I took a breath and nodded. I was thinking of the birds I thought I'd heard yesterday, as we left Roderick Nesbit's shabby little house. "We need to check on Nesbit."

"No." His voice was thoughtful. "*You* need to check on Nesbit."

"Where will you go?"

"There were three of them, according to Maddy." He ran a hand through his hair, tousling it. His gaze went past me, directed inward where I couldn't see. "Jarvis was one, then. And it's possible Roderick Nesbit was another."

"God," I said, as it hit me that I had again been in the presence of one of Maddy's pitiless attackers. "Do you think so?"

"If he is, Maddy has already found him. So you can't do any harm by going to him now."

My blood chilled. I looked at Matthew's face and couldn't help but ask him, "Doesn't this bother you? I feel so angry that these men could have done this to Maddy. And yet—when I think of her, how cold she is, how mad—I don't know what to think of it. Do they deserve the revenge she wants to give them? Can we say that anyone deserves it?"

Matthew stood, paced away, and looked out the window. "It's utterly insane, all of it." He crossed his arms. "I don't know what Maddy did to Jarvis. Perhaps nothing, and we're worrying for no reason. But if she did something to him—if she killed him . . ." He paused for a long moment, his shoulders tensed. "I've seen enough men killed. Good men who didn't deserve it. I shouldn't worry about what will happen to a few rapists. I wish I could call up the necessary heartlessness." He turned and faced me again, lines of strain etched in his features. "Maybe I'll manage. To save Alistair, we have to find Maddy's grave. We have to find where they buried her that day. That's what you're going to get from Nesbit—if he's still alive."

"And you?" I said softly.

"There's a key person in all of this we haven't talked to yet, not really. I'm going to see Tom Barry."

Despite myself, I felt a cold chill of fear. "Are you sure?"

Matthew shrugged on his jacket. "It makes sense. Barry is friends with both Jarvis and Nesbit. He's either the third man, or he has information that will lead me to him. I intend to get that information out of him. I can't do that if you come with me and bring Maddy with you."

"You don't want her to hurt him," I said.

"No." He came toward me, strong and so full of purpose. "She's cut off Jarvis as an interview subject. She may have found Nesbit. I don't want her tracking our movements until we've solved this." He took my elbow, his hand warm through my sleeve, and looked into my eyes. "We can do this, Sarah."

I nodded. "And we leave Alistair to Nan." I stood and brushed at his lapel, lightly, any excuse to touch him. "Do you know, she lost a nephew at the Somme?"

"Excellent," he said. "So she thinks Alistair is a war hero."

I touched his face, ran my fingers down the rough skin of his cheek. "He is."

Matthew pulled away. "Let's go, then. It's already late."

Chapter Twenty-eight

ℛoderick Nesbit's small house was quiet, the windows shuttered under the bright June sunshine. I approached through the thatch of weeds in the front garden, taking in the silence around me. It was the heavy, eerie hush of a house of sickness or death. My throat closed and I stood before the front door, helpless as I remembered the day I had come home to my parents' house with my basket of strawberries. The silence had been much the same.

I raised my hand to knock, but the same instinct that disliked the hush around me would not let me do it. After a brief hesitation, I instead pressed my palm to the front door and pushed. The door swung open, unlocked and unlatched.

The house inside was dark and gloomy, belying the pretty sunshine of the day. I stepped into the main room, where we had interviewed Roderick Nesbit the day before, and let my eyes adjust. The room sat dusty and quiet, undisturbed.

I heard no movement in the house, no voice. I walked through the short hall, past the stairs, to the kitchen at the back of the house. Here was a small bachelor's kitchen, with a compact stove, a single, cold teapot, and mostly empty shelves. A greasy plate sat on the small, heavy wood table, the remnants of a pork chop and a spoonful of peas. Last night's supper, interrupted.

Still, there was no sound. I thought of calling out, forcing words from my stricken throat, until I noticed the door to the back garden. It was ajar, just as the front door had been.

It was too much like what Constable Moores had said happened to Jarvis—the silent house, the interrupted life. I walked back to the sitting room and looked at the wall over the fireplace. Roderick Nesbit's rifle was gone.

I swallowed, took a deep breath, and went back to the kitchen. I pushed open the garden door and walked out into the sunlight, squinting my eyes. The ground here was cleared, the dirt hard-packed around a rough stone walk. No garden was planted, and the wildflowers ran rampant, as they did in the front. The small woodshed stood off to the left, flanked by the woodpile.

I stood for an uncertain moment, listening to the breeze and the faraway larks in the trees. A soft metallic click made my palms sweat and my stomach turn. The sound of the rifle.

"Mr. Nesbit?" I called softly, turning toward the woodpile and walking slowly toward it. "Are you there?"

No voice, but a soft shifting shuffle, the scrape of a shoe against the dirt, told me someone was there.

I came closer. "Mr. Nesbit?"

The click did not come again; whether the first had been the cocking or the uncocking of the rifle, I did not know. I was close enough to the woodpile now to see around it. I took one further step and looked at the other side.

He was sitting there, his back to the pile, his legs stretched before him, the rifle in his lap. He did not look at me, but looked straight ahead. It was Roderick Nesbit, but whatever had happened to him since I had last seen him seemed to have aged him twenty years. His face was as haggard as an old man's.

"Go away," he whispered.

I edged closer to him. "Are you all right?"

"Ssh." He looked up at me for the first time, and I saw his eyes were sunk into his head with exhaustion. "Shut up and go away. She'll hear you. I thought you were her. You're lucky I didn't shoot you."

I crouched down, closer to him, my heart hammering in my chest. "Who will hear me?"

He looked at me. "Do you think I believe you don't know? You're the one who brought her."

My hand flew to my mouth. We had been right, then. Maddy had come. Still, I did not feel her presence, nor did I notice any metallic smell—except for the rifle in Roderick Nesbit's lap. I waited for my breath to come back, as I let all the implications come to me. "So it was you, then. You were one of them."

He closed his eyes and tilted his head back, leaning it against the woodpile, and said nothing.

"You're in danger," I said. I put my hand on his arm. I would take him to Constable Moores, and we would finally close the case on Maddy Clare. "Come with me."

He did not move or open his eyes.

"Mr. Nesbit." I shook him. "You don't understand. The danger—"

A sound came from him then, a low humorless laugh. "The danger, ah yes. It's what she wants, isn't it? For me to run. To think for a moment that I have any hope of escaping her." He opened his eyes, stared tiredly into the distance. "She came to me last night. I thought I heard something during supper. I looked up, and—Mother of God—" He raised the hand not holding the rifle to his face, scrubbed it over his eyes. "I don't know. All night. I knew it was her as soon as I saw her. Jesus God, I've tried everything. Confessing, apologizing. I begged on my knees. I wish to God she'd just say something, anything, instead of looking at me with those eyes."

"Mr. Nesbit, you have to leave. She wants revenge."

"She can have it, then." His fingers curled over the rifle in his lap. "But she'll have to come and take it. Maybe she can't be blamed, but I'm not running like a scared rabbit. I came out here after midnight when I couldn't take it in the house anymore, but I decided not to run. Where would I run that she can't follow? I'm here, but she hasn't come out, not yet. When she does, I'll be ready for her."

I was squatting next to him, and I eased my legs forward to kneel, feeling the muscles unknot. I tried to think. He was a little unhinged; I couldn't use force. He was armed and needed soothing, placating. Besides, what force did I have, a woman, next to him? My only hope was to fetch Constable Moores and bring him back here before it was too late. It would be another wild tale to tell the skeptical policeman, but I didn't care.

The other option was to draw Maddy away. And hadn't she told me herself how to do that?

"Mr. Nesbit." I kept the tremor, mostly, from my voice. "I can help you. It isn't just you Maddy wants. There's something she's looking for, something she can't remember from . . . that day."

He looked at me then, his eyes widening. "She spoke to you?"

"Yes." I touched his arm again. "On that day, you . . . buried her. Where? Where is that grave? If I could find it, I might be able to draw her away. . . . I'll bring the constable to you." It was a wild, unlikely scheme, and I forced myself not to think of its impossible aspects, like how exactly Constable Moores would be able to protect anyone against Maddy Clare. My only hope was to placate Maddy with what she had asked, and hope that protection would not be necessary.

He was not following. His eyes had glazed at the memory of the grave. "God, yes. We buried her. It wasn't my idea—you have to understand that. None of it was my idea. It never was. Not with *them*. Bill Jarvis was a bully—I knew the type from school. God, the way he'd laugh at me." A small, terrifying smile crossed his lips. "Well, maybe he's not laughing now, wherever he is. That's one thing."

I listened, silent. I didn't want to hear it, but in a way I knew I had to. I needed to hear it at last.

"We found her in the woods," he said as he stared into the distance, into his memories. "We were out hunting, and there she was. Taking a shortcut through the woods, down the path by the stream. We'd hardly shot anything all day. And we'd been drinking, of course. I had to keep up with them, always keep up with them, or they'd laugh at me. I was nearly sick with it. And she came along, this pretty girl with long dark hair. No one, really. A servant girl. A bit of sport, they said. Who would she tell? Who would believe her? And so she was—" He faltered, put a hand over his eyes for a brief moment, as some kind of terrible pain wrenched through his body. "It got out of hand in the end. I didn't want to do it, I swear. I think, when she saw us, she had an inkling of what we were thinking. She tried to run, but she didn't get far. She had a small bag of belongings that she dropped when she ran. We never found it. It was the only thing she had on her. I went back into the woods, at night, in the years after, looking for it. I don't know why. But I never found it."

He took a deep breath as the pain wracked his body again, but he had started now, and he meant to continue. "It wasn't me that killed her. It wasn't. It was completely unexpected; even Bill was a little shocked, I think, in that thick head of his, as we watched it happen. But he strangled her, he said, to shut her up. She kept screaming and screaming. And when she was still, he said we had to bury her."

I swallowed my horror. "Who was it?" I said as softly as I could. "Who was the third man? And where did you bury her?"

That humorless smile crossed his lips again. "I thought you knew. It was Tom Barry that killed her, Tom Barry we followed all the time. And we buried her in Tom Barry's woods, six feet from the well behind his house."

My stomach lurched. "No. It isn't possible. It wasn't there. It was somewhere else. The chimney . . ."

"What chimney?"

"Where Maddy was buried. There was a redbrick chimney, visible through the trees. But Tom Barry's chimney is gray."

He looked at me for a moment, and something that was almost wonder came into his face. "You really do speak to her," he said. "You really are what they say. Tom had his chimney rebuilt five years ago, along with the other renovations. The old one was crumbling and rotted through."

The cold, icy bands on my arms throbbed sharply. "And the old chimney was redbrick," I said.

"Yes," he replied. "It was."

Evangeline's husband was the third man. And Matthew was there even now, at Tom Barry's house. Did he know? Had he put it together yet? Was he in danger?

"I hate him," Roderick Nesbit said almost dreamily. "I hate him so. But I've always been there when he calls me, one of his acolytes, Bill and I. There's something about Tom that makes you do what he says, even if it's repugnant to you. Even if he insults you, says you're a queer and a fairy-boy and a coward. You still do what he says. I enlisted because of him, you know. After what happened in the woods that day, I couldn't stand it. I was thinking of killing myself. Instead I enlisted, to get away from him, and because he couldn't. He had those bad knees. I got the satisfaction of saying I was going off to fight while he was staying home. Who was a fairy-boy then? But I saw things over there that seared my soul, burned it away to ashes. I came back with nothing inside me. And he was still here, throwing around his money and playing his foolish games."

Things were falling into place in my mind, so fast I could barely register them. "You saw her," I said. "It was you. You saw her last year, at the Clares' house."

"My God." A dry sound came out of him. "After all that. I'd been suffering, I'd put myself on the cross, and she wasn't dead! I went to fix a broken windowpane for Mrs. Clare. She said she'd be out, Mrs. Macready would be out, to simply fix it while they were away. I came around behind the house and there, on the path between the house and the barn—there she was. She had a metal bucket in her hand. She saw me at the same time I saw her, and the look on her face—like she'd opened a door and seen something inside that tore her heart out."

"We think she had memory loss," I said. "She could feel the effects of the trauma, but she couldn't remember it."

"Is that so?" He looked up, as if pondering the blue June sky. "That would explain it, then. She never left the house in all those years. None of us had seen her, and she hadn't seen us. And we didn't note the comings and goings of servant girls, of course. Not when we believed she was dead."

"But that day—when she saw you . . ."

"Oh, she remembered. She most certainly did. Everything came back to her clear as day when she saw me, and I watched it on her face."

"Did she seem angry?"

"God, no. She dropped the bucket and fell to the ground—it was like her legs gave way under her. She looked at me with such utter horror. Some sound came out of her, almost a high-pitched scream. I was just as terrified, myself. I think I said something stupid—like 'Sshh, sshh'—like a fool. And then she was gone. She got up and ran into the house as if the devil were after her. I left, too. I didn't even fix the damned window."

"Did you tell the others what you had seen?"

"Yes. Bill wanted to see for himself. Tom—I could tell that Tom was already thinking ahead, to what could be done. He was worried she would go to the police. But by the next day it was news that the Clares' maid had hung herself, so she was truly dead then. But I was wrong again, wasn't I? Because she may have been dead, but she still was not gone."

"Mr. Nesbit." My voice was pleading. "You really should come with me. I'll find the constable. This can all be over."

But he was grim now. He tightened his grip on the rifle in his lap. "You go, young lady. It's best. She's teasing me now, but she'll be out soon. She can have her revenge, but, by God, she'll have to fight me for it. I'm not going anywhere."

I stood. I had no more time to waste. Matthew was in trouble, and I needed to find Constable Moores. I looked around me, at the peaceful, quiet, weedy yard. It seemed a somnolent afternoon like any other, the bees buzzing in the straggling wildflowers. I still saw no sign of Maddy.

"I'm sorry," I said, before I turned to go.

"We all are," he said to my back. "All of us."

Chapter Twenty-nine

There was no one on High Street in Waringstoke at this quiet time of day. No matter. I nearly ran to the post office; after an agonizing decision, I determined that I needed to call Constable Moores before doing anything else. The post office had the nearest telephone in town.

Evangeline Barry exited just as I approached the door. She stopped when she saw me, her expression filling with alarm. "Miss Piper, is everything all right?"

I stopped in my tracks. She was as beautiful, as immaculate, as ever; her hair had been freshly marcelled, and she wore a soft, casual, achingly expensive shawl tossed over a short-sleeved dress of dark bohemian gray. I thought of her approach to me in the change room, the panic in her voice.

"Tell me," I said. "Did you know?"

She parted her lips and said nothing.

"All this time," I continued, "did you know? Would you even tell me the truth if you did?" My voice rose and I knew I should fight to control it, but somehow I had lost the will. "How could you not have known? Your own husband? How could you have let her suffer so? Did you think she was dead, like everyone else?"

Her eyes were wide with alarm now, and something that looked like fear. "For God's sake—be quiet."

"My God, you did know," I said, shocked, for despite myself I had hoped it wasn't true. "Perhaps you were even there."

"Be quiet!" She grabbed my shoulders in a tight, painful grip. "Please, for God's sake! Someone will hear, and they'll tell him. He'll kill me if he thinks I know. You don't know him. He'll kill me. I swear to God he will."

I stared at her, uncomprehending.

She pulled me aside, down an alley next to the post office, and dropped her grip. When she looked at me, her face was filled with despair. "Tom did something to that girl, didn't he?" she said. "Something terrible."

I watched her eyes, her face, but if she were not sincere, then she was a better actress than Greta Garbo. "He attacked her in 1914," I said cautiously. "He and Bill Jarvis and Roderick Nesbit. They—" My throat nearly closed on the word. "They raped her in the woods and left her for dead. Roderick Nesbit just confessed it all to me."

Her head dropped forward and she cradled it in her hands, her palms over her eyes. "Oh, my God," she said softly, and then, as if she could not stop, "Oh my God, oh my God. Oh my God . . ."

"You suspected something," I said.

"Not until a year ago," she said into her hands. "When she killed herself. He grew so strange after that. He started to terrify me."

"That's because, until that day, he thought she was dead," I said. "But Roderick Nesbit saw her at the Clare house, and told your husband she was alive." I took a step away from her, remembering

Nesbit and his rifle, remembering Alistair and Matthew. We had no time. "Your husband is a monster, Mrs. Barry. You can claim you don't know it, but he is."

She dropped her hands. "I don't claim any such thing." The pain in her eyes was real when she looked at me. "You have no idea, young Miss Piper. You simply have no idea what a hell my marriage has been." She wiped the dampness from her cheeks. "In the fall of 'fourteen, I was at my mother's house. I told Tom I was going for a visit, but I never intended to come back. I stayed there for over four weeks. But my mother convinced me I was being unreasonable, and sent me back home to him." She looked blankly over my shoulder. "That must have been when it happened. I hated my marriage even then. From the first week, I hated it. But since you and Alistair arrived in town, it has all started to change. I've realized that I simply can't take it anymore, no matter what my family says. And Tom . . ." She shook her head. "Tom laughed at first, when he heard you had come to exorcise that girl's ghost. He said you were fools and charlatans. And then he got angry, and said you should be stopped."

The man watching us from the woods; my room, torn apart. It had been Tom Barry all along. "And you thought—"

"I started to suspect something," she said. "He was so livid. He talked of you endlessly, and of this ghost. Of whether this ghost could talk to you, as the rumors said. Of what she would say. He didn't believe it at first, but he started to become convinced. And I started to wonder what he was so afraid she would reveal."

"And so you came to me in the dress shop," I said.

She looked at the ground. "I'm the worst sort of coward."

"What about that scene in the pub? You weren't afraid then."

She made a short sound. "When I am in public with him, Miss Piper, I am more afraid than ever. I can't show even a hint of what he thinks is disloyalty. If he's displeased with me—" She bit her lip. "I make certain he's never displeased with me."

"And Alistair?" I said.

She looked up at me again, her features softened. "Alistair," she repeated, the word gentle in her mouth. "Alistair taunts me with his very existence. He shows me what I could have had if things had been different. If I had been brave. Alistair is the most wonderful man I have ever met, and I don't deserve him even in the slightest."

"It was you," I said, though part of me had already suspected. "Who hired the nurse. Who spoke to the innkeeper. Who arranged everything for him. It was all you, wasn't it?"

A tear rolled freely down her perfect cheek. "It's amazing what money can do. Money is all I have. It's the only thing I know how to use. Please tell me he's doing better."

It was my turn to grasp her shoulders now. "If you love him, even a little—if you have any good feeling for him at all—you'll help him now."

Her gaze focused on me. "What do you want me to do?"

"Call for Constable Moores," I said. "Tell him everything you've told me. All of it. Tell him that Roderick Nesbit has confessed to me, and is in his house right this moment. Tell him that Matthew Ryder has gone to see your husband. And tell him I've gone after him."

She shook her head. "Don't do that."

"I'm going."

Her eyes met mine. "He's dangerous. Haven't you been listening? He knows you have discovered something. He's an animal trapped in a corner. Your Mr. Ryder may already be injured, or even dead."

My heart lurched, but I was more resolved than ever. I dropped my hands. "I'm going. Matthew needs me. It's the only thing I can do. I know where Maddy's grave is, and I have to take her there. It's the only way to end this."

"I don't know what you're talking about."

I shook my head. "Just find Constable Moores, as I said. Then find Alistair. He's at the inn. He needs you—he has always needed you. I wonder now if you could have helped him from the first."

She nodded. "I'll go."

After she hurried back into the post office, I started off again. It was so random—a chimney gone rotten, and rebuilt, and Matthew and I had missed everything. What if we had found Maddy's grave last night? Roderick Nesbit would not be fighting for his life right now. And what was happening to Matthew?

I couldn't linger on it. I had to hurry now, as fast as my low heels could take me, my shirtwaist dampening with sweat. If Maddy followed me to the Barry house, then perhaps she would leave Roderick Nesbit alone.

Chapter Thirty

The house was quiet as I approached, this time walking up the long drive. I ached to go inside, to find Matthew. But my first business was well away from the walls of the house; and I turned my steps off the drive, through the trees, the weeds stinging my legs, and made for the well.

My arms throbbed where Maddy had gripped me. I stopped, well in the shade, and looked in the direction of the house. From here I could see the gray chimney jutting from the rooftop, visible over the tops of the trees. I stood for a long moment, entranced, as the crickets sang in the weeds around me and the wind blew quietly. I had been here; the feeling was so strong, it simply held me paralyzed as time stretched out unseen. I knew this place. It lived in my memory. I had seen it behind my eyelids, time and time again. My heart thudded slow in my chest. This was a place where something terrible, something truly evil, had happened.

I returned to myself slowly, as the bitter scent of the wildflowers on the warm breeze brought me back to the moment. I was

choked with terror, and I found it difficult to breathe. I was risk-
ing death here. *I cannot do it,* part of me cried. *I cannot do this.* But
still, I stood rooted to the ground.

I felt myself in a dream, as I had been the night I had run
through the woods. I remembered that feeling of dread. I remembered the thing that had awaited me on the path. In my mind's
eye I could see the path again, but it was not shrouded in darkness
anymore; it was bathed in reddish late-afternoon sunlight, and the
birds cried in the trees. I saw a young woman on the path, her
black hair braided neatly down her back. She was twelve years old,
and her family—*always hungry,* she'd said—had sent her away to
service. Her hands had begun to become roughened, and she'd
filled out a little with regular meals. Only she'd been dismissed—
a petty theft, perhaps? An insolent word in a fit of temper? The
mistress of the house watching where her husband's eyes followed?

Where would such a girl go? Home, to her shame, to hunger?
Or forward, somewhere far, where no one would know her former
employers, in hope of getting another position? *I did it until they
bade me go.*

I saw three men, all armed, block her way. I saw one of them
step forward.

I turned and made my way toward the well. It was a dark
smudge at the edge of the clearing. In the dream in my mind, the
girl knew. I saw her turn and run, agile as a rabbit. I saw her small
cloth bag drop to the ground, saw her legs pump, terror giving
them speed, her feet take the uneven terrain off the path as fast as
they could, running for her life. And I saw the three men run after her.

I was running, myself, now. I was getting closer to the well.
Six feet from the well, Roderick Nesbit had said. But in which

direction? In my mind, the men caught the girl, and she fell hard to the ground. She opened her mouth to scream. I was weeping.

Where would be an ideal place for a grave? Not in the open, certainly. Not to the left, where the land sloped downward, became rocky and hard. To my right was a stand of fir trees, outcropped from the forest proper, their trunks dark and dense against one another. No space to dig a grave there. But pinpoints of sunlight showed between the black trunks, like delicate holes of lace. I walked toward it.

This is the place, I thought as I came through the trees.

It was dim, unassuming. A small, natural clearing, perhaps twenty feet square. Two rotted stumps here, where old trees had fallen. Clumps of weeds, thick and forbidding, filling in a depression in the ground, the right size for a human body. The right size and shape for a grave dug years ago, since filled in by nature. A place no one would ever find.

I closed my eyes, searching for Maddy's presence. *This is it,* I said to her in my mind. *I've found it, as you asked. Come.* I focused on this small, quiet place, under the afternoon sun. It felt as if there should be more here, some mark of what a terrible thing had taken place in this spot. But nothing happened; only the birds sang endlessly in the trees. There was no eerie, throaty call of a carrion crow.

Could I be mistaken? Was there another place here, the right place that would call Maddy and ease her grief and confusion? I lifted one foot from the ground to take a step into the clearing, to gain a closer look.

A metallic click sounded next to my ear.

"Don't do that, my dear," came a soft voice behind me.

I froze, put my foot back to the ground. My head buzzed.

"That's it," said the voice. It was a man. "Curious, aren't you?"

I opened my mouth, but my tongue was too dry to speak.

"You're looking for something." The man was amused, his voice as dangerous as acid. "There's nothing to find. Or haven't you heard?"

It was Tom Barry's voice. "Please," I managed.

"Shut up," he said, as if he were discussing the weather. "You're the second person today who has come here, poking into my business. Someone is very, very bad at keeping secrets. Turn around."

I did. I was shaking, my legs hardly obeying me. Somehow, I managed to move.

He stood before me, his dark-lashed blue eyes looking at me with unwavering malice. He wore a chambray shirt under a tan tweed jacket, the casual attire of a country gentleman. Tom Barry, by any standards, was a reasonably handsome man. He had once caught the eye of a young woman named Evangeline. The kind of man who could catch the eye of any young woman at all—except for the fact that he held a long, lethal rifle in his hands, and he was pointing it directly at me.

He smiled. It was the same odd-shaped smile I'd seen at the pub. Perhaps it was only terror making me see things. I was shaking with fear.

His gaze moved down me, then up again. "Now, now." His voice was soft. "You are trespassing on my property, you know. At least the other fellow came to the door."

My stomach dropped. *Matthew.* "Where is he?"

Tom Barry was frowning now. "It's bothering me. Who talked to you? It has to have been either Rod or Bill." He took a step closer, touched the end of the rifle to my sternum, just below my breasts. "It was probably Rod, that coward. But Bill hasn't been reliable since his wife left—he drinks too much, you know. It could have been either." The conversational tone of his voice was belied by the rifle pressed to my body. He gave it a small, unmistakable shove. "Who was it?"

I took a breath, somehow found my voice. "It's too late. You can't do anything to them now."

The smile returned. "Bill, certainly. They found him in the woods a few hours ago, did you know? Keeled over dead in a clump of weeds. Not a mark on him. Some sort of seizure, I'm sure. A shame. But he could have talked to you before he died. And the last I heard, Rod was still alive. The other fellow wouldn't say either." He shrugged. "And now I can't ask him again, as he's not exactly talking." He noted the expression on my face with pleasure.

But fear had brought everything into clearer focus, and now I noticed details I hadn't seen before. The sleeve of Barry's jacket was torn at the shoulder, and—more tellingly—he had a dark red welt on one cheek, an injury too new to have deepened into a bruise. His hair, combed close to his head, was awry over one ear, as if he had smoothed it down and missed a place.

"He gave you a fight," I said.

The amusement left his face and his eyes narrowed. He jabbed the gun into me. "Walk."

I did, trying not to show my fear, my despair. If Matthew was dead—dear God, dear God, if Matthew was dead—at least he had given a fight at the end. I felt my spine tighten. This man would see justice. My life meant less than nothing. I would take any chances I could, pounce on the first mistake this man made even if it meant my own death. I would see justice done for Maddy, for Alistair. For Matthew.

Tom Barry steered me toward the house. The chimney came

closer and closer through the trees. My upper arms throbbed, and I remembered my visions of this place. It had always been this place, if only Matthew and I had found it in time. If only we hadn't put everything together too late.

Maddy, Maddy, this is your place, I thought. *Come and at least one of us can be at rest.*

The house came up before us, expensive and serene, but my stomach would not stop turning at the sight of it. I had suffered too many nightmares; I was too close to the real nightmare that had happened here.

My thoughts went briefly to Evangeline. What had it been like for her, to live here with this man? Perhaps I had misunderstood her, or judged her too hastily. She had been living in a hell of her own for years. I felt a little ashamed, and I wondered if she would be able to find help in time, before I myself died here.

For I was certain I was about to. Alistair was helpless; Jarvis was gone; Nesbit was a prisoner in his own yard. And Matthew, despite a fight as valiant as that of any knight, had fallen. There was no one left. Constable Moores would come, perhaps; but whether that would be in time to find me, or to collect my body, remained to be seen. Tom Barry was not interested in leisure.

He jabbed me in the back with his rifle, prodding me up the steps to the house. "I knew, that day in the pub," he said.

I said nothing.

"You're supposed to be a ghost expert," he went on. "A medium. Eh? Called in special. Well, I could see it just by looking at you. I'll tell you what you are. You're a swindler, that's what, just like the man you came with. Just like this one here."

I stopped where I was, in the front corridor, looking into the front sitting room. I had stopped listening to him. I heard nothing but the blood rushing in my ears, and the beat of my broken heart in my chest.

Matthew lay facedown on the sitting room floor. His arms were raised by his head, elbows bent, as if he were about to catch a ball. I couldn't see his face, which was turned away from me; I could see only the blood pooled on the thin carpet under his head, spreading in a dark brown stain. The sitting room was a mess—a table overturned, a chair thrown back against the wall, smashed glass on the mantel. Barry had invited Matthew into the sitting room for a conversation; then, once he suspected what Matthew was about, he must have surprised him. It was the only way. Matthew was half a foot taller than Tom Barry and a great deal bigger; but if Barry had surprised him . . . if he had used a weapon . . .

Matthew was so very still. I willed him to move, willed him to breathe. A sound escaped my throat, and a small convulsion wracked my chest.

The hard prod of the gun in my back brought me back to the moment. "Move," said Barry.

"Is he dead?" I had to ask.

"I hope so. If he isn't, I'll soon take care of it. Move."

I didn't want to move; I didn't see the point. It all seemed so hopeless, for a long moment. Matthew was lost to me, alone in this awful house; before him, Maddy had suffered here, too. And now I would die, before Constable Moores even put down his teacup and got in his motorcar to come for me—that was, if Evangeline Barry, this monster's wife, had found her courage and run to fetch him at all. Perhaps she had lost her nerve, stripped by years in this terrible place, trapped in a marriage with this nightmarish man. Perhaps she was silent even now, afraid to raise the alarm. Perhaps no one would come until it was too late, if ever.

I felt a deep wrench of pain. There was no one to regret me amongst the living, and that itself was painful, almost as bad as missing someone would be. There was no one except Matthew, who I wasn't sure even lived; without him, there was only Alistair—who would be saddened, I was certain, but would not mourn too deeply. I sensed he would not let himself. He liked me; we were friends. But he had lost so many friends already.

The gun prodded me again, and under this hopelessness I felt a bone-deep chill. It was not fear exactly, but a terror slow and deep, pushing its way out from an icy well inside me, freezing my limbs. I looked at my hands and saw I was shaking. I whistled a breath into my lungs and realized I had felt this fear once before.

"It was you," I managed through numb lips. "In the woods that night. It was you on the path."

I remembered the rush of fear I'd had that night—*There's something on the path.* Something that waited and watched. I had felt it then, this deep unreasoning fear. Because Tom Barry had really been there, in the woods that night.

His hand clamped to the base of my neck, where it met my shoulder, and I felt him move close behind me, his breath in my ear. "Ah, well," he sighed. "I was so close then, wasn't I? You knew it. I was so very close. I haven't done it again, you know, since her. It was a lark. We'd had too much to drink and we wanted a bit of fun. But you . . . I was in the woods, watching the inn, and then there you were. Running like a hare, just like she did. That white nightgown. I hadn't thought of it, but that night—my girl, if only you'd been alone, what fun we could have had. What wonderful fun." His chuckle was hot on my skin. "Maybe we still can."

"You can't do this!" I cried. The hopelessness was gone with his words, and panic started in my veins. "Everyone will know!"

He sighed. "Last time was such a perfect opportunity, really—it couldn't have been better if we'd planned it. Such things don't come often in life. Even my wife was out of town, visiting her mother, or she would have seen something. The circumstances aren't so favorable this time. Still, we make do with what we have, don't we? Your friend here was an intruder—he attacked me. That much is simple. As for you . . ." He tightened his grip on my neck, sending shoots of pain up into my skull. "I've never seen you, and I don't know what happened to you. Perhaps your friend lost his temper. Perhaps the madman did you in. The woods are dense out there. So many people have been lost in those trees. How many people are going to go searching for you, a stranger? And for how long?"

He was so close to me now, leaning in to sneer. I could smell tobacco and sweat. I realized that in his position he had lowered the gun; though his hand was still clamped on my neck, his guard was down for a brief moment. If I could think clearly, if I could control my shaking body, I could take advantage.

I took a breath and drove an elbow backward, into his sternum. He was surprisingly hard—he had almost no fat on him—and I felt the impact up my arm and to my shoulder. At the same time I twisted away from him. He teetered for a split moment, off-balance. I had never hit anyone in my life, and I had no idea how to do it. I could think of nothing better to do than to hit, as hard as I could, the hand that held the rifle and hope he dropped the gun.

He fell backward, but even as he fell, the look of surprise on his face slipped away, and as the gun fell with him, he was reaching for it again. He landed on his back with a heavy thud. I stepped backward to turn to run, but he already had the rifle in his hand again, and he pointed it at me from his position on the floor.

Our eyes locked. We froze a long moment like that, each one

of us taking the measure of the other. A sick humor came into his eyes, and he chuckled darkly. He pointed a loaded, cocked gun at me, and I knew he would use it. I would not run.

"Not bad, darling," he said. "Not bad."

He pulled himself to his feet, slowly, the rifle never wavering. Now I saw something different in his face—interest, and even pleasure. I realized I had triggered something in him, the same instinct that had made him enjoy chasing Maddy. The instinct that had made him enjoy what he did to her. I was no longer a nuisance to him. I was prey.

He came toward me, smiling.

"Don't do this," I said softly.

He opened his mouth to speak, but what he planned to say—whatever it was—I never heard. We were interrupted by a commotion at the window across the room.

It was the low, whirring sound of wings flapping. A crow—a large, dark, long-beaked creature—was alighting on the sill outside the window. As we watched, it gained its balance, scrabbling its feet and flapping its inky wings in a dark tattoo against the glass. Another alighted next to it, the soft thud of its wings hitting the window adding to the noise of the first. The second bird opened its beak and cawed deep and throaty, even as a third bird appeared behind the first two.

The same thing was happening at the other window, near the fireplace; and I could hear the same beat of wings from the other windows in the house. Something large and bony flapped against the front door, over and over, and I felt a new kind of fear come over me.

I looked at Tom Barry. He was gazing around, bemused, but

the aim of the rifle never wavered. He turned back to me and his eyes narrowed. The bruises on his face were starting to darken.

"Please," I said to him as I noticed a familiar metallic smell. "You need to get out of here."

Surprise transformed his face, his eyebrows shooting upward; then he laughed. "Get out of here? What do you take me for, darling? It's just a few birds."

"It isn't. Don't you hear them?"

"I hear birds," he said, but the first spark of uneasiness crossed his expression. The birds were loud now, and unmistakable; they were obviously at every window of the house, and we could hear them calling to one another in their awful voices. I was reminded of the day we had seen them on the barn, covering it like a shiny black shell.

His face hardened, as he obviously pushed the uneasiness away. "Enough about a few birds. I want—"

Again something thumped against the front door, something large and heavy. We both jumped. The sound came again.

"You don't understand," I said, the words bursting out of me. "You're in danger. It's Maddy. It's her ghost. She's still here, and she talked to me, just as you suspected. It was you watching me from the woods, wasn't it? It was you who ransacked my room."

"Shut up."

"You don't want to admit it, but you were worried that the rumors were real. That she was truly haunting the barn. Roderick saw her that day, and told you, and you knew she was still alive, that she hadn't died when you buried her. And then you heard she killed herself, and you thought it was over. But there were rumors that her ghost haunted the barn, and then Mrs. Clare brought us in, and even though you didn't quite believe it, you still worried. What if the ghost was real? What if it said something to one of us? What if your perfect crime was undone at the very end? Well, you were right to worry. *You were right.*"

"Shut up!" He jabbed the gun at me in anger, and it hit me hard in the soft part of my stomach. I gasped in pain, but the sound was lost under the overwhelming whirring of the birds on the house. "I'll take care of this," he said. "Walk. Toward the stairs."

I obeyed, but the words wouldn't stop coming. It didn't matter how wild I sounded; now was no time to worry about sounding like a madwoman. "She didn't remember," I told him. "For years, she didn't remember what had happened. And then, again, after she died, I don't think she remembered—I think she's been living in a shadow world of some kind, unable to leave. But she remembers now. It wasn't Bill Jarvis or Roderick Nesbit who told me what happened—Roderick confessed, but I already knew. It was Maddy, do you understand? It was Maddy who told me, because she remembers what happened now. I didn't want to come to the house, because she follows me. She'd find you. And now she knows who you are. You have to get out of here. It's your only chance. You have to run."

He had prodded me down a set of stairs, into a dark cellar. The sound of the birds was fainter here. I smelled damp, and coal, and the earthy scent of potatoes. The ground was cool through the soles of my shoes.

He glared at me in the gloom. "I've had enough of listening to you. You're completely mad. Just stay still and shut up. I'm going upstairs to deal with those birds, and then I'll be back."

"You can't!" I cried. "You can't! She's come here!" I grabbed his sleeve. "You have to run!"

"Enough!" His face contorted. He jerked his arm away, and brought up the butt of the gun. I had time to glimpse its dark, wood-marbled surface before it connected with my cheek and threw me backward. I lost my footing and fell to the floor. Pain shot through my skull. I rasped for breath and looked up at him from the floor as the warm wetness of blood began to flow down my skin.

Barry blinked, as if unsure for a second who had just hit me; then I watched his expression settle again. The sound of the birds was louder now, and he couldn't deal with them and me at once. "Just stay still, for God's sake," he said. "Just stay still!"

He retreated up the stairs, backing slowly, the gun still pointed at me. He needn't have bothered. I could only lie on the floor, cradling the pain in my face, feeling it overtake me like a living thing. Dimly I was aware of the beating of birds' wings, somewhere overhead, and the strong metallic smell in my nose. I closed my eyes. *Don't go up there*, I meant to say, but I didn't have the words.

The door closed; I heard the click of a lock. I had to stop this from happening. I had to. I searched my mind for Maddy. She was here; I could feel it. *Maddy*, I thought. *Maddy, don't, please don't, please.* But there was no answer. I could not even tell if she heard me.

I heard Tom Barry's heavy footsteps upstairs. I heard him mutter, and curse; he went up a second staircase, out of listening range, and then he came back down. His steps traveled back to the kitchen, where I heard the tinkle of something breaking, and another curse.

There was a sharp cracking sound—almost like the report of a gun, but not quite. Tom Barry's steps came again, running now. He cursed. And then he shouted—a quick, barking shout, hoarse and strangely high-pitched.

A jumble of confused sounds then. Thumps and crashes against a wall. Something crashing down. Once, a curious dragging sound.

But Tom Barry's voice didn't come again—not a yell, not a curse—and he didn't fire his gun.

After a time, all was quiet.

I lay on the cellar floor, cradling my injured cheek. It was over, then. I had done nothing, prevented nothing, and Matthew was still up there somewhere. I cried until the pain overtook me in a sort of fog, and I laid my face against the floor.

I was still there when Constable Moores came, sometime later, to clean up the blood and the bodies.

Chapter Thirty-one

&

Consciousness came slowly, and I thought I heard footsteps and a voice. I opened my eyes.

The voice was big, booming, and familiar. "Police! Police, I say! If you're here, show yourself!"

I stood on shaky legs. My head throbbed horribly, and for a sickening moment I thought I'd lose my balance. I pushed myself forward, up the cellar stairs, trying to make a sound from my hoarse throat. Finally I rattled the cellar door, pounded on it, and shouted for help.

The constable's expression, when he opened the door, went from surprised caution to utter shock at the sight of my face. He had a gun in his hand, though it was lowered to his side. He backed up a step. "Are you alone down there?"

I could hardly speak. I pushed past him and ran down the hall to the sitting room. Matthew was still on the floor, still and quiet, though he had been turned on his back. I ran to him and fell to my knees.

I pulled him into my lap and started to cry again, this time from helpless relief. He was warm to my touch, warm under my hands, though his face was stark white and I could trace the blue veins of his temples. I pulled him to me and bent over him, weeping helplessly.

Constable Moores' steps approached slowly from behind. "He's alive, though it looks like he's had a nasty knock. I'll call for a doctor. Do you mind telling me what happened?"

"Where are the birds?" I asked.

"Birds? I have no idea what you're talking about."

"Tom Barry killed Maddy Clare," I said over Matthew's head. I could feel the beating of Matthew's heart under my hand. "Matthew came to question him about it. Tom Barry killed Maddy Clare with Roderick Nesbit and Bill Jarvis."

"That's what Mrs. Barry said. Her own husband."

"She was away at her mother's. She didn't know."

The constable huffed through his nose. "Well, Nesbit is dead," he said, almost conversationally. His steps moved away to the window. "Shot himself with his rifle, though it must have been damned difficult. I've just come from there. Bill Jarvis had some kind of seizure in the woods. Do you mind telling me where Tom Barry went?"

"I don't know," I said, and it was the truth. "I came for Matthew. Barry found me, took me to the cellar, hit me with his gun, and locked me in."

"Well, something happened in here." His voice told me he didn't quite believe me, but I didn't care. He was quiet for a long moment, and then he said, "There are tracks outside." His steps came closer to me again. "Will you stay here, or will I come back to find you gone?"

I looked up at him. "Are you mad?"

He looked at Matthew and me, his tired, hooded gaze taking

us in. If he thought I would leave Matthew, he was very much mistaken. He would have to tear me away from Matthew with his bare hands, a fact I watched sink into his mind. "Well, then. Just sit tight and don't move, and for God's sake don't touch anything." He turned and left the house.

Matthew shifted in my lap, sighed faintly. His eyelids fluttered. I smoothed the hair back from his forehead and watched his eyes open, his gaze blurred and confused.

I bent down, kissed his cheek, the corner of his mouth.

"Sarah," he breathed.

"It's me."

He looked at me now, his gaze starting to focus. I watched as he saw the injury on my cheek, which I could feel swelling. I had dried blood on my skin. He raised one hand, touched the fingertips gently to the side of my face, his gaze darkening even as I shook my head.

"I'll kill him," he murmured.

"Hush. I'm fine."

He closed his eyes. "I'll kill him."

"No. It's over, Matthew."

"Sarah." I felt the moment he slipped out of consciousness again. I pressed his hand to my face, kissed his palm. His blood was soaking my skirt, and I didn't care.

"I love you," I said to him.

And then, I felt Maddy behind me.

I can't say how I knew she was there. I simply knew. She was standing behind me, where Constable Moores had been only a moment ago. I waited for the crackle of rage, the jolt of fear that always accompanied Maddy, but they did not come. Instead, I heard the quiet shuffle of bare feet on the floor.

I looked back. It was agony to turn my head, and my puffed cheek obscured some of my vision. I saw bare feet, impossibly white, the hem of a simple serge skirt. My gaze traveled up to a cheap white blouse under a bolero jacket that I knew, with sudden certainty, had been the smartest thing she owned. She had worn her best jacket that day—to make an impression, she hoped, when she asked the women of Waringstoke for work.

The face above the bolero jacket was young and elfin, under a mass of long, black hair that fell nearly to her waist. She watched me with big, dark eyes, her arms limp at her sides. I realized I could see, behind her, the open front door through her translucent skin.

"Maddy," I said softly. "Go."

She didn't seem to hear me; she made no response for a long time. Finally she spoke, though I never saw her lips move. But it wasn't the terrifying voice inside my head any longer. She sounded like a nineteen-year-old girl.

"I didn't want to," she said, and her voice was an exhausted sigh. "I'm so tired."

"I know," I told her. "Go."

I peeled my gaze away from her and turned back to Matthew. I was surprised to find his eyes were open again, and he had turned his head to watch Maddy.

He brought his gaze back to me. "She's gone."

I caught a flash of movement from the window, and when I looked up, I saw her briefly, walking away from the house. She was headed toward the woods, the wind lifting her long hair from its heavy place on her back. There was such a pretty sway to her walk, the way her arms swung carelessly, the way her hips moved. A pretty young woman, walking on a sunny day. As I watched, Constable Moores came from the other direction. Her elbow could have brushed his—he passed so close to her—but he passed her without turning his head, without seeing a thing. If he felt a shiver up his spine, he didn't express it.

I turned back to Matthew. "The constable will be back soon," I said to his upturned face. "He said he'd bring a doctor."

"He got me in the back of the head with the butt of his gun. I nearly had him, though. I nearly did."

"I know."

He raised his hand to my cheek again. "He got you, too."

"It doesn't hurt," I said, and he laughed a little, then winced.

He turned serious again. "Don't tell them about Maddy."

"There's nothing to say now."

His fingertips slid over my cheek. "Do you really love me?"

I kissed the corner of his mouth again. "Yes."

We sat for a long moment, his cheek against mine, his hand still cradling my cheek. I felt his breath and knew I would feel every one, down the years, until I felt his last.

"Good," said Matthew finally. "That's good."

Chapter Thirty-two

⟡

Constable Moores wasn't happy with any of it. We could tell. He tried his best to put the pieces together, this way and that, to implicate one of us, but he never managed it. Still, he always knew there was something he was missing, and that we somehow held the key.

Tom Barry was dead. There were queer tracks outside the house, and even queerer ones at the edge of the woods—tracks that looked, to the police who saw them, like the twin lines of a man being dragged. But the angry half-moon marks of heels digging into the dirt indicated this was no unconscious body being dragged into the woods, but a live man, with a size 10 shoe, kicking and, quite possibly, screaming.

The tracks stopped shortly after the edge of the woods. Over a hundred feet away, Barry's rifle was found in a thicket, dropped and unfired. There was blood on the butt of the gun. Scent dogs eventually found Tom Barry at the river's edge, facedown, his head under the water. He'd drowned, but there was no mark on him, just like Bill Jarvis. If someone had held his head as he died, the person had left no sign.

I had been locked in the basement, and Matthew had been unconscious, and no one had been there to hear a thing.

No, Constable Moores did not like it. He thought it was too neatly done. Still, it made no sense. I myself could not have abducted or killed Tom Barry. I was far too small to drag a full-grown man struggling into the woods, and there was no way I could lock myself in the basement afterward. Matthew was, perhaps, strong enough to do it; but for him to somehow dispose of Tom Barry, then knock himself grievously on the back of the head with the rifle, drop it, walk back to the house, and pass out face forward, even Constable Moores could not credit. The constable toyed briefly with the idea that we had been coconspirators, working as a team; but that meant Matthew had also locked me in the basement before passing out, and when the doctor gave his report on the seriousness of the blow Matthew had suffered, he could not make it work.

Still, he made us stay in town until he could reluctantly finish his investigations—for he was still also working on the death of Bill Jarvis, though by all appearances it was an accident, and the suicide of Roderick Nesbit. I had been to Nesbit's house, after all, and had been the last one to see him alive. Nesbit had died alone, sitting on the ground in the yard behind his house, shot with his own rifle. The constable had heard the shot himself as he came through the front door of the house. He would have loved to point suspicion for it at either Matthew or me—to point a rifle at oneself and pull the trigger is almost impossibly difficult, though people have managed it—but he had to admit that I had long left and we must have been already at Tom Barry's house by that time, and when he ran through the house and arrived at the scene only seconds after the shot had been fired, all he saw was a few ugly crows on the fence and a puff of blue smoke.

In the meantime, as the constable's frustrations mounted, and he and the others interviewed us over and over, we stayed at the inn, with Alistair.

Alistair had returned to us.

He was groggy, ill, and impossibly hungry and thirsty; he had a scruffy growth of beard; but he was unmistakably Alistair. Within a day he was washed, changed, cleaned up, and cracking jokes as if nothing had happened, though he was still weak. Nan stayed on and nursed him, and he let himself be nursed, though he told her good-naturedly that she was trying to kill him with an excess of beef broth. A haunted look at the edge of his expression gave him away. Maddy had gone, as quickly as she had come, but she had left a mark in his bad dreams.

My own injuries were relatively slight, though my face looked awful. The doctor shook his head and said I was lucky my cheekbone was not broken, and gave me a salve for the swelling. I was black-and-blue, and sore, but I was happy to be alive. The marks on my arms had disappeared.

I nursed Matthew myself, as much as he would let me. He needed frequent rest, and his wound healed slowly, though he hated to admit it. He had frequent headaches at first, though he took the medicines the doctor prescribed, and recovered with the gradual sureness of a big, vital, powerfully healthy man.

He had been through injuries so much worse. Though he hated being sick, it never truly dragged him down. He could be gruff all day, but at night when I climbed into his narrow bed with him and kissed him and ran my hands gently through the soft darkness of his hair, he would lean into me and put his arms around me. At first he would drift helplessly off to sleep as I held him, but after a few nights he would stay awake, and eventually run his hands up under my nightgown and over my back, and kiss me back hungrily, and we would make love with a pleasure so quietly feverish I felt the bed and the entire room should catch fire.

Though we lived in a kind of limbo of waiting, those days at the inn were strangely peaceful. We spent many hours, the three of us, talking, going over everything that had happened. Alistair wanted to hear everything, of course. He talked little about his own experience, though I felt it weighed on him. He and I spent many a quiet hour, reading and saying nothing at all; sometimes I'd look up and see him staring out the window, his mind far, far away.

One day, Alistair found a map, and the three of us pored over it. It was impossible to know, of course—but there was a train station four miles from Waringstoke. If Maddy had come from there, it was possible she had come through the countryside, from village to village, looking for work. No one would remember, so many years later, a girl—one of many—who had knocked on a servants' door and asked about a position. No one would remember turning her away, watching her walk off into oblivion. No one would now regret not letting her in.

We sat around the map, looking down at it in silence. "We could still do it," Alistair said softly. "We could still see if there is something to find."

"The train station is a dead end," said Matthew. "She could have come from anywhere in the country. We'd never be able to track it down."

"Would she even want us to?" I asked.

"I don't know," said Alistair. All of the old obsession, the old avidity, was gone from his voice. "I don't know whether this is the right decision, or the wrong one. But I think I need to leave off ghost hunting for a while."

"No book?" said Matthew.

Alistair shook his head. "Maybe when I'm eighty, I'll write the book. Maybe then I'll be able to think about it."

So we rolled up the map, and put it away.

Mrs. Clare visited us only once, and briefly. She was quiet and withdrawn. We would have told her the details of all that had happened, but she made it clear she did not want to hear it. Maddy was gone from her home, and all was at peace again; she didn't want to know more than that.

But I did insist that she listen to my theory on the suicide note. It had come to me after I had seen Maddy that last time. *I didn't want to,* she had said so sadly. And the words in the note—*I will kill them.*

I told Mrs. Clare what I thought. The day Maddy had seen Roderick Nesbit at Falmouth House, she had remembered everything. And it had created an anger in her, a murderous desire. She had killed herself, she believed, to stop herself from killing those men. But she had not been able to stop herself, even after death. The murderous desire had lived longer than she had.

Mrs. Clare heard me out. Her face was empty now, empty of anger, empty of grief. She said nothing. Soon after that, she left, and we never saw her again.

One night, unable to sleep, I slipped from my warm bed with Matthew, tied on a robe, and tiptoed to the dark, warm kitchen for a cup of milk. I was just heating it on the stove, stirring as silently as I could so as not to wake the sleeping inn, when the kitchen door snicked open and Alistair came in from outside.

Our eyes met in mutual surprise. He ran a hand through his hair, and looked sheepishly at me. "Hello."

I blinked, the pot of milk momentarily forgotten. "What are you doing?" I whispered.

He looked down and shuffled his feet, for all the world like a servant caught napping on the job. "Sarah, don't be angry. I was with Evangeline."

I turned back to the stove and resumed stirring, taking this in.

"It's the only way," he went on. "We're both under suspicion, and we're watched so closely. I can't not see her. Surely you understand?"

I pursed my lips. I admitted grudgingly to myself that if it were Matthew in that house through the woods, I would be doing the same thing. "How is she?"

"She's . . ." He paused, as if finding the words to describe her. "She came to me, you know, after she telephoned for Constable Moores that day. She came to me and sat with me, even though she didn't know what would happen, if Tom would find out. She didn't care. Now she's getting through things. But she's going to be fine. She's going to be wonderful, someday."

I looked back up at him, at the besotted look in his eyes. "Oh, Alistair."

He smiled at me, his handsome face lighting up.

"Would you like a cup of milk?"

"Yes, I would."

"Sit down, then."

But he didn't. He stood, watching me as I found two mugs and poured a little milk into each. I set his cup next to his hand and as I brushed by him, my body close to his, he put his hands gently on my shoulders. I looked up at him.

"Does he make you happy?" he asked.

I blushed. "Yes."

He nodded. "I can see it. He loves you madly, you know, though it's killing him to admit it. But he's wild for you. The way he looks at you when you're not looking . . ."

I blushed hotter.

"I know Matthew," he went on. "It's hard to explain. We all went to war, all of us, and we all went to the same war. But it seems that every man went to a different war in the end. Even men who fought in the same battles—it's as if every man was in a different place. Matthew's war isn't the same as mine, or any man's. He hasn't let it go. It isn't going to be easy."

I looked at the floor. "I know."

"But he's worth it, in the end."

"I know that, too."

"God." He shook his head. "I'm so sorry, Sarah. You signed on for a temporary assistant job, and look what I put you through. I'm so sorry."

"Don't say that." I looked up at him. Here was the same face I was so familiar with, the face I had first seen across from me in the coffee shop in Soho. The kind eyes, the mussed hair, the handsome smile. "I wouldn't trade it for anything."

"What an extraordinary girl you are," he said, and he pulled me gently to him. I put my arms around his neck and hugged him tightly, smelling his clean, sweet, lemony smell, feeling his welcome warmth. It was nothing like the powerful heat I felt with Matthew, but it was comforting all the same.

"Be happy," I said in his ear.

"I mean to try," he replied.

We stayed there, giving each other quiet comfort, until our milk went cold.

Eventually, there was an inquest. The three of us were summoned to attend. Constable Moores gave evidence, as did the doctor. Evangeline Barry also spoke, her face pale, her clothes somber yet utterly stylish; she testified that she had seen me in the street, and I had begged her to get the police. I feared Roderick Nesbit would take his life, she said, and that Matthew was in danger from her own husband. She testified that she had seen nothing, known nothing, of her husband's possible crimes, that she could think of no reason for him to drown in the stream.

Matthew and I both gave testimony, Matthew to the fact that Tom Barry had admitted to attacking and attempting to murder Maddy Clare before attacking Matthew himself, and finally I spoke, about being held at gunpoint, struck in the face, locked in the basement. The magistrate took me back and forth over the sounds I'd heard while in the cellar. I told him, again, that there had been no shouts, no screams, and no gunfire. I did not tell him about the birds.

Eventually, the judgment was given that Bill Jarvis had died of a seizure, Roderick Nesbit had committed suicide, and Tom Barry had suffered an accident that made him fall in the stream and die of natural causes. The case was closed. Constable Moores was destined to remain unhappy. We were finally free to go.

We packed our bags, and made our plans. Alistair was going home, for a brief time, to take care of some things before traveling alone to a seaside resort. After a few unsuspicious weeks, Evangeline would claim the need for a respite after all she'd been through, and would quietly join him. They were going to try life as a couple, as best they could. I hoped they would be able to make each other happy.

That left Matthew and me.

He came into my room as I packed my few belongings in my little bag. He paced the room, picking things up and putting them down again, staring out the window and turning away.

I packed and waited for him to speak.

He turned back to the window. "I'm thinking of going back to Kingscherry and paying my parents a visit."

"That's nice."

"What will you do?"

I pretended I didn't feel a shaft of pain, a flutter of panic. I smoothed my hand over one of my folded skirts. "I haven't decided."

"You could go back to London."

To my dreary flat, my temporary life. "Yes, I suppose I could."

"You could travel, find somewhere new to live."

Yes, I could do that. Alistair, determined that his guilt was not assuaged, had given me a sum of money, insisting it was restitution for the ordeal I had been through and the injury I had suffered to my face. It wasn't riches, but it was plenty to buy me a little time and a train ticket.

"You must be disappointed," Matthew continued, still looking out the window. "About Alistair."

I straightened at that, and crossed my arms.

He turned to me. "Am I a fool?"

"Yes," I replied. "You are an absolute fool."

He looked down, ran a hand through his hair. I glimpsed the burn scar that showed from under his cuff. I watched his face, the struggle there, his dark eyes so expressive when you learned just how to read them. I watched him struggle with himself, his past, his life. His heart.

Finally he looked up at me. I kept my arms crossed, waiting, feeling the thump of my heart against the inside of my wrist.

Matthew shoved his hands in his pockets. His eyes met mine. "Sarah."

"Yes?"

"Will you please come to Kingscherry with me?"

So many silly words came to my lips. *Do you promise? Do you mean it?* But there was no need to say those things. If Matthew said it, then he promised. And Matthew never said anything he didn't mean.

Do you want me?

I didn't ask that either. I stayed there, with my arms crossed, and looked him in the eye.

"Jesus God, Sarah," he said as if I had spoken. "You know I do."

I crossed the room and went to him. I put my hands on his face, smiling.

"Well, then," I said. "You only had to ask."

Chapter One

Claire Lake, Oregon

The Greer mansion sat high on a hill, overlooking the town and the ocean. To get to it from downtown, you had to leave the pretty shops and the creaking seaside piers and drive a road that wound upward, toward the cliffs. You passed the heart of Claire Lake, the part of town where the locals lived and the tourists didn't usually go. You passed a grid of shops and low apartment blocks, local diners and hair salons. On the outskirts of town, you passed newer developments, built between the foot of the cliffs and the flat land on the edge of the inland lake that gave the town its name.

The land was too wet and rocky to keep building, so the newer developments tapered off into woods and two-lane roads. Along the west edge of the lake were homes built in the seventies, squat shapes in brown brick and cream siding, the gardens neatly kept for over forty years by people who had never moved away. Past those houses, around the other edges of the lake, there was nothing but back roads, used only by hikers, hunters, fishermen, and teenage kids looking for trouble. In the seventies, the houses along the lake were for the up-and-coming ones, the people with good jobs. Everyone else lived in town. And if you were rich, you lived on the hill.

The road climbed on the north side of the lake. The houses were set far apart here for privacy, and the roads were kept narrow and uneven, as if trying to keep outsiders away. The wealthy had come to Claire Lake in the twenties, when the town was first created, looking for a place that was scenic, secluded, and cheap to build big houses. They brought their money from Portland and California and settled in. Some of the houses sat empty after the stock market crash, but they filled up again during the boom after World War II. The people who lived here called the neighborhood Arlen Heights.

The Greer mansion was one of the original houses in Arlen Heights. It was an ugly Frankenstein of a house even when it was built—a pseudo-Victorian style of slanted roofs and spires, though the walls were of butter yellow brick. And when Julian Greer bought it in 1950 with his newly inherited pharmaceutical fortune, he made it worse. He remodeled the lower floor to be more modern, with straight lines and dark brown wood. He also put in a bank of windows along the back wall to open up the house's dark, gloomy interior. The windows looked out to the house's back lawn and its drop-off to the ocean beyond.

The effect was supposed to be sweeping, breathtaking, but like most of Julian's life, it didn't work out as planned. The windows fogged, and the view was bleak. The lawn was flat and dead, and the ocean beyond the cliff was choppy and cold. Julian had done the renovations in hopes of pleasing his new wife, Mariana, but instead the relentless view from the windows unsettled her, and she kept the curtains closed. She decorated the rest of the house dutifully but listlessly, which was a harbinger of their marriage. Something about the Greer mansion stifled laughter and killed happiness. It might sound dramatic, but anyone who had lived there knew it was true.

By 1975, both Julian and Mariana were dead, Julian with his blood all over the kitchen floor, Mariana in the twisted wreck of a car crash. The house watched all of it happen, indifferent.

Tonight it was raining, a cold, hard downpour that came in from the ocean. Arlen Heights was quiet, and the Greer mansion was dark. The rain spattered hard on the panes of glass, tracing lines down the large windows overlooking the lawn. The dark skeletons of the trees on either side of the house bowed back and forth in the wind, the branches scraping the roof. Drops pocked the empty driveway. The house was still and silent, stoic under the wind and the water.

On the lawn, something moved across the surface of the grass. The touch of a footprint. Inside the house, one of the cupboard doors opened in the dark kitchen, groaning softly into the silence.

In a bedroom window a shape appeared, shadowy and indistinct. The blur, perhaps, of a face. A handprint touched the bedroom window, the palm pressing into the glass. For a second, it was there, pale and white, though there was no one to see.

The wind groaned in the eaves. The handprint faded. The figure moved back into the darkness. And the house was still once more.

Chapter Two

Shea

The day before I met Beth Greer was a Tuesday, with a gray sky overhead and a thin drizzle that wet my face and beaded in my hair as I waited at the bus stop. It was unseasonably warm, and the concrete gave off that rainy scent it sometimes has, rising up from beneath my ballet flats. There was a man standing next to me, wearing an overcoat and scrolling through his phone with an exhausted look on his face. On my other side was a worried-looking woman who was frantically texting. I closed my eyes, inhaling the scent of the rain laced with a thread of cologne from the man next to me, overlaid with gasoline and diesel fumes from the street. This was my life.

It wasn't a bad one. I was twenty-nine and divorced. I lived in a small complex of low-rise condos on a tangle of curved streets with the aspirational name of Saddle Estates. In my mind I called it Singles Estates, because it was almost exclusively populated with romantic failures like me, people who needed somewhere to live when they sold off their married house and took their half of the money. The man in the overcoat was divorced, guaranteed, and I'd bet money the woman was texting a kid who was in school while spending a court-designated week with his father.

My divorce was still new. I had no kids. My place was small, smelled of paint, and only contained the bare necessities of furniture. But it wasn't the worst life I could have. I'd known since I was nine that I was lucky to have any life at all.

On the bus, I pulled out my phone, put my earbuds in my ears, and played the audiobook I was in the middle of listening to. A thriller: a woman in danger, most of the characters possibly lying, everything not quite as it seemed. A twist somewhere near the end that would either shock me or wouldn't. There were dozens of books just like it, hundreds maybe, and they were the soundtrack of my life. The woman's voice in my earbuds told me about death, murder, deep family secrets, people who shouldn't be trusted, lies that cost lives. But a novel always ends, the lies come to the surface, and the deaths are explained. Maybe one of the bad characters gets away with something—that's fashionable right now—but you are still left with a sense that things are balanced, that dark things come to light, and that the bad person will, at least, most likely be miserable.

It was dark comfort, but it was still comfort. I knew my own tally by heart: My would-be killer had been in prison for nineteen years, seven months, and twenty-six days. His parole hearing was in six months.

Work was a doctor's office in downtown Claire Lake. I was a receptionist, taking calls, filing charts, making appointments. As I came through the door, I pulled the earbuds from my ears and gave my coworkers a smile, shaking off all of the darkness and death.

"Busy day," Karen, the other receptionist, said, glancing at me, then away again. "We open in twenty."

We weren't bosom friends, my coworkers and I, even though I had worked here for five years. The other women here were married with kids, which meant we had nothing much in common since my divorce. I hadn't talked to any of them about the divorce, except to say it had happened. And I couldn't add to the conversations about daycares and swimming programs. The doctors didn't socialize with any of us—they came and went, expecting the mechanism of the office to work without much of their input.

I took off my jacket and put on my navy blue scrub top, shoving my phone and purse under the desk. I could probably make friends here if I tried. I was attractive enough, with long dark hair that I kept tied back, an oval face, and dark eyes. At the same time, I didn't have the kind of good looks that threaten other women. I was standoffish—I knew that. It was an inescapable part of my personality, a tendency I couldn't turn off no matter how much therapy I did. I didn't like people too close, and I was terrible at small talk. My therapists called it a defense mechanism; I only knew it was me, like my height or the shape of my chin.

But my lack of gregariousness wasn't the only reason my coworkers gave me a wide berth. Though they didn't say anything to me, a rumor had gotten out in my first week; they all knew who I was, what I had escaped. And they all knew what I did in the evenings, the side project that consumed all of my off-hours. My obsession, really.

They probably all thought it wasn't healthy.

But I've always believed that murder is the healthiest obsession of all.

"Don't tell me," my sister, Esther, said on the phone. "You're hibernating again."

"I'm fine," I said. It was after work, and I was at my local grocery store, the Safeway in the plaza within walking distance to Singles Estates. I put cereal in my cart as I shoulder-pinned the phone to my ear. "I'm grabbing some groceries and going home."

"I told you to come over for dinner. Will and I want to see you."

"It's raining."

"This is Claire Lake. It's always raining."

I looked at a carton of almond milk, wondering what it tasted like. "I know you worry about me, but I'm fine. I just have work to do."

"You already have a job. The website isn't paid work."

"It pays enough."

My big sister sighed, and the sound gave me a twinge of sadness. I really did want to see her, along with her husband, Will, a lawyer who I liked quite a lot. Esther was one of the only people who really mattered to me, and even though she gave me grief, I knew she tried hard to understand me. She'd had her own guilt and trauma over what had happened to me. She had her own reasons to be paranoid—to hibernate, as she put it. The difference was, Esther *didn't* hibernate. She had a husband and a house and a good job, a career.

"Just tell me you're trying," Esther said. "Trying to get out, trying to do something, trying to meet new people."

"Sure," I said. "Today I met a man who has a hernia and a

woman who would only say she has a 'uterus problem.'" I put the almond milk down. "I'm not sure what a 'uterus problem' is, and I don't think I'm curious."

"If you wanted to know, you could look in her file and find out."

"I never look in patients' files," I told her. "You know that. I answer phones and deal with appointment times, not diagnoses. Looking in a patient file could get me fired."

"You make no sense, Shea. You won't look at patients' medical files, but you'll talk about murders and dead bodies on the internet."

I paused, unpinning my phone from my shoulder. "Okay, that's actually a good point. I get that. But does it mean that in order to be consistent, I should be more nosy or less?"

"It means you live too much inside your own head, overthinking everything," Esther said. "It means you need to meet people who aren't patients, real people who aren't murder victims on a page. Make friends. Find a man to date."

"Not yet for the dating thing," I told her. "Maybe soon."

"The divorce was a year ago."

"Eleven months." I dodged a woman coming the opposite way up my aisle, then moved around a couple pondering the cracker selection. "I'm not opposed to finding someone. It's dating itself that freaks me out. I mean, you meet a stranger, and that's it? He could be anyone, hiding anything."

"Shea."

"Do you know how many serial killers dated lonely women in their everyday lives? Some divorcée who just wants companionship from a nice man? She thinks she's won the dating lottery, and meanwhile he's out there on a Sunday afternoon, dumping bodies.

And now we're supposed to use internet apps, where someone's picture might not even be real. People are lying about their *faces*."

"Okay, okay. No dating apps. No dating at all yet. I get it. But make some friends, Shea. Join a book club or a bowling league or something."

My cart was full. I paused by the plate glass windows at the front of the store, letting my gaze travel over the parking lot. "I'll think about it."

"That means no," Esther said.

"It means I'll think about it." The parking lot looked like any normal parking lot during after-work hours, with cars pulling in and out. I watched for a moment, letting my eyes scan the cars and the people. An old habit. I couldn't have told you what I was looking for, only that I'd know it when I saw it. "Thanks, sis. I'll talk to you later."

I bought my groceries and put them in the cloth bags I'd brought with me. I slung the bags over my shoulders and started the walk home in the rain, my coat hood pulled up over my head, my feet trying to avoid the puddles. The walk toward Singles Estates took me down a busy road, with cars rushing by me, splashing water and giving me a face full of fumes. Not the most pleasant walk in the world, but I put my earbuds in and put one foot in front of the other. Esther had long ago given up on telling me to get a car. It would never happen.

Besides, I got home before nightfall, so I didn't have to walk alone in the dark. I called that a win.

Simone St. James is the *New York Times* bestselling author of *The Sun Down Motel*; *Lost Among the Living*; *The Other Side of Midnight*; *Silence for the Dead*; *An Inquiry into Love and Death*, which was short-listed for the Arthur Ellis Award for Best Novel from Crime Writers of Canada; and *The Haunting of Maddy Clare*, which won an Arthur Ellis Award. She wrote her first ghost story, about a haunted library, when she was in high school, and spent twenty years behind the scenes in the television business before leaving to write full-time.

VISIT SIMONE ST. JAMES ONLINE

SimoneStJames.com

 SimoneStJames

Ready to find
your next great read?

Let us help.

Visit prh.com/nextread

P.O. 0005418559 202